MANHATTAN
THE RISING WAR

SAL COSENZA

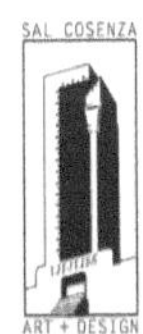

UNUM STUDIO LLC.
Scottsdale, Arizona

For my parents, Belle and Sal Sr.

CONTENTS

My love for the towers ... was for their life.
They were *alive*.
Not many people know that.

—Philippe Petit

PROLOGUE

There once was an island beyond the horizon, past endlessly sloping plains, lush forests, and mighty sand dunes; a slender piece of land, its length triple its width, and blessed with a natural harbor of enviable scale. While such features were undoubtedly distinctive, what came to set this place apart from any other was its skyline of living, breathing, towering giants.

Early inhabitants had first called this strange land of meandering streams and gentle hills *Mannahatta*, but as time wore on, it became known by a more succinct appellation:

Manhattan.

The island's evolution echoed the mindset of its human populace, which meant that immoral diseases like colonization, enslavement, and genocide surrendered to more noble ventures where various faiths, philosophies, and creeds could finally coexist. For only *after* Manhattanites stopped embracing their worst traits could they begin to harness their best ones.

Once that happened, a mythic restructuring became tangible—one that gave buildings the ability to be just as daring, dynamic, and alive as the people within them, and capable of facing any raging threat that might reach their island's shores. So, after years of scientific and spiritual reckoning, Manhattan's era of towering giants began with a breakthrough of statuesque proportions...

PART 1 **MANHATTAN**

LADY LIBERTY'S HEARTBEAT pulsed through her framework as if inside an echo chamber, faintly at first, then becoming more audible to the Manhattanites perched far down below. Such glimmers of life, long in the making, became sparks as the last copper sheets of her robe were attached to her body, their remaining rivets bolted in place to complete a towering new colossus of striking red-orange radiance.

As she began to breathe in and out, strange sounds continued to bellow from deep within her, causing the rest of her body to vibrate vigorously. In short order, the statue's heavy eyelids lifted for the first time, followed by jolting movements in her hands, joints, shoulders, neck, and lips. She felt the cool air sweep up against her metallic skin, a sensation that invigorated the statue further. Blessed with the gift of sight, Lady Liberty surveyed the panorama of her strange new world, admiring the polychromatic skies fit for a painting above just as much as the surging rivers and shifting landscapes that existed below them. Focusing upon the base of the pedestal directly beneath her feet, she took in the throng of curious Manhattanites who were ant-like in scale against her towering profile, numbering a few hundred.

"Such a strange sensation this is," the statue whispered softly while gazing down upon the eager witnesses. Against a steady sound of gasps from the crowd, she summoned the will to speak more audibly in light of the questions running rampant through her mind.

"Why am I here?" she said in a voice warm in tone but steeped in curiosity, unaware that she had been designed this way by forces beyond the physical. As her mind raced, quick flashbacks from some ancient past ran through her head at a frenzied rate.

"And what do you want with me?" she asked helplessly, while cryptic glimpses of erupting magma, colliding landforms, and other visceral flashes soon revealed themselves to her. Such a disorienting flurry of scenes caused Lady Liberty's senses to open further, and her heart to beat faster. Magnetized by the spectacle, the crowd let out greater gasps of excitement, underscored by hints of trepidation, for such life energy had never been seen in anything other than their own kind before.

"My God, that crazy sculptor was right all along!" one witness uttered in stupefied amazement, echoing the same realization of others who saw the birth of Lady Liberty as some long-promised fantasy now made real.

The pressure of the moment, combined with the overwhelming montage of scenes playing inside her mind, began to weigh on Lady Liberty. As the statue flailed her arms to ward off the sensations pouring in, three building inspectors still remained perched on her left shoulder. But they were caught off guard by her rapid awakening during their routine inspection, and struggled to keep their balance. Unable to fasten his safety harness in time like the others, one unlucky inspector plummeted from the statue's shoulder, and crowds below gasped in dread.

"Save him!" a voice in Lady Liberty's mind commanded. Seconds later, the inspector's screams gave way to strange sounds of shearing metal that almost sounded like whale calls, and a giant arm swooped down to catch the man just before he crashed headfirst into the crowd. Plucked from what would've been certain death, the inspector was then safely returned to the ground thanks to the statue's gigantic hand, along with the others who had been dangling from her frame. A noticeable calm soon came over the crowd, as Lady Liberty slowly straightened her posture.

"We seem to share some kind of instinctual bond, you and I," the copper giant said to her audience, as the rescued inspector was whisked away for minor medical attention. While they erupted in appreciation, Lady Liberty sensed her feelings for these so-called Manhattanites growing stronger by the second. With the rush of the moment still flowing through her metal pipes, she didn't realize that her heroic act would repeat itself as the years—and following generations—went on.

During the first night following her dramatic debut, Lady Liberty's slumber atop her pedestal was once again dominated by strange kaleidoscopic visions. And while she certainly felt a newfound bond with her human colleagues, questions still lingered in her mind about the previous day's events.

How had she been able to distinguish the difference between right and wrong so swiftly?

Why were her instincts to reach out her hand and save that perfect stranger?

And perhaps most pressing, how was she able to breathe in the first place?

The next montage of sights and sounds began to answer those questions by painting a telling portrait about who she was and how she came to be. Surrendering to her dream's euphoric persuasion, Lady Liberty closed her eyes tight, took in a deep breath, and saw what looked like a sailing vessel off in the distance, as her surroundings revealed an island heavily forested and wild, quite unlike the urbanized version of Manhattan that greeted her earlier. *This must be from the past*, she thought correctly. Sharpening her focus, the statue noticed several more sailing vessels coming ashore and watched as, one by one, the ships moved in closer to dock near the island's sandy embankment. The symbols and color schemes on their wooden hulls were diverse and eclectic, and the statue suspected that these ships hailed from a number of foreign places. The boisterous sounds of disembarking crew members and passengers echoed faintly in the sea breeze. Judging from their clothing and presentation, which ranged from ornate and gilded to chained up and nearly naked, Lady Liberty figured these colonizers and captives to be just a few generations older than the crowd that greeted her when she first came to life.

But before she could wrap her mind around what she was seeing, from the concepts of human discovery and exploration to even forced servitude, Lady Liberty felt an ethereal whisper radiate through her mind, a strange visitor along for the ride it seemed, as the dream swiftly transported her to an even earlier time in Manhattan's ancient lifespan.

In a flash, the world around her spun into yet another version of itself, one that swapped out those large sailing ships for an assortment of smaller canoes that dotted the rivers and seas, while several cone-shaped wigwams—temporary wooden shelters built by the indigenous Lenape—were perched off the island's embankments. Before anyone else had arrived upon Manhattan's shores, these Lenape were, in fact, the island's earliest known human inhabitants, the whispering voice revealed.

Through a series of successive vignettes, Lady Liberty watched in awe as Lenape of all shapes and sizes gathered outside their shelters to circle around a firepit, where they shared tales of life, loss, and community. Her ears rang as village elders and children alike chanted in worship. From there the scenes expanded, and the more vignettes the dream offered, the more time Lady Liberty had to connect with this vivacious human force. She watched Lenape adults hunt, gather crops, migrate with the changing seasons, and whenever necessary, engage in intertribal battle.

But just as she grew accustomed to the scenes and culture laid out before her, the dream carried her away again, to a period millions of years before even the Lenape called Manhattan home. In this prehistoric glimpse, she could see that Manhattan was not yet an island separate from the mainland, and the landscape surrounding her had neither lush forests nor sloping plains, but rather, darkened marble surfaces and treacherous-looking rock outcroppings. In what became the most rousing sequence of her dreamscape, Lady Liberty soon found herself face-to-face with a mighty spirit called *Schist*, who emerged from the sea with rumbling force.

Gazing upon Schist's towering and stony profile, she watched as the formidable being gathered four elements within his mighty grasp—wind, water, fire, and rock—from which all life derived, the whispering voice proclaimed. Moments later, the sky opened up and Schist began to morph those elements into something lifelike, indeed. As the ground erupted in a flash of blinding light, humanoid shapes appeared in spectacular profusion; a visual phenomenon that formed a direct link in Lady Liberty's mind between the elements, the sea-faring explorers and captives, the Lenape, the building inspector whose life she had recently saved, and Schist himself. Upon seeing such a miracle unfold before her eyes, the statue determined this Schist creature to be a generous creator, a strong and sturdy protector, and a figure to try to emulate.

"That whisper inside your head is mine," the great being then revealed to her in a deafening yet trusting tone. "In doubtful times, never hesitate to call upon me."

Lady Liberty nodded, her thoughts filled with wonderment.

"There is still one more thing you need to see before tonight's journey concludes," Schist told her.

Lady Liberty shielded her eyes as the mighty spirit morphed into a darker, more sinister presence that lingered all around her. This new presence, she soon learned, was Schist's great adversary known as *Pegmatite*—an antagonistic, volcanic spirit, hell-bent on tormenting all life at will. As the dark force coagulated, she took in Pegmatite's horned and twisted form, dreading it more than before.

Suddenly, the dream whisked the statue closer to the fearsome figure, and before she could say anything, Lady Liberty was thrust into Pegmatite's clawed arms. The two merged, and the statue began to see through the eyes of Pegmatite's twisted soul, taking in scenes of raging destruction, persecution, torment, and undeniable suffering. She saw glimpses of random human settlements turned to smoke and ash before her eyes, and such calamity resulted in countless deaths all around her, as Pegmatite's fires spread without remorse. These hellish acts happened across a variety of lands at first, but before long, Lady Liberty noticed through the thick smoke her once gleaming and prosperous island of Manhattan succumbing to the same terrible fate as Pegmatite's other conquests.

Whether these horrible scenes were from ages long ago or times yet to come remained unclear, but so visceral were they that Lady Liberty screamed out for the dream to stop. Thankfully, her request was granted and the statue awoke gasping for breath atop her pedestal, the seas around her calm, and the island beyond resembling the composed place she knew from the day prior.

Upon processing the totality of the visions, the experience was burned into the statue's subconscious. While most of the scenes were undoubtedly from the past, she couldn't help but fear the future, especially when considering Schist's offer to be called upon in doubtful times.

"Will I truly need to summon your aid someday, mighty Schist?" she asked softly to the skies above, aware now of what Pegmatite's rage could do if ever gone unchecked.

"When should we inform her of her significance, sir ... of the many failed years of design experimentation, or her unique role here and all that?" the ambitious Assistant asked.

"Now why would we do such a thing so suddenly?" his lead Sculptor challenged.

"Why? To give her clarity, I suppose."

"Clarity? What do you want me to tell her? That we tried, over and over for years on end, to make this happen, but failed miserably every time? That if Schist is correct, the fate of the city will one day rest upon her copper shoulders?"

"Yes. I guess. Remember, we need to report her progress to our investors, right?"

"May I remind you that we're not doing this for some bottom line, but that we're following a spiritual calling?"

"I know, but..."

"My dear boy, listen to me. You're my brightest helper, my right hand even, but there are two things I need at this moment. First, I need you to get me a coffee with precisely two creams and one sugar. No more, no less. Okay?"

"And the second?"

"Ah! Now we're in business. Second, stop worrying about Lady Liberty, because we're going to take it nice 'n' slow with her. I don't want the symbol of our reimagined city to crack under some kind of bureaucratic pressure. I'll deal with the investors. I'll deal with the public. I'll handle everything. You'll see."

———

"Let's get started," the Sculptor declared the next morning from his perch within the waking statue's crown. "Can you hear me, my dear?" He beckoned toward the nearest copper surface, his Assistant nearby.

"Loud and clear," Lady Liberty replied, surprised by the buoyant human voice inside her head.

"Great! Now, there's plenty of public pressure to get this right, and a lot of people are counting on you. Your extraordinary abilities, once mastered, will earn you a place as one of Manhattan's true beacons of achievement, endurance, and reawakening."

Lady Liberty took in this news with caution. "I had a feeling my place here was of some importance," she said in a shaky voice, processing the magnitude of her purpose.

"Ha! Indeed it is," the Sculptor said. "Those dreams you've been having are just the start of your supersensory abilities, which is why we need to train you to manage them. This is Schist's will, after all."

"I see," the statue responded.

"I'm glad! After all, you truly are the first of a new kind."

The visionary, wildly eccentric, and sometimes hotheaded Sculptor reminded her of this fact often from that point forward, to which Lady Liberty sometimes reacted by asking what her kind *was* exactly.

Over the next week, the Sculptor taught her how to swim the surging waves of the Hudson River, how to walk carefully enough to avoid stepping on humans by her feet, and how to handle questions from any passersby regarding her civic significance. Through it all, Lady Liberty came to learn of her place as the first "towering giant" on record to harness a spirit directly tied to Schist himself.

By the end of her second week of training, the statue perched her tired and aching structure atop her pedestal to prepare for a night's slumber.

"Before you sleep, I've got a couple more lessons," the Sculptor said from within the statue's crown. In small-dose fashion, as per his strategy, the astute Manhattanite proceeded to explain many existential things to her.

"Your dreams and visions were never random," he admitted. "In order to become a link among nations, you first must consider the lessons these dreams are trying to impart to you."

"So why do I exist? Is it by your will?" the statue asked, confused.

"Not really, for that power goes to Schist. But I am here to simply interpret that will."

"Is this why you know so much?"

"I know a lot because I, too, am receptive to Schist's life-giving gift. I believe in it. It's what gave me the capacity to figure out how to design and build you."

Lady Liberty's eyebrows furrowed in bafflement as she glanced out across the harbor for clarity.

The lead Sculptor, sensing the heavy topic had fallen upon fatigued ears, toned down his cryptic descriptions. "What I mean is that you've seen in your dreams what Pegmatite can do ... all that terror and destruction. So, I want you to be a symbolic gift from one to the other, a representation of goodwill in spite of *all* the terrors of this world. Peace and understanding are your ideals now."

As the Sculptor went on, he connected Lady Liberty's special place in history with Manhattan's own dark chapters of turmoil, unrest, violence, and persecution. "This place you live in seeks to redeem itself, because its history is stained with bloodshed. For far too long have people here suppressed and maimed each other. The great Lenape you saw in your dreams, for instance. Do you know what happened to most of them? They were displaced and driven out from here long ago by early Manhattanites, the very same colonizers you witnessed anchoring their ships to these shores. And once those settlers established a foothold on this island, countless others from that point on were either enslaved, eradicated, or exiled. Manhattan knew much discrimination, devastation, disease, famine. The list goes on, but that all had to change and give way to something morally noble for once ... you!"

Lady Liberty exhaled and rubbed her forehead for relief.

"So now, here we stand," the Sculptor continued, "ready to be a place that will rise as an unprecedented bastion for tolerance, acceptance, and plurality this time ... free from our past sins. Coming to terms with this realization was the only way my team and I were able to create you."

These declarations led Lady Liberty to see a much more empathetic side to the often hotheaded and driven Sculptor.

"Over time, it's my dream that you will accept multitudes of people from every corner of this planet. For example, take Manhattan's great harbor, which is fast becoming a gateway for these future generations. It's only natural that you'll be headquartered here on this base, in the heart of the action ...the first thing they would see coming in from their long journey overseas. This pedestal on which we sit was erected here for that very reason, sited south of Manhattan proper, right up there, and north of the harbor below us, for all to hold dear. Do you understand what I mean?"

Lady Liberty's eyes beamed with the prospect of her dignified role in this newly utopian society.

"Now," the Sculptor went on, "understand that many Manhattanites watched you grow higher and higher over these past few months, and that your existence brings them great hope for the future! Love them unconditionally, for they watched with fervor as your feet were first placed atop this pedestal. Then came your legs and torso. Next we erected your arms and hands—one carrying that massive torch of yours, and the other your book. From there, your shoulders, neck, head, and face were assembled and hoisted into position, all on my order. Finally, your adorning crown, complete with those seven pointed rays—one for each known continent—was placed atop your head. Don't ever take it off, because that crown is emblematic of the unifying role you will play."

Lady Liberty nodded as the Sculptor switched subjects. "Respect Schist, the ancient creator who begot you. But fear Pegmatite, who aims to do no good to anyone here by undoing all the progress we've made."

"I understand," the statue said, remembering her recent dreams about life and death.

After a lengthy pause, the Sculptor saved the best piece of information for last as he cupped his right ear with his hand. "And what is that 'thumpity-thump' beating within you, you may wonder? It's your heart, of course, and it's the key to your pulsing energy. It is a seven ton, billion-year-old Schistian stone that exists inside your copper and steel frame—forevermore, I hope. You must guard this energy source, Lady Liberty. Guard it at all costs! If you do that, you will outlive me, my team of designers, every Manhattanite out there right now, and many generations of humanity to come, while ensuring that our legacies are all preserved. I was only able to scratch the surface of that stone's potential, but it was just enough to give us you, thankfully."

The Sculptor took another long view of the budding island city through the windows of Lady Liberty's crown, a land still brimming with unimpressive lifeless timber-frame structures and equally monotonous patches of farmland, and grinned as he returned his gaze upon Lady Liberty, ready with the inevitable next question.

"The key to that skyline will one day be yours, ready to be transformed from its old life, plagued with problems, to a new one ripe with towering giants, just like you. Will you carry this heavy burden?"

Taking her time to answer, Lady Liberty stowed her copper book inside a sculpted pocket of her draped attire and placed her hand on her chest to feel the steady beat of the blessed stone within her; a rare object since so little physical evidence of Schist existed at that point.

Eager for her response, the Sculptor nonetheless recalled his arduous journey in getting to this point. Images, for instance, of the many quarries he and his team had to dig flashed through his mind, as they obsessively scanned the island for the stone's location. It was a search that stretched back to the earliest days of the island's tunnel construction and concluded just recently when the stone was found deep within the island's core. But the find was well worth the sacrifice, the Sculptor knew, for such stones, if unlocked and respected according to Schistian principle, carried life-giving potential from the great spirit himself. Along the way, even Pegmatite-rich stone fragments were located and secured, with the hope that they would never be used for ill intent. Ultimately, his search for these stones had claimed the better part of his career, since the Sculptor's desire to animate the inanimate became a constant driving force. A mantra even. Now it had all led to this, his greatest creation.

Realizing that she was the sole beneficiary of such an involving pursuit, Lady Liberty's growing smile indicated that her mind was made up.

"I accept this gift," she said, "and shall hereafter protect those who carry and honor it with me."

"That's what I like to hear! Good, now get some rest," the Sculptor replied, satisfied beyond measure as he took a long breath and gazed through the windows of the statue's crown once more. "Like I said before, you truly are the first of a new kind."

In the months to come, Lady Liberty dutifully held onto that promise she made to her Sculptor. Now that she was officially a link between two worlds, Manhattan's first towering giant gained a broad spectrum of emotions and behavioral attributes as she matured. And by year's end, she personally met and spoke with each of the thousands of people who called Manhattan home, either through scheduled tours up to her crown, or by crouching down to spontaneously chat with Manhattanites on the streets. Kids adored her, but so did adults, which normalized this other-worldly situation, as many came to feel that Lady Liberty was more than just a strange talking statue. In no time, it was not uncommon to see her face appearing on everything from coffee mugs to backpacks.

"Why do Manhattanites love Lady Liberty?" her Sculptor later opined in an interview marking two years since the statue's birth. "We love her because she's as genuine as any of us. She's also Manhattan's great keeper, and her insightful and tolerant ways mirror our newfound values to their core."

As she rose to dizzying new heights of fame, Lady Liberty's supernatural abilities followed suit, thanks to ongoing training from her Sculptor.

"Close your eyes and harness that innermost Schistian spirit. Closer, closer, closer still. Good! Now, let the will of the *wind* guide you," the Sculptor said one bright and early morning.

The now seasoned statue did as was suggested. She closed her eyes, breathed in deeply, and began to feel herself levitating off the base of her pedestal with newfound buoyancy.

"This is no dream," she said as her power of flight was unlocked for the first time.

"No, it's not. Not anymore, anyway," the Sculptor confirmed with delight.

But her abilities weren't the only aspects to evolve. In time, Lady Liberty's copper exterior also changed from a red-orange to a much more greenish patina. While startled at first by her new appearance, the statue grew to embrace it. "My *green* lady," the Sculptor remarked with affection upon his first noticing the transformation. It was a nickname that stuck.

As well as encountering changes to her patina, Lady Liberty soon confronted changes of other types, too. It was at this time that the generation of Manhattanites who helped bring her into being slowly but surely began to die off. While this happened more often before her eyes as the years went on, the green lady gained deeper value for the life-giving attributes of Schist's story, while coming to terms with death, which she mostly associated with Pegmatite. Despite her best efforts to push it to the sidelines of her mind, death inevitably hit home.

"It seems my journey with you is reaching the finish line, my dear," the dying Sculptor announced one cold December day. With his ever-loyal Assistant by his side, he spent his final hours within the steel frame of the statue's crown to ensure that she received any last teachings he tried to give.

"But why, dear Sculptor, why does this happen? Despite all you know about Schist and, well, everything else, why does death take you and yours so suddenly?" Lady Liberty reacted with frustration.

"So *suddenly*? Ha!" the old man let out with a youthful spark in his eyes. "Who's to say, really? All I know is that I lived a lotta life with very little regret, and I made some friends along the way too. Was I hot-headed at times? Sure. But what could I do?" The Sculptor glanced over at his Assistant, who in turn tried his best to conceal his own sadness.

"Hell, while I'm still here," the Sculptor went on, "I might as well reveal my entire deck. My real name is Bartholdi ... Frédéric-Auguste Bartholdi. Did you know that? I know you used to ask me, but I never wanted to tell you. Didn't want you to get too attached to me, to avoid moments like this, I suppose. Anyway, that's my name if you still wanted to know."

Surprised by this revelation, Lady Liberty nodded and closed her eyes briefly as she sensed her creator continuing to slip away. "Bartholdi," she repeated, before adding softly, "A good name for a good human."

"I suppose you're right. But please, let's not get so hung up on death now, especially since you've got so much more of your own journey to go! And besides, I ... I told you it would one day come to this. Remember, you and yours to come were *always* designed to outlast us."

Lady Liberty sensed increasing fragility in the old man's voice as he struggled and strained to let out his final thoughts. It was a voice, she knew, that grew more precious by the second. Meanwhile, Bartholdi's loyal Assistant, sensing his boss's waning mortality, scrambled to find another blanket to give the old man, hoping it would help in some small way.

Bartholdi pressed on. "Recall from your earliest dreams that if Pegmatite's forces should ever direct their hateful gaze upon this place, you should summon Schist's goodwill. His abilities, after all, know few limits, even in the face of great despair. Never let strange-sounding bells fall upon deaf ears, for they could very well be ringing in freedom."

Perplexed by such a metaphor, Lady Liberty nevertheless treasured the words of her old creator. "I shall not forget these things, for you taught me wisely," she assured him.

"Good, good," Bartholdi let out before coughing up more severely. "You're my legacy, Lady Liberty, but now you must also create your own. That torch you carry ... it's all yours. You are proof that this life-giving concept works, so go forth and construct many more like you. Such is the noble thing to do."

With that, Bartholdi, her great Sculptor, the tireless and eccentric Manhattanite who raised her for so many years, was gone, and a bleak silence permeated the hollow spaces and halls of her immense structure.

"He's lifeless now, Lady Liberty," the Assistant said with equal measures of shock and delivery, as tears began to stream down his face.

"Yes, but he is at peace," Lady Liberty replied. While her expression transformed from one of sadness to acceptance, she slowly processed her creator's dying request until she was sure of only one thing: that the work of this great Manhattanite, his vision and his values, had to continue.

In the wake of Bartholdi's death, Lady Liberty embraced her role as an oracular figure among a cast of architectural characters to come, serving as the missing link between Manhattan's cultures of the past and the present, and as a result, ushering in a new era of towering giants that transformed the city beyond measure.

Under the green lady's direction, Manhattanites went to work in continuing what her creator had started, and the streets of the city soon blossomed with new construction. As technology advanced thanks to the influx of creative minds involved, new buildings were imbued with the same Schistian stones as the type used to give Lady Liberty her spark of life—the one difference being that these stones could now be ground into fine aggregate and mixed directly into the steel, making Lady Liberty's towering successors taller, lighter in weight, and more organically freeform.

In the months following this emboldened effort, various sacred structures, museums, financial buildings, schools, restaurants, office towers, hospitals, theaters, and apartments—each unique in their own special and singular way—sprung from the bedrock with fervor, and the city of tomorrow was in full swing. It was a period called "Manhattan's Big Bang" by the press, and for good reason, since technology, communication, and democratic principles advanced just as fervently.

All throughout this most exciting time, Lady Liberty made sure to be there to officiate each new birth as it happened, and the press had a field day reporting each event. One crisp September morning, for instance, saw the arrival of not one but *seven* new towering giants along the island's eastern border, each reflecting the city's growing and diverse interests.

"Shall we start?" Lady Liberty asked as the excited human builders and design teams of the new towers packed inside her crown.

"Let's do it!" an Architect of one of the buildings called out eagerly.

Lady Liberty buoyantly walked the lineup of new towers as they awoke. First up was Trinity Church, a slender, steeple-topped creation of brick and stone, whose "all-seeing" clock tower was of particular curiosity to the statue. Following him came Masjid Malcolm Shabazz, a boxy little mosque who also touted a stunning bulbous dome that shimmered with golden brilliance against the bright day. Next, she met the tallest of the new batch, St. Patrick's Cathedral, a fascinating neo-Gothic creation composed of smooth, blue-colored stone exterior features, vertically pitched roofs lined with pointed, decorative finials, and topped with two soaring steeples that came to sharp points. Central Synagogue awakened shortly thereafter, her green-and-gold-tinted globes sitting confidently atop her own twin stone steeples. The statue then greeted Apollo Theater, who was much smaller than those preceding her, but who sparkled thanks to her eye-catching marquee. Rounding out the new arrivals were two short but sweet buildings named Puglia Ristorante and

Guggenheim Museum, who became fast friends despite their wildly different architectural styles and programmatic purposes.

"A beautiful skyline stands before us today," Lady Liberty said proudly to both the design teams within her and the nearby crowds gathered on the streets below, before turning her gaze back toward the new buildings. "Your teams of designers, dreamers, and doers have worked hard to get us to this point, my new friends. Now, all they ask, and all I ask, is that you each create your mark on our fair city. So go forth and make us proud. We welcome you to Manhattan."

Indeed, the next several months were chock-full of similar miraculous moments throughout the island, but given the rate in which these towering giants were sprouting, it was increasingly apparent to both Lady Liberty and Manhattan's building officials that their island was no longer the modest place of lifeless one-story structures and low-lying fields that Lady Liberty had been born into, and certain kinks had to be worked out in terms of how the buildings behaved, walked, and functioned on a daily basis. In order to keep a healthy coexistence between buildings and people, the last thing anyone needed was a city of unruly, unchoreographed towers roaming the island without awareness of their impact, be it size or otherwise. As a result, several citywide mandates were in order.

"Firstly, we shall value our neighbors, large and small, with utmost care. This applies to both ourselves and to all human life," Lady Liberty preached to her growing flock. "Secondly, be ever mindful of where you step, for your place in this bountiful city is always a *shared* one. As such, you will each learn how to walk and swim properly. Finally, understand that we are to function side by side with the Manhattanites who live and work within us, no matter what. These are our Schistian principles."

While interpretations among the new buildings were varied, each did their best in abiding by these founding social mandates from the get-go. Given the city's gradual mastery in its own self-management, news of the living, breathing architectural giants spread beyond Manhattan's shores, reaching towns, villages, and cities across the nation at large and around the world. Manhattan's human population, meanwhile, increased nearly as high as its reborn skyline, which of course only furthered construction. Ultimately, for Manhattanites walking any given street on any given day, it was as if God, Mammon, and Nature had decided to work together to create a miracle that trampled all preconceived logic and understanding.

Not everyone was so quick to embrace the new path Manhattan had forged, however. While a great majority of Manhattanites fancied the life-giving attributes of Schist's legend as a proper template for their modern city, the unholy trinity of bigotry, racism, and hatred was still present among certain factions, who felt that such utopian progress somehow infringed upon their personal liberties. Some quickly grew disillusioned by the overwhelmingly idealist and inclusive tone that had been broadcast since the birth of Lady Liberty. Worse yet, they despised the notion of *living* architecture and viewed the new buildings as bastardized interpretations of Manhattan's founding principles. As a show of defiance against the other side, rebelling factions identified more closely with Pegmatite than they ever had with Schist, opting ultimately to take the former's legend to twisted new levels never anticipated by Lady Liberty's creators.

Discontent grew slowly at first, often in underground subway tunnel meetings held by just a handful of organizers—meetings peppered with speeches, statements, and pamphlets decrying how buildings like Lady Liberty were defying the order of Pegmatite. *To give buildings life is to swim in a sea of hubris, one that shall one day incur the wrath of Pegmatite*, typical pamphlets warned.

In the months following the arrival of Manhattan's first crop of towering giants, an alarming polarity began to plague the city due to this pro-Pegmatite sentiment, which was furthered by a small number of brash politicians who went through great measures to legitimize the fringe movement. Anger, in turn, swelled steadily, leading to pro-Pegmatite followers filing a series of divisive and restrictive legal petitions against the towering giants, with 1,988 signatures collected in support of not only *halting* construction of all future living buildings, but also demolishing existing creations like Lady Liberty and her contemporaries. While judges quickly tossed out these petitions on account of low public approval and general empathy toward the towering giants, heated rallies periodically erupted across Manhattan Island, especially near construction sites of soon-to-be-born buildings. "If the law won't fix the problem, then we will!" pro-Pegmatite organizers shouted with growing fervor. It wasn't long before things took an even uglier turn.

The evening of what came to be called "The Great Banishment" was a cloudless and breezy one, as Lady Liberty prepared to settle in atop her base at Liberty Island. It had been another exhausting world-building day for the statue, who remained meticulous in restructuring every aspect of the island according to Schistian principles. The thought of anything coming between her and a good night's sleep was the last thing on her drowsy mind, as was the prospect of enemies hiding out and waiting to strike from right beneath her feet. But as the green lady's eyelids began to close, she suddenly felt faint footstep-like thumps emanating from her pedestal. Moments later, all hell broke loose as a surprise mob of rioters, armed and angry, emerged from every threshold of her star-shaped base, shouting in repeated unison: "Death to Lady Liberty! Long live Pegmatite!"

Following their eerie chant, the perpetrators unleashed a hail of bullets into the green lady, riddling the lower areas of her copper exterior and sending shockwaves of pain throughout her body. Far away from Liberty Island, the sounds of gunfire reached the ears of unsuspecting mainland police, who then desperately sprung into action and prepared to race to the scene by boat. Almost immediately, however, the damage was enough to cause the statue to buckle at her knees and keel over. She collapsed right on top of several offenders, crushing them to death on impact.

"Look at what she's capable of," a pro-Pegmatite organizer said, inciting the mob further. "And if we don't fight like hell, we're not gonna have a city anymore!" With that, hundreds of attackers forced themselves inside Lady Liberty's bullet-riddled lower levels, their weapons drawn, and their motives undoubtedly hell-bent on locating the source of the statue's life-giving power from within—her sacred Schistian stone.

"Get her right in the heart!" one rioter shouted viciously as others poured into the statue's halls and corridors. Those still outside swung long metal cables and chains across her entire body in an attempt to hold her down. Lady Liberty struggled to regain her footing from the stinging snares that pressed down on her from all directions, even as she cried out in terror.

"This is not the answer! Think of what you are doing!" she pleaded to ignorant and angry ears.

"Shut up, you abomination!" shot back an attacker.

"What's taking so long? Let's just kill her now!" howled another.

As the bloody riot continued, the crowds trespassing deep inside Lady Liberty's frame finally found their intended prize. But just before they could pry loose the Schistian stone from her steel framework with the hope of destroying it, police arrived on Liberty Island and began firing back to subdue the angry mob.

Following more resulting commotion, Lady Liberty was freed, and despite considerable structural damage, her life was spared since the stone remained intact. The attack lasted four hours and seventeen minutes, and resulted in the deaths of twenty-one rioters. Each was labeled as either a martyr by fringe, pro-Pegmatite media, or as a domestic terrorist by nearly everyone else. The next day, newspapers across Manhattan screamed with the headline:

ASSAULT ON LIBERTY ISLAND! MANHATTAN HIGH COURT ORDERS PRO-PEGMATITE BANISHMENT IN WAKE OF SURPRISE AMBUSH.

While most of the perpetrators were arrested at the scene of the crime, others slippery enough to escape quickly arranged to flee overseas. In the weeks following the attack, the small band of radicals, including certain politicians, organized plea deals with a handful of sympathetic governments far beyond the jurisdiction of either Manhattan or any other national authority—ones that still favored the business of war and oppression. Surely, this pro-Pegmatite movement sought to regain its footing and influence elsewhere. While that on its own was not immediately consequential, the movement soon metastasized into something far more cult-like and sinister. Successive adherents reinterpreted the relationship between Pegmatite and death with notions of *justified* violence in the name of righteousness. Inevitably, their philosophy planted the seeds for Manhattan's greatest challenges to come.

During her recovery, Lady Liberty couldn't help but take into account the anger and ferocity of her perpetrators, and what this might mean for Manhattan's future. To her, these attackers were a reflection of Pegmatite's most destructive traits; a direct foil, she believed, to the life-giving ways of Schist. As she ruminated on this distinction, flashbacks of Bartholdi, her Sculptor, reminded her of such reprisals.

"Not everyone will agree with what we're doing here, my dear, so be wary of those who express words or acts of hatred against your kind. Most value Schist's story, but you will likely come to know others who don't," he had once warned her. Despite those early signs, or any of Lady Liberty's periodically nightmarish premonitions, she hoped that such destruction would never actually hit the island so forcefully. In essence, she hoped Bartholdi was wrong. But given her recent brush with death, the severity of it all was more palpable to the green lady in the days and months following her assault.

"As our city continues to grow, and grow it must," she cautioned her fellow towering giants soon after, "we need to be aware that there are many who support our existence even as others oppose it. This means that we need to look after each other with greater vigilance."

Far from Manhattan proper, Lady Liberty's calls for mindful coexistence were countered by ones of growing divisiveness, as pro-Pegmatite sentiment continued to evolve. Most people and buildings of Manhattan returned to their daily routines and largely forgot the horrors of "The Great Banishment" over time, but the situation became dire a world away, and piecemeal reports of whole villages being wiped out by mysterious raging infernos reached the city. Largely overlooked by the global community, such incidents overseas were in fact laying waste to hundreds of people and scores of structures, all in the name of Pegmatite.

And as this pro-Pegmatite phantom continued to take form, it became fueled by three burning desires. The first was to strike down Manhattan's most prominent towering giants, still viewed as a particular affront to the order of Pegmatite. These calculated assassinations served as a symbolic critique of their enemy's hubris. The second goal was to ultimately conquer Manhattan Island and its national sister cities with full force, to eliminate any opposition and ensure that the creation of living buildings could never happen elsewhere. To date, Manhattan was the only place to have unlocked such a Schistian-inspired phenomenon, and they wished to keep it that way. Following the takeover of the city, the third burning desire was to establish a new headquarters in the enemy's place—an act that would be viewed as a restoration of Pegmatite's so-called "Lost Kingdom."

The *enemy*.

This was what Manhattan and its ever-growing number of towering giants were characterized as in the eyes of the growing darkness, vilified because of why they were created, what they represented, and how they so freely embraced free thought and altruism. Such rage was most evident in the hate group's messaging, such as "Living buildings breed societies of mockery, pride, and ignorance against Pegmatite, and supporters of such deception must be turned to ruin."

All things considered, the new darkness viewed the city as a corrupt embodiment of tendencies and traditions that deserved no sympathy. Sadly, as the global attacks began to demonstrate, their viewpoint was proving to be more than just an abstract construct. It was only a matter of time before this fringe group of escaped ex-Manhattanites assigned a new moniker to their cause:

Territorial Reclamation and Restoration of Righteousness.

To anyone who either survived their wrath firsthand or opposed their militant interpretation of Pegmatite from a distance, that long name became an even more apt acronym:

The TERROR Group.

Five short months after the events of "The Great Banishment," Manhattan welcomed the fast-tracked arrival of one particularly notable towering giant, whose knack for diplomacy served as a key sign of the uncertain times.

"Welcome to Manhattan, UN Building," Lady Liberty proclaimed as she stared into the reflective curtain wall of the brand-new waking tower, whose distinctive rectangular profile, consisting of refreshing aqua-colored glass and white concrete trim, became another unique silhouette in Manhattan's skyline. The statue shifted her focus up toward UN Building's roof and noticed the presence of many flagpoles but only one lone flag on display thus far—a circumstance she hoped would soon change.

"Thank you! I see you and hear you quite clearly," UN Building responded after stretching from side to side.

"I see myself too, actually!" Lady Liberty said as she caught her reflection from UN Building's glass façade. "Now, are you mindful of your intended calling?" the green lady added, knowing full well that the newest generation of towering giants were pre-instructed by their design team to follow specific civic virtues.

"Yes, my designers have done their job. When can I start mine?" he replied with zest.

Lady Liberty nodded at UN Building's design team as they listened from within their creation's top floor. "You can start today," she said, "for our matter is urgent. We must learn all we can about this so-called TERROR Group. From within my crown we are joined by Manhattan's top defense personnel, and their general can share with you what is known so far."

UN Building stood by attentively while the top-ranking Manhattanite official began to report through an intercom that transmitted to all participants, his voice amplified for them to hear.

"Thank you, Lady Liberty, and welcome aboard, UN Building. At this moment, our intelligence gatherings on the matter are limited at best," the General admitted. "But we do know a few details. Firstly, the TERROR Group is not a stationary enterprise with set headquarters, which makes it increasingly difficult to track. Secondly, the movement continues to grow at a fervent rate, according to our data from other intelligence experts across the planet. Reports indicate that this group sweeps through a region, clearing its resources and kidnapping potential new recruits in the process, before destroying the area and moving on to the next place. As such, UN Building, total destruction is often the only evidence that the group was there at all."

"As you might gather, knowledge of this menace must no doubt expand," the green lady added. "Such chilling conduct signifies a movement interested only in consumption and death. The virtues of Pegmatite are these."

"As opposed to Schistian ones, I presume?" UN Building asked.

"Very good. Your instincts are on the mark," Lady Liberty replied. "Which is why we need you, and those working within you, to establish as many diplomatic ties as you can with faraway partners and regions. Manhattan is quite insular, but this needs to change, and once a global partnership is more evident, it is our hope that the TERROR Group will cower against this watchdog strategy."

UN Building looked around his new home with a sense of purpose in his demeanor, heeding Lady Liberty's call wholeheartedly.

"Those flagpoles of yours are mighty bare, my friend," Lady Liberty quipped, trying to alleviate the heavy task at hand.

"Well, let's just see what I can do about that," her new friend replied.

His directives clear, UN Building and his occupants began their arduous task of engaging in regular long-distance dialogue with various towns, villages, and governments sympathetic to Manhattan's ideals. At the same time, the TERROR Group's overseas ascent escalated as it swallowed up enough resources to mobilize its own underground army. Led by self-appointed Chieftains who carried out the order's agenda in the name of Pegmatite, there was now a structured hierarchy to this global threat, as Chieftains made sure to categorize themselves just a few rungs below Pegmatite in terms of divine veneration, and the mythic nature of their leadership evoked authority that cast a shadow over the entire network. To keep the movement growing, the Chieftains used their incredible influence to enlist new recruits from conquered lands, on a rolling basis.

As it expanded, the TERROR Group went to work weeding out its recruits, whose traits and characteristics were keenly observed. Composed almost entirely of young adults, the recruits were plucked from their homelands before being systematically tested for loneliness, anger, disillusionment, and susceptibility to outside influence. Candidates who met all criteria found that they were no match against the psychological and physical forces that worked to bend their wills. These were the candidates who advanced in the program while other more reluctant souls were either killed or saved for future sacrificial demonstration. This practice added another level of dread to the TERROR Group's tactics.

Radicalization often played out in a predictable way. During a lengthy period of indoctrination, branded as the "Spring of Life" by the TERROR Group, new recruits were subjected to extensive psychological prodding that began to transform their fears and animosities into self-conviction, replacing preconceived social conventions of right and wrong with newly established directives. While seemingly self-empowering, these directives cleverly pointed the finger toward anything deemed to be an "enemy of righteousness and an affront to Pegmatite."

Chieftains groomed their recruits in an itemized fashion. "You shall eschew all forms of earthly distraction," they instructed their flock, "including artistic, scientific, and emotional expression, acts of passion, bartering with the enemy, democratic feelings, and a love of anthropomorphism—the sin of bringing life to inanimate things."

Once the initial shock had subsided, and with enough forceful encouragement, recruits usually came to connect those perceived vices with their own personal inadequacies, and in so doing, they came to feel that anyplace fostering such concepts was a bastion of immorality and a direct threat. "Do as *we* say, for it is the will of Pegmatite," Chieftains repeated.

Such grooming was how the TERROR Group justified any carnage it unleashed. For those earliest qualifying recruits, the end of their indoctrination consisted of one final and terrifying task before they were considered to be "Soldiers for the Order of Righteousness." If carried out correctly, there was truly no going back from that point.

"It is time for your physical transformations from old to new," Chieftains often explained cryptically, and the recruits were left to anticipate what this entailed. "Once you complete this final step, you shall be free of the constraints that plagued your former selves, including your names and physical forms, and as a result of such purification, all traces of your so-called humanity shall be shed in light of your newly idealized likeness to Pegmatite."

When the time came for this to occur, groups of recruits were systematically divided up and escorted, two at a time, into secret caves deep within their given territories. For those who made it to this point, the halls and chambers that greeted them were dark and brooding, echoing in their resonance, with textured surfaces of hardened lava accented by smoldering pockets of fiery light that peeked from behind the cracked walls like red veins. In addition to the crackling sounds of unseen fires, periodic screams howled from every direction, permeating the halls at a trembling speed. If Hell ever needed to expand, these spaces would do just fine.

The recruits were then led past the halls and into a network of smaller rooms. Upon entering these rooms, the first thing they saw were three Chieftains in the center of the space, each perched atop a throne of charcoal-colored rock. The Chieftains, always composed in their posture, looked upon the recruits with somber expressions and a fiery gleam in their eyes.

As the recruits stood mesmerized, a strong white light shone on the subjects. "Remove your clothes," Chieftains ordered. The recruits were then told to look down and observe their human features for one last time. "Sentiment is dead now," they were then informed. Once enough time had passed to let that idea sink in, the Chieftain seated in the center, seemingly the highest ranking of the three based on his animated nature, waved his fingers gently as if to indicate that he was driving the proceedings. With his contemporaries staying seated, the lead Chieftain stood up from his chair and approached the two naked recruits, towering over them.

"What is your sole purpose, my slaves?" the Chieftain asked, his voice echoing throughout the room.

"To serve the order, honorable Chieftain," the recruits replied in unison.

"But why serve the order?"

"So that we are one with Pegmatite, sir."

Satisfied with their response, the lead Chieftain grinned and gestured toward a cage that emerged from the darkness behind the recruits, where two other prisoners were being held. "Wonderful, my slaves, wonderful! Now, I want you to open this cage and free these prisoners," he commanded, his voice still bellowing. The recruits obliged, yanking open the cage door and pulling out the prisoners with force. Now side by side with the frightened captives, the recruits awaited their next order. The lead Chieftain paced as he spoke, while his contemporaries continued to watch from their thrones in relative silence.

"These two prisoners have decided *not* to follow the order as you have," the lead Chieftain said, and stopped in his tracks to look directly at his audience. "Nor have they chosen to accept the will of Pegmatite. Does this make them our friends or our enemies?"

While the terrified prisoners looked around nervously, the recruits faced each other with knowing grins. "They are our enemies," they then replied in unison.

"I see. So what must we do with *any* enemy of righteousness?" the Chieftain asked while his seated colleagues focused on the two recruits, who in turn replied with a statement that had undoubtedly been hammered into their minds.

"Enemies must perish. Righteousness must prevail. Such is the will of Pegmatite."

Satisfied still, the lead Chieftain smiled at his seated peers and each nodded back approvingly. He then returned to his throne, cleared his throat, and gave the recruits one final command. "It is time then, my slaves, to help restore righteousness by laying waste to its enemies."

Then the three Chieftains watched calmly as the four grown men—two recruits and two prisoners—fought to the death. Shadows on the wall depicted swirling motions of figures brutally scratching, kicking, punching, biting, and tearing each other to pieces, while the sounds of grunting, shouting, and screams that only happen when flesh is torn from the body greeted the Chieftains' ears. This continued for several long minutes until the carnage subsided and the two recruits stood over their lifeless conquests.

No going back, indeed.

The Chieftains laughed in shared amusement, gleefully congratulating their newest members.

After a strange calm permeated the hollow darkness all around them, the lead Chieftain then moved into the next phase of the nightmare. "Now you know what it's like to taste victory, and surely, with our guidance, you will taste it again. But before that happens, you must summon this victory into a power greater than your human flesh. Release your wildest rage, I command you, and become the agents of Righteousness that you were meant to be!"

Following this, the Chieftain lifted his right hand to aim it at the two recruits, and they felt a growing tremor in their chests as their muscles began to pulsate, causing them to quiver abruptly. They grabbed their chests with alarm, nearly keeling over from the increasing pain, and as their eyes bulged from their sockets, each recruit howled. The shadows on the wall again revealed animated figures, only this time, ones that contorted into strange new shapes, their proportions stretching to three times the size of normal humans. Their legs, arms, and torsos protruded out, while bending bones let out horrific sounds all their own. Hands and feet morphed into talons, while skin turned gray as ash, seeming to dehydrate. Facial features became devilish, as eyes enlarged and morphed into irregular, glowing red pupils. Noses, ears, and hair all but disappeared or fell off. Teeth, much like the jawbones they were set in, grew into needle-like spikes with piercing tips. Sounds from the bodily transformations bounced hauntingly off the chamber walls, transitioning from abrupt and painful cries to deeper moans, as the recruits' lungs changed shape.

As the transformation neared completion, the pain ceased, and following the event, the two figures stood upright, towering higher yet over the recently dispatched prisoners at their feet.

The Chieftains remained seated and admired the spectacle before them. "Flawed human flesh no more," the lead Chieftain remarked with ease.

And there they stood before their masters, transformed by the twisted goals of a new identity fed by the deceitful tongue of the Chieftains whom they served. All this resulted in a new kind of militaristic monster, something both treacherous and alarming, and remade in Pegmatite's image. It was as if their passions and lusts took hold of them, to the point where hellish disfigurement was the only answer. Slaves no more, or so they thought. In fact, the recruits had become something far worse.

Similar transformative episodes took place all throughout the TERROR Group's hidden territories, and with each new recruit who surrendered their individuality, the order added to the growing number of obedient troops at its disposal. As more lands were conquered, these Soldiers for the Order of Righteousness became the organization's ultimate symbol, pure in intention and dutifully focused on their mission.

The TERROR Group's militaristic muscle couldn't depend on ground troops alone, for Chieftains knew that cities like Manhattan wouldn't go down quietly. So began the authorized creation of a vast and deadly TERROR Fleet to help carry out the order's ultimate vision. Infused with Pegmatite-rich stone fragments that had been secretly smuggled off Manhattan Island following the assault on Lady Liberty and "The Great Banishment," the very steel used to construct the new mechanical army was further transformed using dark magic associated with Pegmatite himself. It was a recipe that directly foiled Manhattan's towering giants in terms of their own supernatural origins, used here with a more sinister intention in keeping with Pegmatite's destructive ways.

What resulted was the design of three ultra-durable attack vehicles, ranging from stealthy TERROR Cruisers, building-toppling Cyclops Bots, and a spine-chilling series of lava-spewing hovercraft known as Death Rays.

The smallest crafts in this lineup, but lethal nonetheless, single-manned TERROR Cruisers were designed to lead the charge into enemy territory with calculated effort from the skies above. Only the best of the TERROR Group's Soldiers were selected to pilot these swift airships, to ensure a strong initial attack that would then set up the TERROR Fleet's next assault, its terrestrial offensive.

The towering Cyclops Bots were designed to lead that phase of the assault, and they acted as monstrous mechanical representations for the TERROR Soldiers operating inside them. Standing nearly four hundred feet tall, Cyclops Bots' large, hulking bodies were supported by two thin legs with taloned feet. Their insect-like mechanical heads functioned as cockpits that featured a single, giant red "eye" that was bright enough to strike fear in the hearts of opponents from any distance. While formidable in appearance, their destructive power came from a pair of bright-blue glowing arms, capable of releasing energy so powerful that they could level their target in seconds. Often dispersed in groups of five to ten, the Cyclops Bots were intended to obliterate objects many times their height with a single show of force.

If TERROR Cruisers and Cyclops Bots weren't enough to paralyze any enemy, the Chieftains had one last key player in their arsenal, and those were the Death Rays. The devil-ray-shaped hovercrafts, composed of the same Pegmatite-rich steel as Cyclops Bots, sported a pair of red, reptilian eyes and had two primary tasks. The first was to transport Chieftains and soldiers, the second to cover conquered territories with a quick-hardening lava that burned through the ground to form new caves and corridors, readying it for immediate occupation.

In just three months following its initial design phase, the TERROR Fleet was ready to carry out what was envisioned as a slow but sure manifestation of Pegmatite's will over the planet.

"All the pieces have fallen into place now," one Chieftain remarked to his peers at the sight of the new mechanical creations towering over them, waiting to be activated. "In time, let them go forth to do Pegmatite's bidding."

And go forth they did, systematically sweeping through villages and settlements with largely unnoticed fury over many months, reducing landscapes to ash in the process, and taking full advantage of the fact that most parts of the world were not as technologically developed as Manhattan. All the while, the order remained extremely elusive and difficult to track by intelligence agencies and other networks. Such elusiveness, coupled with the tactical patience to lay low for long stretches of time, gave the TERROR Group an eerie edge over its opponents, which it continued to nurture even as subsequent years were hindered by unrelated fascist aggressors, global conflict, economic turmoil, and, particularly for Manhattan, a new generation of towering giants fueled by deep-pocketed Manhattanites whose aspirations were more dizzying than ever before.

With so much going on, the attention-seeking Chieftains knew that any future victories wouldn't get the attention they deserved from the media, which led the TERROR Group to patiently hibernate until the planet sorted out its other troubles.

"I've got some questions for you, Bill. We've seen what Manhattan's towering giants are capable of so far, but could they ever possess that most human ability to be romantic? And if so, why can't *my* new towering giant do that?" Chrysler Building's namesake owner asked his Architect over a bottle of bourbon and a poker match.

"Well, sir," the Architect said, "it's never quite been done before, buildings falling for each other. It will take careful planning, revisions, Lady Liberty's blessing, the strongest steel with the most Schistian magic we can get our hands on, and th—"

"Yes, great, whatever it takes, Bill," Mr. Chrysler buoyantly interrupted, and took another large gulp of his libation. "I'll leave all that to you. Plan, revise, and get all the blessings you need. Remember, I've got more bucks than there are oysters in the Hudson. That's a lotta oysters, Bill."

"Well, Lady Liberty can't be dazzled by money, so…"

"I know that, Bill! Everyone else could be though. Just throw my cash around and see where it sticks is all I'm saying. Find me the best steel we've got and mix it with as much Schistian magic you can get your hands on."

"Okay, I'll just throw it around then. Business is good I presume, sir?"

"Business is *very* good, Billy. So, you just make it work, ya hear? Give me a building who *loves* and who *is* loved. And while you're at it, make her the tallest damn towering giant in the whole damn city … I'm talking about a real showstopper now!"

"You certainly know what you want, sir," the astute designer replied. "I'll see what I can draw up."

With that, the quest for romantically-minded architecture began. It was just one delirious idea out of many during those high-horse years before the Depression would ultimately force the city to shift its priorities. Such speculative chats between architects and building owners set into motion the phenomenon of towers experiencing mutual love for the first time—making the link between humans and buildings even closer.

From the moment her shadow first loomed over the city, Chrysler Building's physical form alone was enough to mesmerize legions of human artists, writers, and poets, but there was so much more to her than that. When she awakened for the first time—her steel frame blessed, of course, with plenty of that miraculous Schistian magic—Chrysler Building stretched from her lower to upper floors with casual delight. Gazing about, she heard the gasps that permeated the air from throngs of onlookers as they peeked out the windows of nearby buildings. The crowd's delirium, it seemed, had already set in.

"Well done, Bill. She's an absolute showstopper. An absolute showstopper!" her proud owner boldly proclaimed from within Chrysler Building's gleaming crown of starburst walls and triangulated windows, as his Architect stood nearby, basking in the afterglow of his mighty creation.

"I'm a showstopper, am I?" Chrysler Building said with curiosity as she overheard her owner's praise. "If you say so. And thank you, everyone! I'm most grateful for this kind reception." The building paused to take in the applause and noticeable whistles emanating from the streets and buildings all around, a reaction that further stroked her ego.

"You seem to rejoice at my slightest gestures," the tower noted while she seductively surveyed her new home. As Lady Liberty looked on with approval, many other buildings stood by with transfixed admiration for the Art Deco beauty.

Perhaps their trance could be traced to the fact that they felt a bit flabby when compared to Chrysler Building's gleaming sheen, which was accented by thin strips of windows that ran up her brick and steel body with sinuously lacey perfection. As the finest example yet of Art Deco to grace the city, Chrysler Building's design blended multicultural motifs and materials into one all-new, rich, expressive *zeitgeist*.

Certainly more visually flamboyant than any building that came before her, it was possible that she'd even outshine any soon-to-be lover's take on the same style. Striking chrome eagle gargoyles on her upper floors, for instance, were both dynamic and eye-catching, but they only hinted at the majesty that was Chrysler Building's topmost crown. Designed as a series of radiating stainless-steel arches, her highest floors were punctuated by rows of triangulated windows that rose along with it, and when the light caught the tower just so, her crown seemed to float above her body with heavenly splendor. Whether she glimmered in the morning sun or became illuminated at night by her neon lights, Chrysler Building was a wonder to behold at any time of day. Given her Owner's desire to capture romance in a bottle, no building ever looked the way she had before, and the starstruck crowd was something Chrysler Building fully embraced from day one.

Following the dizzying reaction that accompanied Chrysler Building's debut, her need for engagement and pleasantries with others was in order. Aware of Chrysler Building's romantic nature, and intrigued by it, Lady Liberty jumped at the chance of introducing her to potential candidates that could win the tower's heart.

"It is time to meet your cohorts." the green lady announced as she introduced Chrysler Building to a host of fellow towering giants, each more anxious than the next to greet her.

First up to the plate was Rockefeller Slab, another soaring Art Deco contemporary born just weeks prior, with a more chiseled and streamlined design. He moved up hastily and gazed upon Chrysler Building's shimmering crown with immediate attraction. "It's a special pleasure to meet you. I hope we'll be able to interact often," the media-savvy tower said.

"Now, I don't want to influence you, but he's a real keeper, that one," Mr. Chrysler opined from inside his tower's crown, aware that such a towering union would mean headlines galore for his business empire. "Just imagine it! Chrysler and Rockefeller ... a match made in architectural heaven!" he said to his Architect.

"How 'bout it?" Rockefeller Slab said anxiously, expecting Chrysler Building to immediately return the compliment. But contrary to her Architect's intent, the new tower was proving to be a free-thinking rebel from the get-go.

"The pleasure's mine, Rockefeller Slab. I'll think about it, for sure. Now, if you'll excuse me," she said with a certain coolness before moving on to the next building with equal aplomb. Lady Liberty had no choice but to move along with her, while Mr. Chrysler and his Architect stood by, flabbergasted.

"Oh, uh, certainly," Rockefeller Slab replied, his shock apparent but irrelevant.

The next to greet Chrysler Building was St. Patrick's Cathedral, whose large stained-glass windows caught the tower's attention as she took in their stylized depictions of human hands holding green clovers and other unfamiliar yet intriguing scenes. Scholarly by nature, St. Patrick's Cathedral entertained Chrysler Building with exploits from the city's storied past as they spoke. She even learned that the cathedral's bell towers, once among the tallest markers on Manhattan's skyline, featured bells that still rang at the stroke of each hour. "Not to signify the passing of time, though," the cathedral maintained, "but rather, to welcome times ahead."

While they spoke, other sacred houses greeted Chrysler Building with equal reverence. First came Masjid Malcolm Shabazz, then Central Synagogue, followed by Trinity Church.

"These sacred buildings hold a special place in Manhattan's heart," Lady Liberty noted with pride. "Our city has room for followers of Allah, Buddha, Christ, Schist, Shiva, Yahweh, and, well, most others."

Chrysler Building sensed that each of them proudly wore the badge of their particular faiths. But that was a love of a different variety, she deduced.

As she processed the green lady's statement, Chrysler Building also couldn't help but remain curious. "This sounds incredible, indeed. But I'm sorry, Lady Liberty, did you say 'most' others? Whose followers are not welcome here, I wonder?"

"Easy one. That would be Pegmatite's followers, those bastards," a booming voice added, and surrounding buildings turned in attention.

"Oh dear, here we go. More about that later, Chrysler Building. For now, allow me to introduce one of our more *boisterous* emissaries," Lady Liberty noted with a playful tone as she gestured toward UN Building, whose flagpoles now displayed a multitude of banners and symbols from sister nations far and wide. From his appearance, Chrysler Building could see how the diplomatic tower's design differed considerably from her own Art Deco style. As they interacted, Lady Liberty explained how UN Building had been created some time ago as an International Modernist symbol for the city.

"And with international modernist intent, mind you!" UN Building reaffirmed. His specialty being tough but well-intended dialog, Chrysler Building learned that UN Building was born out of a desire for greater cross-cultural understanding and diplomacy; relevant attributes for sure, but not necessarily up her alley. "The planet's a mad, mad place sometimes, Chrysler Building. I'm here to help it from getting too far off track," UN Building summarized with a sense of pride in his tone.

"Well, it sounds like truly daunting stuff, indeed!" Chrysler Building said.

"Oh it is, but he does a fine job!" Lady Liberty added. "He is actually a very good diplomat, and we are lucky to have him. Those flags do not lie. But aside from all that, he is very funny!"

Lady Liberty stopped herself after that last point, sensing from Chrysler Building's body language that her sales pitch simply wasn't sticking. So, following the spirited and concluded interaction with UN Building, the green lady became more desperate as she scanned the lineup of remaining buildings, wondering if perhaps the highly cultured Guggenheim Museum could be the one to light Chrysler Building's romantic fire.

"He's very wonderful, but a bit too short for my taste, for one," Chrysler Building soon admitted, much to everyone's chagrin.

Next, Puglia Ristorante tried his best to charm the Art Deco tower just as he'd done many times over for human lovers young and old, with his red, white, and green façade enticing all to enter with empty stomachs and leave stuffed to the gills. But alas, no dice.

As the meet and greet strained along, Chrysler Building came next to the dubious and divisive Wall Street Tower, who, given a powerful career in high finance coupled with his current mayoral duties to the other towering giants, displayed a certain narcissism in his voice and mannerisms.

"Trust me, as both a mayor and a financial guru, I've dealt with some of the most beautiful and exotic things over the years, so those qualities are not new for me. But as I look at you now, I see that nothing matches your glistening beauty. I'm damn sure about that, my dear," the column-and-pediment-clad building boasted.

Right off the bat, Chrysler Building knew better than to get intimate with such a building type, and Lady Liberty was secretly relieved to know that those two hooking up probably wasn't in the cards.

"Well, nobody's ever compared me to an exotic thing before," Chrysler Building replied with a dash of sarcasm, her fire still unlit.

"Okay, I think we should move on," Lady Liberty said as she quickly introduced Chrysler Building to the last assortment of towering giants in wait, including Metropolitan Life Tower, Sony Building, Citicorp Center, Apollo Theater, several neon-tinged towers of Times Square, and finally, that curious creation called Ladder Tower.

Perhaps the most bizarre looking of all buildings, Ladder Tower's architectural features were particularly avant-garde, even for a city as stylistically diverse as Manhattan. Chrysler Building couldn't stop gazing at Ladder Tower's long, brass-clad exterior that resembled a giant insect antenna, coupled with his out of place cathedral-like entryway, and she noticed the tower's mysterious glowing red orb, way up top, accessible only from a rickety ladder that spiraled around the building's exterior.

"That red orb of yours must be quite the tourist attraction, yes?" Chrysler Building asked in an attempt at casual conversation.

"My red orb and I are one and the same. My red orb is for me to know and others to wonder about," Ladder Tower replied cryptically, while an inevitable awkward silence followed.

"That's, um, interesting. Well then, good luck with everything," Chrysler Building offered with slight embarrassment in her tone.

Lady Liberty stepped in yet again. "Ladder Tower is quite the unusual one, right?" the green lady said, desperate to encourage some kind of romantic progress.

"Oh, quite unusual for sure, a little *too* unusual for my taste, I'd say. But it was certainly nice meeting you, Ladder Tower," Chrysler Building determined with as much politeness as she could muster, but ready to move on.

Given the totality of lukewarm assessments, it became clear to Lady Liberty that neither Ladder Tower, nor *any* of the other towering giants present, possessed what was needed to make Chrysler Building's heart skip a beat. Despite Lady Liberty's best efforts, Manhattan's tallest building would stay single for the time being. Nevertheless, she embraced her title as the tallest towering giant to grace the city's skyline.

"I suppose we'll have to wait a little longer before we bust out the champagne, eh, boss?" Mr. Chrysler's Architect observed as evening drew upon the city and their twinkling new tower.

"I suppose we must," the mellow millionaire conceded, his dream only half complete. "For now, anyway. But hey, at least we've got the tallest one out of the bunch. We'll drink to that, Bill!"

Records were made to be broken, of course, and just ten months following Chrysler Building's glitzy and glamorous arrival, Empire State Building's first glimpses of life evoked adulation from Manhattanites as they strained their necks like never before to take in his towering profile.

Taking his first breaths, expectation and anxiety greeted him right from the start, for unlike the bucolically rustic version of Manhattan that Lady Liberty had been born into forty-five years earlier, or the dreamy days of the so-called Skyscraper War that had welcomed Chrysler Building just ten months prior, the city that greeted Empire State Building was riddled by an economic depression of unprecedented scale.

And while it gripped the nation and planet at large, it was a particularly bleak event for Manhattan itself. Manhattanites and their towering giants were the ones to suffer the worst, as misguided stock market calculations and greedy aspirations sent the city into a financial abyss just days after Chrysler Building's birth. Nearly overnight, new building construction dried up as fast as jobs had, and as a side effect to the financial turmoil, a sudden sense of purposelessness permeated in and around the living skyline. Even Lady Liberty was powerless to stop the dire situation.

This was why, the green lady recalled as she stared up at Empire State Building, from day one of his construction, tremendous expectations were placed upon him, and his creation was heavily documented. Week after week, while she and the other buildings watched anxiously, so too did waves of media personnel and spectators, who crowded the streets below in feverish anticipation of Empire State Building's birth. Everyone, it seemed, wanted a glimpse of their next "tower of tomorrow," as the press so hopefully hyped him to be.

Such anticipation, however demanding, was nevertheless embraced by many who saw Empire State Building as a savior who would spare them from further misery. As such, nearly every aspect about his creation was dissected and interpreted by the eager public. The numbers relating to his design were staggering: 57,000 tons of Schistian-infused steel, 450 tons of aluminum, 200,000 cubic feet of flexible exterior limestone, 100 stories of leasable office space, and sixty-six elevators. From his cylindrical base to the tip of his soaring spire, Empire State Building was born to stand an astonishing 1,450 feet tall. Even Chrysler Building had no other choice than to look up like everyone else, while her brief reign as world's tallest came to an end.

"Don't worry, sweet pea, he'll get us out of this gloomy time for sure," one mother said to her child from the street below on the day of Empire State Building's birth. Lady Liberty, overhearing that remark and others like it, sensed the air thick with expectation, and couldn't help but wear a look of concern on her face as a result. Straining her neck to gaze upon this "tower of tomorrow," she trembled at the thought that so many of her contemporaries expected Empire State Building to single-handedly rid the city of the Depression's nasty grip.

"Let us give him room to awaken," the statue said to an anxious crowd of people flashing cameras, while curious buildings huddled in a bit too closely. "Can you see us, Empire State Building?" she asked him, to which the new tower contorted a bit and rose higher still until he became, without question, the tallest among them.

"I ... I can hear and see you," he proclaimed as he surveyed the audience of humans and towers. Upon hearing those first words, the crowd erupted in boisterous applause, and from their reaction, Empire State Building sensed that he held some kind of importance to them. Such feelings had an instant and profound impact on the building's psychological makeup, which could explain why his life would be forever marked by an obligation to lead and protect, no matter the cost.

Like others around her, Lady Liberty admired both the earnestness as well as the sturdy design of this brand-new towering giant; qualities that would aid him greatly, she foresaw. "You have quite a presence, Empire State Building, and a strong one at that," the green lady said, not losing sight of the fact that Manhattan's *other* tallest towering giant was still seeking a mate.

Formidable as he was, many in the crowd admired his broad-shouldered appearance which seemed classically masculine for a skyscraper. Others took note of his uniform window "rings" that rose up Empire State Building's tubular façade in rhythmic fashion. The design terminated at the top with a series of recessed setbacks which were capped off by a soaring, lit spire that doubled as an antenna. As a potential mayoral prospect to serve Manhattan's towers down the road, it made sense to all that Empire State Building's Art Deco appearance be more toned down from Chrysler Building's aesthetic, which lent a more sturdy feel to the former's design.

After coming to terms with his existence and later as he greeted some contemporaries like UN Building, Empire State Building became increasingly aware of the hardships the city was facing. Aside from the eager crowds, the tower's first impression of Manhattan was that the city looked, smelled, and behaved quite badly. And his assessment was on the money, as he would soon be briefed about the financial hardships facing most Manhattanites, many of whom had lost everything to the fickle stock market. Inevitably, he was told, such financial detriment meant a domino effect on general civic upkeep.

As a result, buildings cracked and leaked when they moved, maintenance crews worked in limited capacities or sometimes not at all, and garbage bags piled up on the streets to heights that almost rivaled the buildings they came out of. Crime and disease spiked in the face of such unrest, too, while the number of unemployed Manhattanites grew by the day. And as fed-up Manhattanites frantically recalled or reshuffled their elected officials, Manhattan's building population also yearned for new governmental representation.

For years leading up to the Depression, Wall Street Tower, a short in stature but otherwise domineering financial structure, presided as the longtime mayor to the buildings. Initially voted in because he was designed to understand the city's hard-to-navigate stock exchange, his otherwise tone-deaf leadership skills and distant demeanor led him to focus on everything else but the buildings he was supposed to serve. While adored by elite Manhattanites who felt their money to be in good hands, nearly everyone else, including most buildings, complained often during his divisive tenure, despite his frequent assurances to Lady Liberty that he remained the best tower for the job. With the onset of the Depression, though, the joke finally wore thin, and Wall Street Tower struggled more than ever to keep a tight leash on the buildings he was supposed to be governing. Seizing upon this, agitated towers with nowhere else to turn heartily sounded Lady Liberty's calls for new construction and better leadership.

Such were the strenuous circumstances that greeted Empire State Building's arrival, and with a recall election very much in the cards, buildings expected a strong showing out of any potential successor. His design allowing for such instinctual desires, Empire State Building was game to contend.

"Why do workers within me grumble that they've got little to feed their families with? Why are there so many bread lines dotting the streets below us? Why does every other tower I talk to groan about how vacant their floors have become? Too many questions and not enough answers. I really don't like what's going on around here, Lady Liberty. There's gotta be a way to lift everyone's spirits. How could I help?" he remarked to the green lady days after he came to life.

Lady Liberty, ever the spiritual sage, kept up her longstanding tradition of having one-on-one sessions with each new towering giant following their birth, in order to assess their feelings and to get a sense of their aspirations. During their first such session, Empire State Building's proactive statements resonated with the green lady, and she related to his mindfulness of the city's pulse. "What did you have in mind?" she asked.

"Well, I'd love nothing more than to call a citywide meeting to try and tackle some concerns. Can I do that?" he replied.

"We think alike, you and I. The only difference is that you were designed to handle these matters from a political standpoint, and

I was not," Lady Liberty said. "However, you can call meetings so long as they are unauthorized, since only UN Building and current mayors are allowed to hold official gatherings. I trust UN Building will have no problem with it, but our mayor on the other hand..."

"I see. Then I guess I'll just have to get this mayor on board too," Empire State Building replied. Lady Liberty's expression went from empathetic to incredulous in the blink of an eye.

"Wall Street Tower will not budge, unfortunately, and I cannot enforce that he do so, given his original design intent," she admitted. "But if you call a meeting, unauthorized as it may be, I know buildings will come to hear you out. I will help summon them to attend, too."

Heeding the green lady's advice in the coming days, Empire State Building went to work trying to inspire his fellow towering giants to see past their present-day problems. "Things are rough around here, but I know that we can combat the ravages of this Depression if we approach it logically," he preached to a modest crowd during his first unofficial meeting. "To start, I suggest we push for a general city-wide scrub-down of each and every tower, so that we look our best despite our current conditions. From there, I'll work with each of you in formalizing a plan to get us out of this economic downturn as quickly as possible. I'm calling it the Manhattan Infrastructure Plan, and I think it can succeed."

As Empire State Building held more of these unofficial meetings, an increasing number of down-and-out buildings tuned in. By his fourth "fireside chat," as they came to be called in the press, he began attracting the likes of UN Building, who roundly supported his ideas for civic reform, and Rockefeller Slab, who began broadcasting his messages directly into Manhattanites' living rooms.

"Starting tomorrow," Empire State Building said during one such meeting, "I'm pitching the strategies we've laid out in our past few chats to both Wall Street Tower as well as Manhattan's human leadership, with the aim of setting them into motion. I will also formally back the long-languishing initiative that all buildings older than ten years of age receive thorough maintenance and top-to-bottom retrofitting with the latest technological upgrades, so that we can fully compete when tomorrow's economy comes knocking. This would also put plenty of Manhattanites to work, so let's get this going!" he proposed, with growing support.

But as Lady Liberty correctly anticipated, Wall Street Tower was having none of it. "You want me to meet with him and discuss this, Lady Liberty? No can do, sorry. I mean, who does this new kid on the block think he is? What the hell kind of a building did you approve to be built, with all due respect to Schist or whatever? Your new tower's destined to drive us off a financial cliff!" the vain mayor scolded, using every effort he could to avoid the real elephant in the room—his own shoddy leadership.

"We seem to be halfway off that cliff already, Mr. Mayor," Lady Liberty retorted, her tone indicative of her disappointment with Wall Street Tower's handling of the situation. "Besides, I believe that Empire State Building is well intentioned. If you would just talk with him, there could be serious bilateral solutions for us."

But Wall Street Tower remained skeptical. "Oh really?" he chided. "He's advocating for city-wide scrub-downs, retrofits, upgrades to even the lowest-income apartments and the like. Does he have any idea what these things are going to cost, Lady Liberty? And how dare he go against my preset vetoes!"

"Well, again, I believe in his intent," she added sternly.

"You do, huh? Then, go! Support him. But I tell you, I will never support this fourteen-hundred-foot-tall fiend, do you hear me? He will *never* get the votes to override my arrangements, I'll see to that. I have friends all over ... Many, many friends," Wall Street Tower stood taller. "Now, you tell Empire State Building that he's playing with fire," he barked.

"What happened to you?" Lady Liberty asked, feeling miserable as she walked away from her unshakable opponent.

As the Depression only continued to intensify in the weeks ahead, so too did the back-and-forth between the two warring architectural ideologies; one being Wall Street Tower's one-percent approach to the problem, the other a "fair share" philosophy as argued by Empire State Building and his growing constituency.

True to his combative nature, Wall Street Tower vetoed all new proposals drafted against his current policies. "In the name of fiscal priority," he said to his dwindling base of former millionaires, "by no means will we ever invest our precious dollars into anything else but the market itself. Building upkeep is a choice, not a right, and our own upkeep is trivial compared to the ebbs and flows of the market! Don't believe me? Well then, just look at how I keep myself so well-groomed, and I *certainly* don't need handouts."

Despite Wall Street Tower's grumblings, growing public support of Empire State Building and his Manhattan Infrastructure Plan meant that Lady Liberty and the other towers finally had the momentum they needed to override the mayor's tone-deaf delays, and to get their measure on a recall ballot for all Manhattanites to consider supporting.

"With respect to our current mayor and his strategy," Empire State Building countered during his latest press conference, "Wall Street Tower's got it backwards. Building upkeep is a *right*, not a choice, and we should invest in improving ourselves now, so that we open the door to future investors and tenants who want to start new businesses without having to worry about extra distractions. Morale and momentum are a winning combination for any startup business, and throwing our precious dollars back into a corrupt and insecure market is irrational."

Empire State Building's words were reaching a growing number of legislative ears, and given the options, his plan soon won out. Just four weeks later, Manhattanites overwhelmingly voted in favor of spending emergency dollars to approve the infrastructure measure, the hope that buildings would regain their pride by housing new startups within their walls.

In a matter of days following the approval, plumbing, sewage, and electrical systems were retooled across the city, building façades repaired, and the skyline started to gleam more brightly again. Soon enough, the transformation gave Manhattan much-needed national notice, with relief aid trickling back into the city at rates not seen since the days before the Depression took hold. While a long road ahead remained, Manhattan was on a path to recovery, and for his part, Empire State Building was just what the city had needed to get back on track.

Lady Liberty put it best. "Your actions have helped tip the axis away from Wall Street Tower's sordid and self-serving mismanagement, my friend," she told him on the day that the Manhattan Infrastructure Plan was resoundingly approved by Manhattanite leadership. "You did a very good thing."

Given his early political victory, Empire State Building's relationship to the buildings and people of Manhattan took on a more personal meaning to him, and he further embraced his role as the last great towering giant from this very tumultuous period. In fact, so honored was he to be a part of Manhattan's skyline that he often switched out his topmost floodlights to signify his mood or any number of historic occasions important to the city. Red, white, and blue, for instance, evoked national pride, while blue on its own could signify anything from mournfulness to diplomacy to religious observance. Red and green represented citywide holidays like Christmas, while green by itself signaled the advent of spring. On and on it went. Thanks to such chameleon-like lighting, Empire State Building's role as a visual exclamation point on the skyline was established.

Even beyond his image, though, it was apparent to many that the tower understood the heavy burden placed on his shoulders by the unprecedented Depression.

"As we press on together," he announced to onlookers at the first press conference since the approval of his plan, "I won't be just another sideline tower who forgets your problems. Rather, my words and actions will be *driven* by those problems, and I will work with you, while also expecting you to work with me."

True to his candor, the building followed up the early triumph of the Manhattan Infrastructure Plan by working directly with Lady Liberty, UN Building, and other towers to redefine the roles each of them played for the city's people, eventually pushing for every building to provide a certain amount of housing for evicted or displaced Manhattanites while maintaining their original responsibilities. And much like his first legislative triumph, this idea took hold without the official support of Wall Street Tower.

Despite the current mayor's ongoing public dismay, dialogue between humans and buildings was closer than ever. Everyone stepped up accordingly, even as the Depression raged on. To average Manhattanites, it seemed like jobs were being created from out of the smallest corners and cracks of the city. Because of this, the buildings that housed jobseekers maintained a sense of purpose in their own daily lives. Lady Liberty and others assessed the mood of their fair city on a regular basis, and a greater sense of community seemed to be in place despite the lingering challenges. The heroic aura Empire State Building emitted in his first few months was evident in everything he supported and argued for. Since he truly put the city and its buildings first and found a better way to relate to them, he won the respect and admiration of his peers on a near-unanimous level.

"His designers did a fine job. I sure wish he was our mayor!" UN Building remarked openly whenever asked by the press, echoing the general public's sentiment about their mighty new tower while not missing a chance to throw some shade in Wall Street Tower's direction.

And yet, despite all the raging complexities that the Depression incurred upon their city, and aside from her genuine admiration for Manhattan's new tower, a dogging thought often reentered Lady Liberty's mind during this time. For while Empire State Building became more comfortable with his civic and political duties, it remained to be seen if he was capable of any romantic achievements. *I wonder if he will finally be the one for her*, the statue pondered silently.

Lady Liberty's speculation, while worth entertaining, was definitely a longshot scenario given the rivalry between the city's two biggest structures and their owners. During her brief reign as the tallest towering giant, Chrysler Building basked in the limelight as not only the victor of the Skyscraper War, but also as the most *eligible* tower on the skyline. Rarified air, indeed, at least until Empire State Building came along.

On top of that, Empire State Building's design team tried to upstage Chrysler Building's reputation any way they could. For instance, many recalled the time leading up to Empire State Building's birth, which was an event so amplified in the media that pictures of his construction lived on as a symbolic celebration of the enduring *might* of the city. As the Depression kicked in, Manhattanites admired public service announcements describing how Empire State Building's creation employed so many of those who would otherwise have been waiting on bread lines. Buildings, meanwhile, saw the tower as some kind of legend before his own time, even as Manhattan sunk deeper into financial ruin.

Meanwhile, rather than being personally financed by just one owner as in Chrysler Building's case, able financiers were so eager to see Empire State Building rise that they contributed millions of their own dollars toward his creation. All of this was to ensure that the tower, as one article put it, "did his part in saving us all." Given such efforts, combined with his out-of-the-gate heroics, Empire State Building's actions meant that the Depression remained a stubborn yet slightly manageable problem for both Manhattan and the nation at large.

"As if we don't have enough problems right now," UN Building said on the morning of his next scheduled briefing with Lady Liberty and several others. "I've got news from overseas about that conflict we've been tracking. It appears to be getting much worse. Now, I just informed the mayor of this too, along with Manhattanite authorities, that the President's House is sending more troops to the battlefields this week."

"I see. That national order will include many Manhattanites," the green lady said while Empire State Building and Rockefeller Slab looked on.

"Almost undoubtedly," UN Building agreed.

"Is this that TERROR Group I've heard about from time to time?" Empire State Building asked.

"No, my friend. We haven't heard from them for a while as they've been hiding out for years. They may not even exist anymore. This one's something else entirely that we've been tracking for a few weeks," UN Building said.

"I see."

"Equally as menacing though!" UN Building added, referring to reports of non-TERROR-Group-related conflicts kicked off by a far-right fascist party that had invaded various overseas cities—events that dominated headlines as of late.

"Thank you for the updates. Rockefeller Slab, please distribute this news to our buildings. In the meantime, we will stay vigilant," Lady Liberty said.

In the weeks ahead, the foreign events escalated into what became known as the Modern Global War. While this conflict eventually helped bring an end to the ongoing Depression, it also forced the very architects, engineers, and designers responsible for Manhattan's rebounded skyline to exclusively create objects of defense for the entire nation. Wartime manufacturing reawakened the city's economy, as factories and other buildings were put to work serving as venues for the creation of everything from munitions to tanks and aircraft. At the height of this wartime economy in Manhattan, Empire State Building's leadership continued to be a welcome presence for the city. Coordinating tirelessly with UN Building, Lady Liberty, and Manhattanite representatives, the city's tallest tower sharpened his reputation as a safe and secure voice in an otherwise uncertain time and gained what Wall Street Tower had failed to—trust from his peers. In turn, Empire State Building inspired them to not only overcome the last traces of the Depression, but to also ride through the Modern Global War with relative confidence.

Amid immense global events at play, time and circumstance were what ultimately made Chrysler and Empire State Buildings go from rivals to romantic partners, and even kindred spirits, for while Chrysler Building was never as fully engrossed in the political workings of the city, she was far more apt at social affairs than Empire State Building could ever be.

While most agreed that Chrysler Building remained the more visually scintillating of the two, she'd just have to get used to sharing the spotlight with her taller rival. Despite any initial enmity this provoked, there was also something special about him, or so Chrysler Building came to feel.

Their first meaningful encounter happened at an official Manhattan Building Conference. Created just after the start of the Modern Global War, these weekly gatherings were moderated by UN Building as a way for the city's towering giants to come together and share any wide-ranging concerns they had about the conflict and its ongoing impact. Notably, this was also the first conference immediately following Empire State Building's latest political victory.

Lady Liberty excitedly broke the news to him several hours earlier. "The votes of the recall election have been tallied, and they overwhelmingly declare you as our next mayor. Congratulations, my friend!"

With this sudden changing of the guard, along with a plethora of economic and wartime topics to be addressed, the conference was understandably jam-packed with attendees. As was customary for mayor-elects, Empire State Building spent the first few minutes greeting Lady Liberty, UN Building, Rockefeller Slab, St. Patrick's Cathedral, and other buildings in attendance.

Just as speeches were set to commence, Empire State Building happened to notice Chrysler Building as she arrived fashionably late and with no shortage of reluctance in her pace.

Wow, I can't believe she actually came, the tower thought as he continued to glance in her direction, before abruptly turning back to face the proceedings. It was just obvious enough to earn the attention of Lady Liberty, who stood nearby.

"Okay, everyone, quiet down," UN Building announced to the crowd, who seemed abuzz with adrenaline. "As we begin our latest Manhattan Building Conference, I'd like to first call Wall Street Tower to the fore."

Caving to tradition, Wall Street Tower—quite hesitantly of course—had to comply with the ritual of publicly acknowledging the peaceful transfer of power from one mayor to the next. "Two days ago, my constituency informed me that the city decided it's time for a new leader," the outgoing building conceded. "And since that time, Empire State Building's supporters have told me that they've got *just* the tower for the job. Well, my fellow Manhattanites, to them and to you, I can only say that I did the *best* I could. Let's hope that this shining new knight of yours will do the best that *he* can."

Following the remainder of Wall Street Tower's outgoing speech, which brimmed with falsehoods and self-congratulatory remarks, it was time for Empire State Building to accept his new role. In his debut speech as mayor, the new tower inadvertently reminded viewers that he was the *right* building for the *right* time. With an energy that riveted the crowd further, he outlined his strategy for crawling further out of the Depression, while maintaining morale as the rest of the planet engaged in the Modern Global War overseas. At the close of his speech, long-dormant feelings of good cheer finally had a reason to be let loose, and it was apparent to everyone that Empire State Building was in the right state of mind to lead them to long-term renewal. So, despite no lack of potential "gotcha" questions from the hungry press, such as when the city would be back in the clear financially, or how long it would take for buildings to switch back to a pre-wartime economy, the new leader maintained his composure under fire.

"I challenge everyone here, and everyone watching from home, to exercise masterful patience in the weeks ahead, as we navigate the last leg of this crisis through intelligent planning and careful coordination," the tower said with determination, often looking directly at Rockefeller Slab while he spoke, as if asking his media-savvy colleague to stream his words into living rooms across the city as swiftly as possible. "Inaction ends with the outgoing administration," Empire State Building added in a justified dig at Wall Street Tower.

Following his triumphant Q&A session with the media, a fundraising gala for Manhattan's lower-income apartment buildings was held along the city's southern waterfront. Many buildings joined the event, and music permeated the skies above the affair with moonlight melodies. As buildings mingled, it seemed as if destiny had worked in Empire State Building's favor, and he spotted Chrysler Building in a rare moment of solitude.

How is she not being slobbered over by Rockefeller Slab? he pondered, suspicious of the situation. If there was ever a time to make a move, Empire State Building knew this was it. The tower moved in on her slowly, all the while deflecting passers-by with polite disregard. When she turned to notice him, all Empire State Building could do was gaze blankly as everything in his field of vision besides her seemed to blur.

Seeking to end the prolonged awkwardness, Chrysler Building initiated their first conversation, albeit one served with an undercurrent of sarcasm. It had to be that way, she felt, for not only were they encouraged to not get too cozy, but Chrysler Building was also still reeling from the fact that he'd bested her in height. Being seen mingling with such a building wouldn't sit too well with her owner, who, despite maintaining a desire to have his tower fall in love, nursed a bruised ego from no longer owning Manhattan's tallest. Chrysler Building knew she needed to keep her guard up during their chat.

"You certainly promised a lot to these buildings today," she challenged, "but will you deliver, I wonder?"

Empire State Building snapped out of his trance, realizing that the press had nothing on Chrysler Building's intimidating personality, and that engagement with her wasn't as easy as he'd expected.

"Of course ... of course I will," he stumbled. "I mean, I intend to, you know, keep my promises, if that's what you're asking. I think that's what you're asking. *Is* that what you're asking?" Breathing more heavily, Empire State Building took a step back to reclaim his bravado, while Chrysler Building stood patiently. Seeking to save face, Empire State Building had to say *something* to get out of the hole he'd dug. "What I meant to say was that I promised we'd get out of this jam, and so we will," he declared confidently.

But Chrysler Building could never resist a clever retort. "Which jam do you refer to? The Depression, the war, or this conversation?" she toyed.

"Well, I suppose I walked right into that one," he said playfully. Unprepared for Chrysler's ways, and quite turned on for that reason, the newly-minted mayor revealed himself to be far more fragile than his peers perceived. "I apologize for my rambling. I didn't expect our first conversation to turn out this way," he admitted, realizing just how well Chrysler Building could see through him. Such was one of her talents.

He expected her to walk away right then and there, but Empire State Building was shocked to see that Chrysler Building lingered.

For her, perhaps it was Empire State's genuine, albeit imperfect charm that stood out in a sea of arrogant towers. In truth, pomposity never interested Chrysler Building. Nor did power or ego, for that matter. Besides, she was not about to fall for Rockefeller Slab's charm, no matter how the media-savvy tower lusted for her. Even if she and Rockefeller Slab had been seen together at past functions, none of it was ever meant to go anywhere as far as she was concerned, no matter how badly Rockefeller Slab wanted it to.

And he did want it to. They all did. But Chrysler Building yearned for someone with something truly special, and the more she thought about it, the more she came to admire the fact that the building standing right in front of her was created *for the city*, rather than for a corporation or captain of industry. Whether or not she admitted it, Chrysler Building was a staunch supporter of altruism. It was this fact that finally set off a spark in her heart—one that allowed her to see past Empire State Building's stutters and stumbles.

Making up her mind, Chrysler Building broke character right then and there. "Could we start over? I realize it took a lot for you to come here and talk to me, and I'm sorry for my rudeness. I have a confrontational way with words at times," she admitted quite uncharacteristically.

Empire State Building, appreciating her sudden candor, eased back into the conversation. "I don't find you rude at all. Your words, I mean. Besides, such criticisms are good practice for my new role!"

Chrysler Building let out a small laugh before leaning in about a hundred feet closer to him. "I suppose you've got me there. You'll likely be dealing with more confrontations than I on a daily basis, anyway," she said.

The two shared another laugh as they moved in closer still, and it was clear that they had no problem keeping their conversation unforced and authentic. Such was a sign that they were becoming more equals than rivals.

"Is it weird to say I feel like I've known you for much longer than is possible?" Empire State Building asked without restraint.

"Not at all. Just don't say that too loudly," Chrysler Building quipped, sensing that something unprecedented was indeed happening between them. She knew it and so did he, yet both wondered if others would just as easily accept it.

Despite the desire for their initial spark to play out naturally, the two towers soon detected whispers from Manhattanites within them, and buildings all around turned to watch their interaction with some alarm.

"They're starting to stare at us, Mr. Mayor," she noted softly.

"Let 'em stare," he replied with newfound liberation.

"But don't you remember who our builders are? They can't stand each other as it is. The last thing they'd want to see are their two prized towers getting on so well," Chrysler Building said as more eyes and windows turned toward them.

"Who cares about any of that?" he protested boyishly.

"I do. We can't keep this up right now," Chrysler Building said, as the two towers instinctually moved apart from one another. Not long after, Chrysler Building was summoned by a group of buildings hoping to socialize, Rockefeller Slab among them. Watching her move away to go greet the others, Empire State Building felt compelled to arrange another meetup, but in private next time.

"Wait. Can we see each other again? Just us?" he called out. The blunt request seemed to float in the air for what felt like an eternity before Chrysler Building granted him a response.

"Why are you asking me that?" she said.

"Well, because I'd like to see you again, that's all," Empire State Building replied honestly.

Motioning to the other buildings to wait for her, Chrysler Building revealed the obvious as she approached Empire State Building once more. "We're supposed to be sworn rivals. You know that, right?"

Empire State Building thought about the question for a moment before replying. "Yeah, I know that. But can I see you again?"

Realizing that it was useless to go against her own romantic instincts, Chrysler Building obliged as she whispered her directive. "Okay. Tomorrow evening. Up across the river from Inwood Hill, there's an access path into the Manhattan Forest."

"I know that area," he said.

"Good. Head about two miles in. The trees and cliffs there are just high enough for us not to be noticed. At seven o'clock sharp, we'll meet. And bring no one within you. Not a janitor, not a security guard, not a soul. Got it?"

Empire State Building nodded just before Chrysler Building hurried to join her friends.

For the rest of the evening, the thought of seeing Chrysler Building alone put an extra pep in Empire State Building's step. When the next day arrived—a Friday no less—he powered through various meetings and press conferences, while his forbidden date with the gleaming beauty remained in the back of his mind. And as the skies over Manhattan surrendered to dusk, he beamed as he saw the moon make its first appearance. At half past five, the building took note of the last handful of enthusiastic Manhattanites exiting out his lobby doors for the weekend.

A half hour later, he felt his maintenance crews empty out too. *They always head out quicker on a Friday,* he happily reminded himself. Once the last of the workers were discharged from his main doors, Empire State Building felt more grateful than ever that he hadn't been designed to be a residential building. He hoped Chrysler Building felt the same way.

As he made his way past Inwood Hill and across the river toward the still-wild Manhattan Forest, Empire State Building was reminded of how much more serene Manhattan's northern areas were compared to the rest of the island. No congestion. No noisy business districts. Just unassuming apartment buildings who largely kept to themselves and generous acres filled with old-growth trees and wilderness. In other words, it was a perfect spot for secret love, or whatever it was that Empire State Building had gotten himself into.

Soon enough, the tower reached his destination past the access path and was in the steepest topographic point of the forest. Almost immediately, the whistling of the wind through the trees combined with the sounds of the nearby waterway cleared Empire State Building's anxious mind. Looking out toward the fast-moving river, with much of his body hidden by the towering old-growth trees, he admired the jagged and rocky cliffs that met the waves with a crashing splash.

"Two opposing forces colliding as one. If they can do it, why can't I?" he said in a low voice. Beyond the cliffs, the tower gazed out at faraway dunes that seemed to multiply forever. An incredible sight, he knew, at the same time acknowledging that his admiration for them paled in comparison to his newfound feelings for Chrysler Building.

The tower waited for a long while, and his mind wandered more. He stretched up his highest floors to look at Manhattan Island's faraway southern tip, barely making out the silhouettes of his friends among the skyline as they prepared for their slumber. He watched while their twinkling lights all switched off one by one, save for a few floodlights. Fearful of being seen by any nosy buildings, Empire State Building followed suit and dimmed his own lights even further. He knew that Manhattan's tranquility mirrored his own. It was his city, his past, and his future all in one. Everything he experienced up to that point had happened on that small, narrow island. But now, as he stepped away from it for a while on this nature-filled escape, the tower felt he was about to add something new to his life.

But at five minutes to seven, his anxieties returned with a vengeance. Was he doing something wrong by falling for Chrysler Building? What if she had feelings for Rockefeller Slab and just wasn't broadcasting it? Even Empire State Building's political instincts grappled with the prospect of Rockefeller Slab turning the media against him in light of this potential soaring affair. What could happen to their reputations if word of this leaked out? What if some random cleaning person was still working inside Chrysler Building when she arrived to meet him, and witnessed this unfolding scandal? Breeze or no breeze, the scenarios jabbed at Empire State Building from all sides while he waited in the woods.

By the time he could rectify all the possible outcomes, however, seven o'clock on the dot arrived and like clockwork, so did Chrysler Building. "She's actually here," Empire State Building quietly uttered, and his negative emotions were washed away by her presence. "And this is actually happening." He watched her curved and gleaming form approach ever closer. The moment was all that mattered now.

Chrysler Building moved in closer still, her triangulated windows dimmed, but her crown still aglow with moonlight as she zeroed in on her subject. She said nothing, and Empire State Building, transfixed by the moment, did nothing to ruin it. Catching a reflection of himself in her polished crown—connection through reflection—he admired Chrysler Building's Art Deco form with growing fervor, lusting in silence but still saying nothing. Restrained and *in control*, as was she. This dance continued for a few moments more, and the distant crashing waves were all either of them could hear.

"Do you feel okay being here with me?" he finally said. Chrysler Building remained silent, but nodded approvingly.

"Me too," Empire State Building continued before adding, "I thought about this moment all day, you know."

Chrysler Building processed his words as she gazed out toward the river. "I hate to admit it, but so did I," she seconded after another long silence, her words providing Empire State Building relief from any nagging speculation. With the ice now broken, he inched in closer.

"Tell me, have you ever been one to experience loneliness?" she inquired.

It was a question that led Empire State Building to revisit the few moments in his brief life that could qualify as such. "I think my public role doesn't allow for much of that. Still, you could say some part of me has been lonely. Sure," he answered truthfully, and Chrysler Building appeared pleased by his response.

"Public roles aside, Manhattan can be a lonely place for any building," she admitted. "Even buildings like us." Her self-reflection provided Empire State Building with a revelation, though he couldn't believe for one second that such a beautiful, flawless figure of architectural royalty could be dogged by something like loneliness.

"I would have never imagined you felt this way, Chrysler Building. You're the shining star of this city. You've got the whole town's reflection in your crown, and I mean that literally and figuratively," he gushed.

Chrysler Building looked away.

"But I can say the same about you, can't I, Mr. Mayor? And yet, here we are, two lonely towers living among a crowded skyline."

"You mean two of a kind?"

"Perhaps," she said.

However they interpreted their situation, it was clear that all preconceptions and biases about what buildings should and shouldn't do faded from their minds. "Maybe being lonely was the greatest thing to happen to us, then," Empire State Building suggested playfully.

"Maybe," Chrysler Building replied, beaming with the idea while her triangulated windows briefly lit up before dimming back down again.

Suddenly, their symbolic bonding turned physical, as their bodies locked together with mutual desire. Following his instincts, Empire State Building slid his upper stories along Chrysler Building's side with unbridled liberation. In response, Chrysler Building's lights flickered uncontrollably, and she returned the favor by swaying across her partner's broad, tubular façade with sensual ease. Gone were any traces of their contentious past. Chrysler Building surrendered any lingering thoughts she had about Rockefeller Slab, and Empire State Building, in turn, did the same.

"What is this strange new sensation that overtakes us?" he asked, sounding ecstatic.

"I don't know, but let's not have it end," she said, and each tower continued to act on their desires.

Many nights like that one followed, always at the close of another work-weary day when the city was dimming its lights, and always with the forest as their secluded backdrop. For a while, these erotic sessions were theirs alone, but seclusion could only last for so long in a place like Manhattan.

In time, word of their unexpected union unleashed all kinds of reactions. Chrysler Building's owner ranted in frustration, flabbergasted by the idea of his tower getting involved with an archrival instead of, say, with a safer bet like Rockefeller Slab. But others embraced the idea.

Lady Liberty, relieved that their union had finally materialized, saw to it to smooth things over in the minds of her colleagues. Besides, the statue had suspected the romance long before anyone else, and her public embrace of it made a world of difference for the budding couple. "It is simple, really. They love each other," the statue said whenever the topic came up. "Who are we to deny them that?"

With the green lady's public blessing, the shock soon subsided. Chrysler and Empire State Buildings grew more comfortable with professing their union, and an increasing number of critics, including Chrysler Building's boisterous owner, came around in their favor. And just like that, life went on as usual in The Wonder City.

Two-and-a-half years following Chrysler and Empire State Building's towering union, the Modern Global War came to a most-welcome end and word reached Manhattan that the fascist powers overseas had finally surrendered. While many other cities were virtually in ruins from the ravages of war, Manhattan remained a largely unscathed urban paradise, its positive morale reinforced by the prospect of becoming a post-war boomtown as Manhattanite soldiers returned victorious from battle. All things considered, Chrysler and Empire State Building's once-scandalous romance wound up becoming just another curiosity in the cosmology of curiosities that made Manhattan unique.

For any given Manhattanite to look up and take in the sights of their fair city was a singular experience, as they'd get to experience a moving skyline of buildings that walked and talked, sharing life and love in the most human-like sense. This reality provoked a feeling of childlike wonder in even the most jaded observer, for these towering giants seemed to reflect every facet of human emotion, leading many to feel that people and buildings were one and the same.

However, in spite of their larger-than-life qualities, this also meant that buildings, like people, could die too. Lady Liberty was always aware of this, but since a building's life span was designed to surpass a human's by many generations, neither she nor any of Manhattan's other towering giants had yet to experience such a loss first-hand. As the post-war era unfolded, this circumstance was set to be tested by a long-dormant threat, neither detected nor thought about for years, that prepared to reemerge with newfound vengeance.

From the moment they first sprung to life, the Twin Towers appealed greatly to the youngest Manhattanites, given that the buildings' size dwarfed any others in sight. They also appealed to the city's super-elite, who equated size with economic might. But to nearly everyone else, from the average working stiff to a building not designed for financial matters, the Twin Towers left a mixed first impression when they came into the world. In fact, in a city that practically deified its tall buildings, there rose a tide of backlash against these two, who like their predecessors Empire State and Chrysler Buildings, were born to rise above yet another economic downturn.

But times had changed since their forerunners first graced the skyline decades prior, and the notion of height no longer defined a building as importantly as it once did. Instead, the latest crop of towering giants now had to showcase a variety of other traits, since the new perception was that the higher they stood, the less concerned the towers were with the people they were designed for. But the Twin Towers came anyway, forty years after the great

Skyscraper War, each seemingly more unwelcome than any other before or since.

Empire State Building was one of many who felt conflicted by news of the Twin Towers' arrival. In a professional sense, he saw them as a chance to pull the city out of its first economic crisis since the Depression, knowing that they were created partly to draw new businesses to Manhattan's shores. But if history was any guide, it taught him that *no* building, no matter how tall or charismatic they were, could harbor enough energy to positively alter an economic situation with the flip of a switch. Now, not one but *two* were expected to try it.

Whether or not the Twin Towers could pull it off remained to be seen, and Empire State Building saw it as a huge gamble. He also foresaw the tightrope the Twin Towers had to walk in order to please other buildings. Manhattan's architectural scene was more crowded than ever by that point, increasingly difficult to manage, and among the most harshly critical to boot. Based on their height alone, Empire State Building knew that these new towers were about to have every eye of judgment cast sharply upon them, scrutinizing their every move. Manhattan was a real gossip column in that sense.

Empire State Building also expected to work with the Twin Towers on all things concerning world trade, and should their strategies be incompatible, or their generation gap too wide, it could add to the latest pressures facing the city rather than alleviate them. This was the nervous but pragmatic side to Empire State Building, who had learned to anticipate problems that hadn't arrived yet. Chrysler Building had been on his case for years about this habit.

His ego, meanwhile, was another matter entirely. After four decades of being Manhattan's tallest towering giant, he now had to hand that title over to the Twin Towers. On a public level, he would show no signs of concern about it, of course, and brush off questions about his feelings on the matter with ease whenever asked. But Chrysler Building knew that, on a private level, her lover was struggling with the idea, just as any Manhattanite might when faced with a midlife crisis.

"Swallow your pride," she often whispered to him. "They could very well turn out to be good friends." As usual, Empire State Building eventually realized what Chrysler Building already knew.

So, despite the city's early grumblings, higher and higher the Twin Towers rose with each new week. First beyond the spires of St. Patrick's Cathedral, then past the shimmering crown of Chrysler Building, and finally, they rose taller than Empire State Building himself, who felt strangely relieved the moment the Twin Towers surpassed him. His role as "world's tallest," for better or worse, was officially behind him.

Crowds were noticeably smaller than in similar times past, but they still gathered in sentimental awe as the Twin Towers took their first breaths on a cool and breezy Tuesday morning. Lady Liberty was present, as were Wall Street Tower, UN, Chrysler, and Empire State Buildings, plus a handful of others. But the noticeable lack of turnout alarmed the green lady, who believed all buildings to be gifts of Schist's good graces, and therefore deserving of proper celebration. Such were the times, however, and rather than get swept away by the Twin Towers' impressive observation decks or their clean, streamlined Modernist designs that lent a whole new stylistic dimension to the skyline, the media seemed more preoccupied by the idea that these twin brothers had come late to the party by about forty years. Resultant grumblings from Manhattanites watching the ceremony came in all varieties.

"They're way too blocky for my taste," one Manhattanite remarked bluntly.

"And they cast so much shadow! God help us in the winter," complained another.

"Can they even *see* us from that height? What an impersonal gesture. Who designed these things, anyway?" questioned yet another spectator in been-there-done-that fashion.

Indeed, the city's negative reaction was just beginning. To her dismay, during their birth Lady Liberty was confronted not by comments of praise from the press, but rather loaded questions such as whether or not the Twin Towers could restore the city to its former glory.

"Former glory is a misnomer, but to entertain such a question, yes, I believe they can ease the tension," she replied patiently. "We are Manhattan, remember? We face struggles big and small, and so, too, will these Twin Towers. They are as special to us as any."

But the public wasn't buying her comments, and for their part, the Twin Towers had to endure unwelcome ridicule from the moment they took their first breaths.

"We're happy to be here and stand among you," they stated graciously, with a form of vocal back-and-forth that allowed them to complete each other's sentences. It was a speech pattern so foreign that laughter could be heard from the unaccustomed crowd.

"I realize they're twin brothers, Lady Liberty, but this is ridiculous. You didn't say they'd be so connected that they can't even speak on their own!" Wall Street Tower lampooned without a trace of good taste, as usual. "I mean, I've seen inanimate bridges smarter than these two!" His observations were rewarded with naughty laughter from the audience.

The Twin Towers' drooped posture indicated their sensitivity to such remarks, and as they turned to look around nervously, more stately towers like Chrysler, Empire State, and UN Buildings stood startled by the cold reception.

"No need to worry, my twin brothers," Lady Liberty cut in as a show of crowd-control. "Some just need to warm up to you, and each will in time, for it is the *respectful* thing to do." The statue directed a sharp glance in Wall Street Tower's direction.

"So you've told us. I guess we'll just wait and see how useful these Twin Towers can be," Wall Street Tower said as he and several others walked off, cutting the ceremony short.

"Why does Wall Street Tower always have to act like an over-privileged fool?" Chrysler Building remarked to Empire State Building under her breath, trying to keep some dignity over the proceedings.

"Nothing changes after all these years," her lover whispered back, shaking his head in equally restrained embarrassment.

As authoritative as they were, Lady Liberty's words in defense of the Twin Towers still seemed powerless against the current mood of the city.

"We don't want to be a nuisance, Lady Liberty," the Twin Towers admitted, following the ceremony.

"Pay such thoughts no mind," Lady Liberty said. "We have an economic storm happening right now, caused by a spike in people leaving the city for suburbs across the nation. It has created a fiscal crisis for our banking systems, which is the *real* nuisance driving such poor behavior, but it is also why we needed to construct you two. Your colleagues will come around, not to worry. For your presence among us is a gift from Schist. Come now, let me begin to acquaint you with your new home."

In the days following their unceremonious arrival, the Twin Towers worked with extra fervor to quell low public opinion. They were, as Lady Liberty noted, created to boost the city's morale from its latest economic calamity, much like Empire State Building had been expected to do in years past. But with the crisis worsening to the tune of a surplus of office space and mounting citywide debt, speculators and the press now had twin targets to heap unfair blame upon. Such actions seemed to place the dire situation almost entirely on the Twin Towers' shoulders, and the tabloids had a field day printing such crude headlines as:

TWIN FOLLIES: CITY'S TALLEST GO LIMP
AGAINST MARKET'S LATEST WOES.

If their Shistian existence itself couldn't shake the recession, perhaps their intellect could.

"Lady Liberty spoke of times like this, Tower Two, but she also said not to lose our moral purpose. We'll find a way to get through to everyone," Tower One said to his downhearted brother after another long day with little to show for it.

"I hope you're right," Tower Two replied doubtfully.

"We will, you'll see," the more upbeat brother continued. "Tomorrow I plan on promoting our highest office floors, which are our most flexible-use spaces. With Lady Liberty's help, we've been cleared to have Rockefeller Slab send out a huge press release to all active real estate agents, and I'm told our owners just secured a meeting with prospective investors and two interested companies who may be willing to lease some floor space from us. After that, we'll follow up with Empire State Building to see if he has time to collaborate with us this week."

As he listened to such prospects, Tower Two juggled feelings of possibility and exhaustion. "That all sounds great," he said, "but I'm so tired. Let's get a good rest and be fresh in the morning."

Despite their best intentions, neither tower could have anticipated just how stubborn Empire State Building was to work with in the coming days, especially on matters regarding free trade and reaching out to other global markets to foster long-distance trade partnerships. Results from their early collaborations were moderately successful at best and forced at worst, especially since Empire State Building went out of his way to exclude the Twin Towers from most building conferences, his still-bruised ego hiding behind the excuse that the newcomers lacked credible experience.

"Listen, the best thing you guys can do right now is focus on leasing out more of your square footage to Manhattanites, okay? Once enough of your floors are occupied, then report back to me and I'll be happy to include you in more pressing discussions. You're almost ready," Empire State Building instructed in an unconvincing fashion.

But Chrysler Building was growing increasingly perturbed by her partner's uncharacteristic disregard, which felt more *Wall Street Tower* in approach than *Empire State Building*. Equally frustrated by the situation was Lady Liberty, who still clung to the hope that the Twin Towers would one day rise to the occasion and win over their agitated city, because in these twin giants, the green lady sensed a genuineness she hadn't felt in new buildings for about forty years.

"You two are *more* than what everyone perceives you to be," the statue encouraged them one evening, sensing their hidden anguish emanating from their home near the southern tip of the island.

"We're doing everything we can to fit in here, Lady Liberty, and yet most buildings still largely avoid us. Why is this so?" Tower One complained, as he and his brother hung their upper floors down in defeat, indicative of another day posted in the loss column.

The situation hurt Lady Liberty's Schistian heart for several reasons, the first being the dire nature of the current climate, the other being the unavoidable trend of Manhattan's towering giants generally being taken for granted by that point, their innovative and mystical qualities all too familiar to their audiences. These realizations were written all over Lady Liberty's countenance as she gazed at the Twin Towers' silhouettes, knowing that despite the best intentions, she and her kind were slowly becoming relics from another age.

The Twin Towers carried the weight of these changing times with immense frustration. While their titanic forms towered over the city, broad-shouldered and seemingly indestructible, their inner thoughts explored the darkest and most fragile existential questions.

"What if Lady Liberty's mistaken? What if Schist was wrong to create us?" Tower Two asked one evening.

"I actually wonder that myself, but it just can't be," his brother replied.

Such weariness was the natural byproduct of being cast into a fractured world that expected overnight results, coupled with the fact that most buildings remained distant toward the Twin Towers, as if not quite sure what to make of them. Lady Liberty, while increasingly careful not to overwhelm the two brothers with false promises, deduced that only one building could be able to help them, whether he wanted to or not.

"I need you to swallow your pride and reach out more warmly to them," a decisive green lady instructed Empire State Building one morning thereafter. "They could use your mayoral guidance."

"It's not about pride, Lady Liberty. I've just been incredibly pre-occupied with things," the former world's-tallest building retorted, sensing that his answer wasn't what the green lady wanted to hear. Chrysler Building soon approached, gazing at her lover with the same sternness that he saw in Lady Liberty's expression. Capitalizing on the intervention-like atmosphere, the statue then reminded Empire State Building of his own past struggles and challenges as a young leader.

"Think about your early days, Empire State, and how you were *expected* to turn things around instantly, but how you had practically the whole city on your side," she argued. "Now, think about what the Twin Towers have to contend with, and how the city is *not* behind them. How frustrating do you think that would feel?"

Empire State Building thought about this disparity for a moment, hesitant to reply but realizing that Lady Liberty was, once again, on the mark.

"She's right, you know," Chrysler Building added before turning to face the green lady. "And one other thing. Empire State Building will be *more* than happy from now on to take the Twin Towers under his wing, Lady Liberty. Won't you, my love?"

Empire State Building took the hint. "You're asking me to swallow my pride," he said. "Well, maybe I can for once. When you're right, you're right. I'll talk with the towers tomorrow and do my best to turn this whole thing around. You both have my word."

Lady Liberty and Chrysler Building knew that their little nudge would be all it took to change his mind, and sure enough, come the next morning, Empire State Building made good on muzzling his pride in order to start building some metaphorical bridges.

As he approached the Twin Towers near the southern tip of the island, there was an air of unease among all parties involved.

"Oh no! Did we miss an appointment, Empire State Building?" said Tower One, before his brother asked with trepidation if there was something they should be working on.

"That's alright, nothing at the moment; it's early in the day yet anyway. But it's gonna be a nice day out, I think," Empire State Building awkwardly replied, hoping to break the ice. "So, I, uh, was asked to come and speak with you two about, well, fitting in here and such. I understand that Manhattan can be a cold place without a little insulation in our walls to keep us warm."

The Twin Towers looked at each other dubiously, unsure of where Empire State Building was going with this.

"Anyway," he continued, "what I mean to say is that I'd like to, well, help guide you two going forward, as a kind of mentor. It's good to have a mentor, as they say. Does that make sense?"

The Twin Towers couldn't help but sway their highest floors from side to side in unified curiosity, as if to weigh the possibilities of such a proposal.

"That ... would be so amazing!" Tower One finally let out, while his brother agreed.

"Okay then, good! Come, let's take a little stroll," Empire State Building offered, his mind somewhat relieved. As they walked, the rest of the towering giants began waking for another day. "Manhattan, you know, is a thriving place with all kinds of wonders besides us buildings," he noted. "You've got Breuckelen to the south, for example, where Manhattanites grow their crops to eat and such. Things like apples, lettuce, cotton—it's all harvested right over there. And look up here, just north of Manhattan Island, where you can see the great Manhattan Forest. That's where our own structural parts— our steel, stone, and wood components—are quarried and collected. Without that forest, and without divine help from Schist, of whom I'm sure Lady Liberty told you about, we just wouldn't be here."

As the three towers made their way about the island, ever mindful, of course, not to step on smaller buildings, streetlamps, or pedestrians below, the Twin Towers began to brim with a newfound curiosity for the city around them. All the while, Empire State Building took extra care in reacquainting them with the buildings they passed, directly defying dubious critics like Wall Street Tower and signaling that the Twin Towers deserved much better from their fair city.

"These are our twin brothers, so let's be good to them from here on out," Empire State Building advocated to towers large and small, as more began to greet them. It was a small gesture that made a big difference, and after a few more mornings of these get-togethers, the childlike wonder that the Twin Towers exuded began to rub off on Empire State Building, taking him back at times to his own youth. Clearly, everyone benefited from their talks.

"You know," Empire State Building admitted one day in a fatherly tone, "for every bad day you might have around here, there's usually two or three really great ones. And the great ones, well, they almost make the bad ones worth it." It was an astute observation that stayed with the Twin Towers, who, while no strangers to rejection, finally had a relatable colleague at their own scale; one who provided a unique window into the worlds of daunting public role-play and civic management.

"How do you not get overwhelmed by hurtful words or deeds?" they asked their mentor with grave concern, to which Empire State Building took his time to give a worthwhile answer.

"First, learn to swallow as much criticism as you both can, which will always be there in one form or another. Also, *always* try to have something to look forward to at the end of a hard day. For me, that certain something is being with Chrysler Building, but it's different for every tower. You'll each find yours in time."

As the three continued to open up over the following weeks, nothing was off limits. Feelings of periodic depression were brought up and discussed outright. The concept of falling in love, too, was dissected, as were topics like relating to Manhattanites versus relating to buildings.

"We have much more in common with humans than you realize. I can't describe it, but I just feel it," Empire State Building said as their bonding continued.

"Here's a story I never tell anymore," Empire State Building shared one morning, recounting the time when a small plane accidentally crashed into his side, killing fourteen Manhattanites and nearly ending his own life. "It was the single most painful thing I ever felt, something I hope no building ever has to endure," he said.

"Will that ever happen to us?" Tower Two asked fearfully, while his brother looked on.

"No, no. Don't worry about any of that. It was a long time ago. We're safe here in Manhattan." Empire State Building nodded in a gesture of confidence.

As a result of their open and honest dialogue, Empire State Building and the Twin Towers grew in ways none of them had anticipated. Even as the city continued to struggle financially, each tower continued addressing problems by day and talking about them together the next morning. Benefiting greatly from this new regimen, the Twin Towers started handling themselves more masterfully in public. They clicked more naturally with random buildings, conducted everyday business more professionally with tenants occupying their floors, and took a page out of Lady Liberty's playbook by occasionally bending down to the streets below for a quick chat with everyday Manhattanites.

Little by little, the city's general optimism was also clicking back on again. Businesses reopened. Housing and employment numbers went up. Foreign and national aid poured back in, and all across the island, buildings long vacant were starting to fill with people once more—fast enough to avoid calling this latest crisis an ongoing recession. Even the Twin Towers, once regarded as unrelatable, unnecessarily tall follies from yesteryear, became active players among the skyline, with office space that was finally leasing at an enviable rate.

But the greatest catalyst came in the form of acrobatics. One morning, the legend of the "Magical Little Man on the Wire" was born. In a bold and brave gesture, this gutsy high-wire artist managed to sneak up to the roof of one of the still-sleeping twin giants, swing a tightrope between them, and walk the line with nothing above or below but sky. It was the kind of moment that was only possible in Manhattan, where dreams often crossed over into reality.

While it was happening, the Twin Towers awoke to a slight tugging sensation, alarmed at first before soon admiring the boldness of such a diminutive daredevil. As the rest of the city began to notice what was happening, a host of Manhattanites piled onto the streets below, and buildings all around were equally transfixed by the spectacle. Amid loud "oohs" and "aahs" from the electrified crowd, the Twin Towers stood their ground with care so as not to sway too severely while the gutsy little artist performed his feat. For forty-five heart-racing minutes, the whole city watched his every turn and acrobatic gesture with wonder. It was said that even Lady Liberty looked on with tears of joy in her eyes. After eight nail-biting passes across the wire, the performer took one last bow in the sky, stepped off the wire and back onto the roof, and smiled as he walked into the waiting arms of police officers.

The event quickly became the stuff of legend, remembered by buildings and Manhattanites alike as one of the greatest moments of dialogue between their scalar worlds. It was also the perfect gesture at the perfect time, for any last criticism of the Twin Towers was soon swept away. And to the relief of Lady Liberty, Chrysler, Empire State Building, and a growing host of others, the Twin Towers were finally seen as role models and friends who added richly to Manhattan's long-standing traditions. They became, as Rockefeller Slab publicly put it, a "new one-two punch of heroic proportion."

So, despite all the early drama, it turned out that their arrival was a great thing for Manhattan, as they added two more stars to the city's enviable constellation. Each of them grew into their roles with the ongoing encouragement of Lady Liberty, Empire State

Building, and others, and the city's latest financial crisis fizzled out completely by year's end. It wasn't long before most felt secure that they had seen their city triumph over yet another obstacle, basking in a prosperity known to few other places once again. All was calm, all was right, and Manhattan functioned as the perfect amalgamation of civility and exchange, at least for the moment.

Skeptics of Manhattan's latest upswing began to wonder how much longer such good fortune could win out. Was there truly no limit to the city's ability to overcome obstacles? As the island rode high on the wave of its most recent renaissance, news that places overseas were once again falling victim to a mysterious menace barely made the evening editions. The threat was enough to spark discussion among those tasked with protecting Manhattan, with words like *national security* and *terrorism* sprinkled into meetings held by the Manhattan Military, the city's premier defense alliance. But their analysis barely grasped the role the city played in the eyes of its enemies, and as a result, long-term security solutions remained vague and hypothetical. With the exception of Lady Liberty's first-hand brush with domestic terror many years back, time seemed to diminish any sense of urgency among Manhattan's other buildings who never experienced such a direct assault. After all, any rumored dangers were over *there,* and not *here,* or so was the common disposition—a troubling sign to the green lady that Manhattan had become too complacent, too insular, and too preoccupied by its own universe.

Elsewhere, creating a militaristic presence was just the first piece of the reawakened TERROR Group's tactical puzzle. In the decade following the birth of the Twin Towers, the order was back to its long-dormant destructive ways, gaining unprecedented and unnoticed momentum across vast swaths of continental landforms.

As its fires raged once again, its *join or die* strategy increased with startling results. For instance, smaller villages and cities, virtually unprotected against the TERROR Group's growing might, surrendered their resources as an act of compromise against their larger foe. But upon such surrender, and despite pleas from village elders, TERROR Group forces unleashed their destruction anyway, killing many and wiping out whole communities without remorse.

Through a series of hostile acquisitions, aggressive pro-Pegmatite fervor, and dishonest deals, the TERROR Group's membership quadrupled, with no signs of slowing down. Despite UN Building's best efforts to establish a global watchdog group over the years, there remained an underwhelming reaction to the horrors transpiring, and it was still nearly impossible to pinpoint the location of the phantom network. But the TERROR Group's fires were indeed spreading in ways not seen since before the Modern Global War, nearly five decades earlier. While the true scope of its grip was a mystery, the latest reports compiled by a handful of analysts within UN Building estimated that the TERROR Group likely controlled up to 244,706 square miles of the planet's known land mass, a number relatively modest compared to the planet's total mass, but alarming nonetheless.

As soon as critics began to question these estimates, the floodgates opened for all kinds of misinformation to circulate through the media, which only meant further inaction and misunderstanding among the masses. Intelligence reports continued to reach higher echelons of Manhattan Military leadership, but it was hardly enough to provoke citywide concern. Weekly Manhattan Building Conferences should've been ripe with talk on the matter, but that, too, wasn't so. UN Building, for one, could only say so much on the issue since he received so little from Empire State Building, who in turn was fed almost nothing from the Manhattan Military. By that point, even Lady Liberty couldn't predict the storm to come, her visions clouded by an overabundance of rumor and speculation.

Manhattan existed in a sort of vacuum in the meantime, with its towering giants, technology, diverse population, and commanding grasp on free trade serving as distractions from any potential horrors that plagued other places.

While the city struggled to grasp its importance as the center of a changing geopolitical landscape, all the way on the other side of the world there existed a small village where a young man lived. One day, this boy, a privileged only child of nineteen and son to the village's wealthiest family, relished his latest acquisition which adorned his bedroom wall. Having pined for this new poster for quite some time, he jumped at the opportunity to secretly purchase it from a friend that morning.

"Do not tell *anyone* where you got this, or we're both dead!" his friend warned once the transaction was complete.

"Yeah, yeah, don't worry. Just give it to me," the young man said impatiently. With the poster now his to enjoy, he couldn't get home fast enough to hang it up in his room and pour over it like some kind of sacred document. Almost immediately, the young man was swept away by its romanticized depictions of four towering giants in all their glory. On the left stood a gallant Empire State Building, his top floors aglow in red, white, and blue. In the center, Lady Liberty held her torch high up in the air, while at right, the radiant profile of the Twin Towers completed the composition with soaring majesty. The boy processed the bold proclamation that hovered at the top of the poster, as if ready to jump off the paper:

MANHATTAN: THE WONDER CITY

The poster's combination of words and imagery alluded to a place vastly dissimilar from the village the young man knew, for his was still a world of small-scale, inanimate buildings, a modest human population, and an economy still driven by bartering and handshakes. It was a place where the tallest buildings were no more than two stories high, and where news was given life by actual storytellers.

To any Manhattanite, that poster was nothing more than a proud propaganda piece, not unlike the thousands of others found in gift shops. Yet the fact that this souvenir had reached the young man's remote village in such pristine shape meant that it took on a greater role in his mind—a little piece of Manhattan in a far-off world, it was.

But his victory was short-lived once his mother found out what he had obtained. "Where did you get this?" she asked the following day, with dread in her tone.

"I found it," he lied.

"Take it down at once!" his mother ordered as the boy's father noticed the poster.

Despite his parents' agitation, the young man remained steadfast in his resolve. "No!" he said.

"Son, do you have *any* idea what would happen to us if a soldier, or worse, our Chieftain, ever saw this? We'd either be banished from the village, or killed on the spot!" his father said.

"Don't you remember what happened to our neighbors when the Chieftain found out their daughter was writing to relatives in Manhattan?" his mother anxiously brought up. "We still don't know if any of them are alive or dead!"

"Well, I don't care! It's my poster and I'm keeping it," the young man insisted.

"Our Chieftain is supposed to be here later this afternoon. Take it down now! We haven't time for this nonsense," his father urged.

But his request fell on deaf ears once more, and he had just about enough. He stormed toward the bedroom wall, ripped the poster down, and shoved it into the trash.

"I hate you!" the young man lashed out.

"That's fine, son. I don't expect you to understand just yet, but I've worked too hard to remain in the order's good graces to throw that all away," his father said, resolved. The young man burst out of the room and his mother ran after him.

"Son! Turn around and listen to me," she commanded, and the young man complied. "Okay, now just let me remind you. Whom do we serve above all else?"

"We serve Pegmatite," he replied, angry yet obedient.

"That's right," his mother continued. "And *why* do we serve him?"

After another pause, the young man reiterated what he was taught since birth. "Because we are false, but Pegmatite is truth."

As the boy's father joined them, his mom had one more question. "Why are the buildings on that poster an abomination, then, my son?"

Shifting his attention to the torn and crumpled poster that now lay in the filth of the garbage can, the boy knew the answer to that question too. "Because, mother, they go against the will of Pegmatite."

At that moment, a knock on the front door resounded throughout the family's mansion, causing each to turn in swift attention.

"My god, the Chieftain's already here! Now, listen to me, son, we are *not* to discuss that poster anymore. I want you to go to your room now," his father commanded as his mother raced to let the feared guest in.

"Welcome, Excellency! I have tea warming in the kettle. Please, come in and make yourself comfortable," his mother offered as she made way for the unnaturally tall, horned creature. Ducking to enter through the doorway, the Chieftain's towering frame dwarfed the human occupants once he stood upright in their palatial home.

"So good to be back here, Number Eighty-Five," the Chieftain said to the young man's mother before casually adding, "Now, where is my favorite businessman?"

At that, the young man's father walked hastily into the living area. "I'm here, my Excellency! Sorry, I was just sending our boy off for a nap."

"Ah! No problem at all, Number Eighty-Four. Good to see you again. And now that you're both here, I want to personally thank you for making the land acquisition of this village more peaceful. The Order of Righteousness is much obliged," the Chieftain said as the boy's mother stretched up to hand him a cup of tea.

"Remember," the Chieftain said in between sips, "that the work you're doing ensures our continued peace arrangements. After all, we don't seek to torch *every* place we conquer. As you know, villages like yours can offer benefits in other ways. I'm talking training facilities, mating areas for our troops, munitions centers, the list goes on. So again, thank you for making it as cooperative as possible."

While the young man's mother listened in from the kitchen, his father answered the only way he knew to be allowable. "No problem at all, my Excellency. Anything to please Pegmatite."

The Chieftain chuckled with appreciation. "Yes indeed! Now to business. I'm here to inform you that I shall require your services for the next two weeks to discuss the swift acquisition of more land just to the south of us, along the bay. I trust you'll be ready for me, won't you, Number Eighty-Four?" Allowing no time for the boy's father to respond, the Chieftain placed his teacup on a nearby table and circumnavigated the living area as he continued. "So with that, let's meet your boy, shall we? I always look forward to seeing how our future recruits are shaping up."

Left no choice but to please the Chieftain, the young man's father obliged with reluctant obedience. "He's likely asleep now, my Excellency, but I suppose I could let you look in for a moment."

"That's fine by me!" The Chieftain gave the young man's mom a creepy grin, as if joyous in knowing how his behavior was never to be questioned.

With that, everyone made their way up to the young man's room, but as his father carefully cracked open the door, the Chieftain insisted on swinging it out more to get a better look inside. As he did so, light poured into the space to reveal the sight of the young man standing next to his bed with a look of defiance on his face, the crumpled poster of Manhattan back on the wall for everyone to see. His mother gasped with dread at the sight, while the boy's father swung open the door and erupted at his son.

"I told you we are not to keep this!" he shouted before turning back to the Chieftain. "Excellency, I apologize that you had to see this. My son ... he, uh, was given that poster by me for educational reasons. I told him to destroy it once he was done with it, which he certainly will, I promise. I just wanted him to be made aware of our enemies, that's all." The young man's father continued to plead for understanding as the Chieftain's red eyes beamed with a new kind of glow, and his long, spindly fingers stretched into the room to snatch the poster from the wall.

"Not to worry, my dear friends," the Chieftain assured them as he inspected the poster in a composed manner. "Not to worry at all. I see you and your wife have a curious young man on your hands, and a worthy future recruit at that. You're perfectly wise to show him this blasphemy on educational grounds, Number Eighty-Four, since you know, I trust, that any other reason for possessing such an object would result in my need to declare this village as an affront to the order, and then call my men to burn it all to the ground. But I waste my words of course, yes?"

The young man's father responded as best he could. "Of course, my Excellency! We would *never* have this for any other reason than to know the enemy better," he said.

"I admire your dedication, Number Eighty-Four. And you know, such commitment will be highly rewarded in time," the Chieftain replied. "In any case, I shall return tomorrow morning so we can begin our work as discussed. I'll show myself out, and thank you for the tea, Number Eighty-Five! Ta-ta."

With the poster still firmly in his grip, the Chieftain left the mansion, and as the young man walked out of his room to confront his parents at the front door, he could see that their faces wore a new kind of concern as a result of his conduct. But there was little time for reprimanding.

"We need to pack essential items," his father ordered, "and leave here within the hour."

As the three scrambled for the next fifteen minutes, knocks at the mansion's door sounded with a sudden vengeance.

"My God, they're already back! It's alright. I'll get the door. Just hide the luggage and stay calm," the young man's father said.

Even so, as he opened the door, a look of horror overcame his face at the sight of the Chieftain and three armed TERROR Soldiers, who quickly forced themselves inside.

"I think you take me for a fool, Number Eighty-Four," the Chieftain said as he held the crumpled poster up. "You and I both know this wasn't here for some kind of *educational* motivation. Rather, it's a sign that I'm being too lenient on you and your family."

"We would never insult your intelligence like that, Excellency!" the young man's mother interjected.

"Oh, but you already have, my dear!" he shot back. "At least now I see that this village is no longer secure and we must take our business elsewhere. Am I wrong?" The Chieftain paused as the young man and his parents stood silently, unable to come up with any other excuse.

"You can't even defend yourselves," the Chieftain uttered in pity before signaling his soldiers. "Very well. Take the adults but let the young one be. I want him to reflect on the outcome of his actions."

Just like that, the young man's parents were rounded up and escorted out of their home without the chance to say good-bye to their only son, never to be seen or heard from again.

"Always obey the order my dear boy," the Chieftain told the newly minted orphan before casually heading out the door.

As he stood in shock from such sudden horror, the young man experienced a watershed moment that day as his psychosis burgeoned. Natural instinct should have either induced mourning or a steadfast desire to seek revenge for such terror, but this young man shed very few tears in the days and nights that followed the loss of his parents. Instead, he became wrapped up in what he viewed as liberating power.

"My thoughts carry consequence," the young man repeated aloud in mantra-like fashion as he wandered the empty mansion, reinforcing the Chieftain's parting wishes. But rather than cry over something or someone he'd never get back, the young man became corrupted by the power of his own actions, and enraptured by a world where he could unseat anything, from authority figures, to his past, to even seminal things he once exalted—Manhattan among them. Never again would he cling to posters or people. Now it was only about a future world in which his actions alone would have the final say.

The young man isolated himself for weeks following his parents' abduction, all the while shaping and perfecting his newfound fixations and orienting his place at the center of this new world. Behind the walls of his mansion, he cultivated his contempt for the policies driving the village he once called home, thereby sympathizing with the TERROR Group as a logical alternative. As he embraced this mindset, he came to believe that the pursuit of happiness was a fabricated dream, for corruption and falsity surrounded the world he knew. Filling his head with a host of anti-democratic literature and ideas, he came across points of view that seemed to validate his fears and feed into his desires—much of that literature coming from pro-Pegmatite propaganda.

About a month after the swift erasure of his parents, fate came knocking at the village's door again, making good on the Chieftain's recent change of heart. With the TERROR Fleet in full assault-mode, sirens wailed and screams inevitably followed. Awakened by the commotion, the young man ran out of his mansion to take in the chaos coming to his once peaceful village.

Casting himself as the central hero because of his newfound worldview, nothing fazed the young man, even as people fled every which way in the face of walking mechanical beasts that loomed tall above the village. While others around him screamed, cried, or begged for mercy, he did none of this, choosing rather to embrace a calmness that permeated his entire body. As more homes and people were blown to shreds, he just stood outside his mansion, waiting.

Amid the chaos and destruction, one Cyclops Bot took notice of the tiny passive figure as it towered over the young man's diminutive frame, its single red eye glaring down at him with curiosity. His heart ready, the young man stared deeply into the Cyclops Bot's red eye and thrust his hands up in surrender—the only one in the village to do so. This was not an act of forfeit, though, but one to signal the merging of two like-minded creations, for the young man knew he had found his salvation and thereby happily gave his soul to it. Following this fateful convergence between man and machine, the young man took the TERROR Group's existence as the final component to his own transformation.

The TERROR Group took note of the fact that this young man wasn't just another victim, but something quite different. After his capture as the sole survivor of the now-destroyed village, the order devised ways in which the young man could grow within its ranks. It was a time coinciding with the strategy to plant sleeper cells right into Manhattan and select other cities.

So, just a few weeks later, plans were put into action, and three lone spies—one being the young man—headed to the city by way of concealed overseas transport, bypassing necessary checkpoints. They then set up temporary living conditions in small towns just beyond Manhattan's shores.

In short order, the young man and his two fellow recruits went to work surveying areas in and around the city, but their mission didn't stop there. After sufficient study, the best routes to Manhattan were identified and meticulously studied, while the Manhattan Military's security strategies and locations were also obtained and deciphered. Lastly, the city's living buildings—the Twin Towers among them—were visited, documented, and analyzed.

During his numerous trips to the buildings, the young man couldn't help but remain impressed by Manhattan and all that it offered, even though he now saw it through a warped lens. Looking out over the city from atop one of the Twin Towers' mighty observatories, he ruminated on the buildings. They swayed gracefully, he experienced, while each tower periodically greeted a starstruck tourist or two, and engaged in chatter with other nearby buildings. The whole scene was surreal to the young man, who for so long had romanticized and idealized such a place. But there he stood, shoulder to shoulder with other eager tourists and free to take in Manhattan's riches for himself, yet unable to look past his new-found interpretation of the world surrounding him.

"No matter how elegant or soaring these Twin Towers appear, it is all a lie," he quietly reminded himself.

Naturally, in order to carry out such a delicate mission, the young man and his fellow spies remained in their human forms to minimize suspicion. They had been promised that their physical transformations would be finalized upon completion of their duties, and that the most *effective* of the three recruits would then be elevated in rank. It was that second promise that motivated the young man further as he carried out his mission with infinite care.

When the spies' research tasks came to an end, they got out of Manhattan with the same level of obscurity that they had come in with, their actions detected by no one. Such a productive mission meant dramatic repercussions for the ambitious young man's career within the TERROR Group's network. Upon his return to TERROR-controlled territories overseas, the young man was officially ranked a "Commander for the Order" for his efforts, and as the Chieftains sought out their most capable members to lead the intended charge against Manhattan and its sister cities, focus turned to their newly minted member.

But the young man's rapid ascent to a senior rank wasn't the only transformation he experienced in the days following the mission, for his allegiance to the order meant that he would receive a new physical form, as had been promised. So, the once handsome and well-toned body of his youth morphed into something frightening and unnatural, a hyper-reflection of his twisted thoughts and feelings. As he shape-shifted, the young man, now a Commander, grew to a height of over thirty-seven feet, a little taller than most of the others, and developed grotesque, spindly features that reached demonic proportions. His eyes became red as fire, while his shoulders, hips, and ribs jutted through his skin to create sharp points. The transformation was particularly slow and painful, taking several agonizing hours. Upon its completion, however, his new body felt as natural and normal as any, and his modified look had shed any last traces of his former self.

His influence and profile ever rising from that point forward, the TERROR Commander took to the idea of preaching his worldview to a growing flock within the order.

"There is no good to be found in past days," he proclaimed with passion, reinforcing the reasons why he had succumbed to the TERROR Group's methods in the first place. By this time, anger and ego drove much of the TERROR Commander's assumptions, which in turn, fed his appetite for destruction. "Protection in any form is afforded to no one," he stressed, "and those ignorant enough to believe they are protected will fall to a greater depth than the rest."

Followers were hooked by their new leader's presence from the very start.

Despite his growing power and legions of new adherents, however, his preoccupation always seemed to circle back to Manhattan. From the time he began filling his mind with anti-*this* and anti-*that* propaganda, he grew ever incensed by the same "wonder city" that he had revered in his former life. Something had to be done, he knew, while also recognizing that taking Manhattan required total and absolute devotion.

But Manhattan was no village or settlement like the order's usual conquests. It was on a scale far larger, and this stirred him to arrange the inaugural attack to a tedious degree. After all, for the effort to be worth his time, Manhattan needed to then be transformed to fit *his* new vision. To not do so, he felt, would be counterproductive to the whole project, no matter what anyone else thought. Indeed, while the current Chieftains were still the spiritual leaders of the enterprise, in the mind of this up-and-coming Commander, they were also Old Guard remnants from the original pro-Pegmatite supporters who had attacked Lady Liberty so long ago. As such, the TERROR Commander felt that it was he, not the Chieftains, who held the keys to the order's future.

During his regularly scheduled strategy sessions, the TERROR Commander surrounded himself with a dedicated flock unlike any previously seen within the order. As soon as he was officially granted the task of taking Manhattan, the Commander released propaganda to every area within the TERROR Group's sphere in order to attract more eyes to his cause. In widely disseminated videos, future TERROR Soldiers watched in awe as their charismatic new leader presented his messages with a fervor that seemed to burst through their television screens. In these masterfully calculated performances, no gesture or word was wasted as the TERROR Commander sold his vision to the masses, while cleverly rebranding the order's intended "Lost Kingdom" of Pegmatite to something far more apropos. "Manhattan's Salvation," as he called it, proliferated rapidly, as intended.

Never a one-trick pony, the TERROR Commander always looked two steps ahead. In his grand scheme, the vile ruler planned to extend "Manhattan's Salvation" well beyond its publicly understood intent. If worked out properly, the plan would allow for one final power grab *away* from the order's highest ranked Chieftains—an ultimate act of supremacy to surpass all others, as he envisioned it.

For the time being, though, popular approval was what the TERROR Commander sought, and popular approval was what he received. During countless rallies, he reminded his viewers that the taking of Manhattan was "the most important single act that shall be carried out in the name of Pegmatite," and also provided other justifications. In another blatant act of contempt for the city, he offered a biased (and often fabricated) comparison between an average recruit's mental illnesses and a typical Manhattanite's prosperity.

"Manhattan's established schools of thought are to blame for any financial, ethical, or moral hardships that plague you here and now!" he told his susceptible flock.

The effort worked well, and to those believing in his messages, Manhattan's towering giants came to epitomize this great disparity. As the TERROR Commander's words continued to fall upon receptive ears, he attracted the most capable soldiers from far and wide, forging alliances with dedicated troops who would have otherwise been sent to conquer less formidable lands.

Second only to a handful of Chieftains at this point, the Commander carried out violent and swift practice runs in the years leading up to "Manhattan's Salvation." Under his watch, TERROR forces leveled over a dozen settlements, villages, and towns, murdering several thousand in the name of righteousness, and leaving the scene each time with no other trace but fire and ash. It was all useful practice, the vile leader reasoned, in advance of the ultimate goal, and if murder and violence earned him more devotion, then he accepted that as well.

Within the first year of the Commander's reign, TERROR Group territories nearly doubled. This resulted in throngs of new recruits, new soldiers, new spheres of influence, and continued frustration among other governments and armies. For his efforts, the Chieftains presented the Commander with an honorary "Staff of Righteousness," a specialized version of the weapons carried by his troops. But while theirs were merely practical, his staff carried even more power since it was said to have once belonged to Pegmatite himself.

As a bonus, the victories under his watch afforded the Commander near total immunity by his superiors. Therefore, his strategy for conquering Manhattan saw little internal opposition. The grand assault against the Twin Towers was being planned, while the Commander's reputation rose to almost spiritual proportions. For those in his inner circle, *he* was the figure to fear and obey in the order. The young man had come a long way.

Thanks to its charismatic new leader, the TERROR Group became emboldened like never before, and few others across the planet suspected the clock to be ticking so rapidly against Manhattan Island. In the months leading up to the unthinkable, there remained surprisingly little success by the Manhattan Military or any other global watchdog in understanding the motivation of TERROR forces. The media continued to speculate, UN Building and other officials kept debating, and security precautions went nowhere. Globally, the TERROR Group maintained its rigor by successfully burying its tracks beneath mountains of hardened lava and inaccurate headlines, even as civilizations continued to be erased by fire—gobbled up by a beast of darkness with an insatiable appetite. At this point in the beast's journey, only the taking of Manhattan could satisfy.

On the eve of the fateful day, Manhattanites were brimming with excitement over a nine-thousand-piece orchestral performance in Central Park, staged in conjunction with the Manhattan Philharmonic and Rockefeller Slab. The evening concert—the largest ever assembled in the city's illustrious history—capped a weeklong celebration commemorating Bartholdi's discovery of the Schistian stones that gave life to Lady Liberty and the rest of the towering giants. Live-streamed and brightly lit, the spectacle was met with a marvelous turnout, as filled-to-capacity buildings pressed against each other along the park's seemingly endless perimeter, careful as always not to crush people within their walls as they took in the sights. The program brimmed with musical pomp of the finest order, and included such ancient works as *Concerto in F*, *The Firebird* and *Nutcracker Suites*, as well as a surging, triumphant rendition of *Rhapsody in Blue*. All the while, soaring strings and thumping brass reverberated off the façades of the transfixed buildings, making for a singular aural experience for human and tower alike.

After a nearly four-hour performance, the cymbals clanged one final time and the orchestra went silent. Rapturous applause traversed the entire length of the park for about twenty minutes, and the musicians rose to take a bow from the park's massive meadow. It took another half hour for the crowd's appreciation to fully subside, and when Central Park finally emptied out, the cool September skies still hummed to the tune of a constant breeze. It had been a day befit for royalty, perfection even. A thousand days hath September.

As crowds dispersed, Manhattan's favorite architectural couple took a slow stroll uptown before their evening rest. Nestled beside his lover, Empire State Building felt jovial and upbeat; the pressures of his mayoral duties temporarily lifted in the face of the evening's fun.

"What a marvelous concert. I sure needed that one," he said.

Chrysler Building, having cherished a rare opportunity to be alone with her overworked companion, replied, "I'm glad we caught it, love." Turning to look at him, she slyly added, "I wish we could have more carefree nights like this. You've been working later and later, it seems."

Empire State Building got the message, peering at his lover with trepidation, a bit intimidated by her presence even after all these years. Just how he had managed to win her heart remained a mystery to the tower. It couldn't have just been unwavering confidence. It had to have been luck, too.

In any event, what a sight she was, with those meandering lines that danced along her sinuous form like some kind of kinky stitching, and that breathiness in her voice which suggested a no-nonsense, streetwise allure. Empire State Building couldn't get enough of it. Chrysler Building pivoted slightly, causing a burst of light to flare off her crown. It was further proof in Empire State Building's mind that even the universe was transfixed by her. There was no escape, for Chrysler Building's ornaments were in all the right places.

She caught him staring and he turned away bashfully, knowing that she wanted him to assure they would have more nights like this. Or better yet, Chrysler Building would have loved to hear him say that he planned to hand off his mayoral tasks to someone else in the foreseeable future. Perhaps the Twin Towers were finally ready to fill that position, as she often suggested. But whatever Chrysler Building was expecting to hear at that moment, words were failing Empire State Building.

"I don't have to remind you yet again that I want you all to myself, do I?" Chrysler Building said, filling in her companion's silence.

Still speechless, Empire State Building caught something even more complicated coming into view. It was the sight of Rockefeller Slab, that suave and lean ringleader of fun, approaching the couple with zest. "Oh, hey there!" Chrysler Building let out flirtatiously, keen on rattling her lover's foundations for a bit longer.

"Looking magical as always, Madame Chrysler," Rockefeller Slab called out, before directing his gaze up toward Empire State Building. "You are one lucky building, Mr. Mayor! Pretty flowers like her bloom once in a millennium. Hold onto her."

"I'm sure he intends to," Chrysler Building said as Empire State Building nodded sheepishly.

"Very lucky, indeed," Rockefeller Slab repeated as he redirected his attention back to Chrysler Building, his thoughts as unfiltered as his floodlights. Sure enough, the ostentatious tower's presence got to Empire State Building, taking him right back to when he was younger and more insecure.

"You're so right. I'm *very* lucky," Empire State Building let out with slight agitation in his tone. "Thank you for the heartfelt advice as always, Rockefeller Slab. What would I do without you?"

Sensing her lover's shifting mood, Chrysler Building interjected as only she could. "You outdid yourself with the production tonight, Rockefeller Slab. We had a wonderful time." She gazed at her lover once more. "Both of us."

"Oh, please, it was the least I could do, for *both* of you, I mean."

His disdain brewing, Empire State Building cleared his throat in a plea to end the awkward encounter. This time, it was Chrysler Building who got the message.

"Well, it's been fun, but we should really head uptown. We're very tired. Thank you again, Rockefeller Slab, and good night," she said, even as the casual conversation was enough to dampen the rest of their stroll.

"What exactly does Rockefeller Slab get out of this? I'm just trying to understand. Every time he sees you, it's as if I'm not there. Have you noticed that?" Empire State Building fumed.

Chrysler Building defended her friend. "Oh, please, he didn't mean anything by it. Relax. It's not like I'm having an affair or anything. Where could that even happen anyway, in such a public city?" she replied, in a joke that turned sour fast.

"How about the Manhattan Forest, for one? Plenty of acreage up there," he pressed.

Chrysler Building wanted no part of this sudden interrogation. "You're ridiculous. I shouldn't have to answer that question! Maybe if you were around more often, you'd get it."

Empire State Building looked up with revelation. "Ah! So that's what this is about. You're upset because I'm not available enough to go with you to parties, swanky dinners, and all that other jazz! Well, I've got a nearly thankless job to do. Do you realize how difficult it is to manage this place, with every single building out there having an opinion about how things should be run?"

The two towers reached their uptown destination in the midst of a long, painful silence. All around them, most of Inwood Hill's residents were asleep, as hardly a light was on. A rude breeze brushed against Empire State Building's upper floors, triggering him to realize his foolishness.

"Look, I'm sorry. I've been under too much stress lately. Tonight was fun, and I just didn't want anything to ruin that. The housing council has only three more conferences this week. The apartment community really wants me to back their initiative because it would finally help convince Manhattanites to chip in and fix them again. Lady Liberty thinks my being there will help sway some minds. After that, I'll have more time for us, I promise. This time, I really promise."

Following another pause, Chrysler Building decided to ease her lover's fragmented universe. "Dear Lord, I *am* in love with a politician," she conceded. "Be that as it may. Give me a kiss goodnight, and I'll give you another four years."

Order restored.

Back on Liberty Island, the green lady ascended her pedestal with intent as she looked forward to a night of deep meditation. Reaching the top, she took another glance at the panorama of her resting neighbors among the skyline before peering toward the expanse of towering sand dunes just beyond the city's borders. "Another day taken with the tide of history," she noted. Like everyone else that night, the statue remained floored by the concert in the park.

Soon enough, her copper eyes felt heavy and she took a deep breath, closed them, and drifted into unexplored channels of her mind. The sound of crashing waves all around her base encouraged this transition, and as she continued to give in, Lady Liberty began to dream. She felt as if she was being carried off her perch on Liberty Island, across those vast sand dunes, and into an unknown realm beyond Manhattan. Against the limits of time and space, she hovered just above changing landforms and topographies, while the sky became ablaze with every known hue.

She journeyed across what seemed to be billions of miles, even as visions of her friends back home appeared, beginning with Empire State Building, who greeted her with kindness. Chrysler Building then shimmered while the sun grazed her crown. Next appeared St. Patrick's Cathedral, that ol' spiritual one, Lady Liberty recalled fondly. More towering giants entered her subconscious, and the green lady smiled as she distilled each down to their respective essence. Next, she saw the humans, those Manhattanites whom she swore to accept with fidelity, in all their variations and shades. The people of the city and the green lady were parts of a whole, after all. At peace with that Schistian arrangement, Lady Liberty did little to repel any of the images that flashed by her. Her circuitous journey continued on, taking her across many more canyons, oceans, crystal-clear ice, and sun-cracked clay, before bringing her to something more familiar again.

"Wait, I know of this place. I was here before," she exclaimed with eyes shut, as the dream hurled Lady Liberty toward a rapidly appearing object in space. While she moved in closer, she began to recognize the formations of a city. Her city. With increased velocity, Lady Liberty caught fragmented glimpses of her friends yet again. But something was amiss this time, and the faster the dream propelled her, the more alarmed she became.

"Please, slow down, make it all stop!" she uttered helplessly. But her plea fell upon deaf ears. By that point, almost everything looked like a giant blur, except, she noticed, for two monumental figures: the Twin Towers, Manhattan's tallest and proudest beacons, who stood dead-ahead of her with no sign of moving out of her way. "Wait, stop, stop, STOP!" she begged, to no avail.

Seconds later, the impact between the accelerating statue and stationary towers was swift beyond sensation, causing everything to be enveloped in blackness.

"Why?" Lady Liberty gasped as she awakened from the maddening experience, inadvertently letting her torch plummet to the ground and crack. Trembling, she clutched her shoulders and biceps in nervousness, hoping to ensure that she was, in fact, awake. "If it was just a dream, why did this one feel more real than the others?" She focused her eyes upon her patinated and weathered hands, frustrated by her inability to unpack any lessons the dream was foretelling.

Across the river, Tower One awakened from his perch near Manhattan's southern tip. Looking out over the great harbor as he often did, he noticed Lady Liberty staring out toward the ocean beyond, and her body language seemed uncharacteristically somber to the tower.

"She's sure up early," he whispered while his twin brother stretched himself awake.

"Who is?" Tower Two asked a few moments later.

Before Tower One could turn to reply, however, he caught the strange sight of what looked like a shooting star, flying quite low but coming in fast from the southwestern skies. "What could that..."

Back atop her perch, Lady Liberty heard a piercing sound that whizzed by, far too harsh to have been waves, as it sliced through her thoughts with disorienting force. The sound rose in pitch until it gave way to a loud explosion, and the sky was illuminated in a flash of blinding light. The statue felt afraid to turn her head in Manhattan Island's direction, for she already suspected what she would see.

Following the sound, a ferry captain called out to the green lady from his window on the bridge, his ferry docked just behind her immense pedestal. "What can ya see from up there?"

Summoning the courage to turn around and look, Lady Liberty's eyes became filled with the sight of her two friends, consumed in flames and appearing to be in great pain.

Looking back down at the captain and his crew, she quickly began to instruct them. "Manhattan has just been attacked. Alert the mainland to prepare for the worst. We need first responders to get to the Twin Towers at once."

The captain was perplexed at first, but then a look of dread came over his face. "Good God," he said, before turning to his crew. "All passengers must stay on this ship, and alert authorities of Lady Liberty's report, on the double!" The faint sound of wailing sirens began to gather from afar.

"It was a premonition!" Lady Liberty announced in frustration as she realized the gravity of her dream despite being powerless to stifle it. But while that dream's hellish scenario had ended, a new nightmare became all too real. Nevertheless, given her Schistian heart's intention to help out any way she could, the green lady knelt to clear her mind before summoning the ancient spirit that would allow her to fly into the devastation.

***

In the hours leading up to that sinister explosion, while Manhattanites and buildings alike were still resting up from the concert, there was nothing to indicate that their day ahead would be so radically different from the previous one. The sky, after all, was up to its usual tricks, and seemed to radiate with an optimistic palette composed of baby blues, turquoise, and streaks of pink. Indeed, an optimistic forecast. Central Park's trees, meanwhile, were beginning to shed their leaves, gracefully anticipating another Manhattan winter that was right around the corner. Meanwhile, the buoyant neon glow of Times Square was still visible, lending an additional radiance to the soft morning light which blanketed buildings far and wide in a rich, golden magenta.

Back uptown, Chrysler and Empire State Buildings woke to sounds of commotion and confusion as nearby buildings speculated whether there was a gas explosion, a subway collision, or something else.

Fearing the worst, Chrysler Building peered to the south and caught a huge plume of rising smoke. "Everyone needs to head inside the closest building now!" she shouted to nearby Manhattanites on the streets below.

"All buildings, unlock your doors so that more people can get inside easily," Empire State Building instructed.

Moments later, a second shearing sound ripped through the air, and buildings looked up in horror toward the blinding sky. By that point, it was clear that whatever was happening was no accident.

"Everyone get as low to the ground as possible!" Empire State Building said, as the white light shot past his upper stories and toward the smoldering ground to the south of the island, appearing smaller and smaller while it hurled toward its target. He watched as the object then disappeared into the other plume of smoke, which triggered a new explosion. Skies above the targeted area were filled with even heavier clouds of smoke and ash as a result. Watching from a distance, Chrysler and Empire State Buildings turned to each other in trepidation.

"Stay and look after these buildings," Empire State Building instructed. "I've gotta get down there."

Sensing her partner's call to duty, Chrysler Building did little to dissuade him. "Go," she said, "but *you* be careful."

Following that second explosion, panic gripped the island's southern tip with renewed fervor, and smoke traveled up the streets like a ghostly, devouring force, causing nearby buildings to rush uptown in droves. In the chaos, taller towers tripped over smaller ones, triggering a domino effect that put multitudes of fleeing Manhattanites in further danger.

Injured from having been trampled, Trinity Church crawled away from the stampede and toward the relative safety of the island's western edge, all the while keeping his doors open for any desperate Manhattanites who sought cover. Before the dark cloud swallowed up the skies above his steeple, the church caught a brief glimpse of one of the Twin Towers, surrounded by smoke and shaking violently from the choking carnage. At the same time, he noticed along an adjacent street numerous firetrucks and emergency personnel racing with determination against the frenetic path of panicked crowds, and right into the ground floors of the Twin Towers.

"God be with them," he uttered helplessly.

Just then, Lady Liberty swooped onto the scene, intent on rescuing as many people as she could. Dodging fireballs and clouds of ash, she surveyed the growing devastation before descending right into the plume of smoke. Flying low, she scooped up as many ash-covered Manhattanites as her hands could manage, and dropped them off farther uptown to safety. But the heat and low visibility soon disoriented her as she tried to continue her flyovers, which caused the statue to collide headfirst into a fleeing tower's antenna. It was enough of an impact to send the two buildings careening to the ground, leaving Lady Liberty unconscious.

While panicked towers continued to clamber uptown, Empire State Building did everything he could to maneuver around them and head in the opposite direction. Making it to within a few hundred yards of the impact zone, he caught UN Building and Rockefeller Slab attempting to prevent the stampede of many more frightened buildings.

"Form a tight cluster so they don't run along the streets and kill more people!" UN Building directed, hoping to form tower chains perpendicular to the path of the panicked evacuees that would give Manhattanites below a clear means of escape.

"I hear ya," said Rockefeller Slab. "Citicorp, Ladder Tower, come and help me with this!"

Many of the city's largest towers followed suit, and UN Building's solution worked to prevent more casualties, since stranded Manhattanites were able to enter buildings without risk of being crushed to death. Meanwhile, Empire State Building pressed on toward his intended destination.

The Twin Towers couldn't bear the ungodly pain for much longer. It ran through their bodies with sharp and paralyzing force, and under such immense structural strain, mobility was almost impossible. The towers struggled even to look down and assess their injuries, not realizing that the sudden impact wiped out their internal fire suppression systems, thereby exposing their Schistian-rich steel framework to an enraging heat of no comparison.

"This feels ... horrible!" Tower One cried out, despite his instinctual resolve to battle through the pain.

As they prepared for the inevitable, a collective desire flashed through the towers' minds, which was to remain upright for as long as possible to ensure that more people could escape. Despite their brave and defiant heroism, the unfamiliar sensation of eroding walls and collapsing floor plates became increasingly difficult to overcome, like a rabid cancer eating away at its host from within. Clinging to their goal, though, both towers managed to stay upright for well over an hour—an act that saved many lives.

"I ... can't ... hold on much longer," Tower Two strained as his injuries hit a new level of indescribable agony.

"It's almost over," his brother said.

Finally, each giant let out one last deep and sad moan, and after using every ounce of their collective strength, their lower floors began to give way. All across Manhattan, buildings and people watched in horror while their two tallest icons surrendered to the inevitable. Their collapse was at once catastrophic and unforgiving, and it crushed injured adjacent buildings and vaporized countless Manhattanites within them. As soon as the towers gave way to mountains of dust, the sky was filled with another soft rumble that built to a thundering crescendo, while the ground trembled throughout the entire island, and the harbor's waves crashed violently on account of falling debris. The destruction generated another plume of smoke that seemed to put the initial explosions to shame, as it enshrouded Manhattan further in blinding darkness.

Following their fateful and cataclysmic collapse, the landscape became increasingly quiet and eerily still, and the silence was so void that nothing seemed to exist anymore. The shock of the devastation rendered the once-teeming island with few words to spare but many tears to shed.

Away from the chaos, Chrysler Building anxiously waited uptown with unspoken dread as she took in the sights of a city transformed. All around her approached injured buildings, many of which could barely stand upright, and deep within her frame could be heard the cries of thousands of Manhattanites, a horrible sound that multiplied from inside other nearby buildings. Gone were the Twin Towers and missing was Lady Liberty, as well as a host of others. And Empire State Building was still out there, his whereabouts uncertain.

"You better come back to me," Chrysler Building muttered helplessly.

Pressing on but greatly fatigued, Empire State Building slowed his pace as he approached his destination. The tower found himself surrounded by smoke, strange lights, and almost no sounds. The occasional ash-covered building walked past him in a daze. Among dense clouds of dust, he made out the silhouette of Trinity Church, who stumbled toward him from out of the darkness.

"Are you hurt? Is anyone still inside you?" he asked the church with alarm.

"We're okay, but you don't want to see what's past this point, Empire State Building. It's just too horrific," the church warned.

But Empire State Building had come a long way to see whatever he was destined to see.

"Forget about that. Just keep heading north, and tell any others you see to keep moving in that direction," he instructed, and the two separated.

With each passing minute, more hope was being sapped from Empire State Building's heart. "Is anyone out there?" he shouted into the persisting darkness. The silence was haunting yet deafening, as Empire State Building felt with certainty that death was all around him.

There's no one alive around me, he thought as he pressed on. Walking farther still for what seemed like an eternity, the tower noticed an orange haze in the distance. Like a moth to the flame, closer he went toward it, even as the heat intensified with each step. Suddenly he stopped in his tracks, for the terrible sight Trinity Church had promised was now in front of him.

Against the crackles and pops of cindered remains, Empire State Building recognized a weeping Lady Liberty, crouched on her knees among piles of ash and debris. His heart weakened as the statue looked up at him with a sense of fragility in her eyes.

"I was unable to stop it, Empire State. This TERROR Group took them from us," she said. "Now darkness runs rampant."

Empire State Building couldn't believe what he was hearing and from *whom* he was hearing it. Lady Liberty, ever a proud beacon of hope, she who was there during his own birth, she who had opened his eyes to many things over the years, was now crouched in deep grief. With this realization, he surveyed the horror that surrounded them. Just beyond Lady Liberty, the last structural remnants of their young friends, the once mighty Twin Towers, stood half-buried among the smoldering embers of twisted metal parts. It was a sight so devastating in its rawness that it weakened Empire State Building's heart even further, while sudden memories of his two friends ran through his mind.

"They had so much life to live," the tower muttered. As he processed what he was seeing, a new kind of rage ran through Empire State Building's pipes like a liquid fire. "We're going to hit them with everything we've got, Lady Liberty. Whoever did this, mark my words, we're going to hunt down every last one of them!" the building howled.

Lady Liberty wiped the tears from her cheeks, gently lifted herself up, and turned to face her vengeful friend. "We can try, and it might calm your rage for now, but that hurt you carry cannot be put to rest so easily."

Processing her words, Empire State Building took another deep sigh and turned away in shame, his rage giving way to total helplessness.

"If we stick together, however, no matter what happens to us," Lady Liberty added, "we may find a way to move past this somehow."

Atop the heaping ruins, the two icons stood and cried, joining in a collective grief insurmountable in its scale and united in meaning. Lady Liberty's tears were as real as any that a human ever experienced, and Empire State Building's deep, cavernous hallways and floors bellowed in pain as he quivered in sadness. Their feelings were irrepressible, lacking any sort of composure or self-awareness, and they were crying not only for their twin brothers, but also for the countless human lives lost, including hundreds of doomed first responders who had run into the burning towers while everyone else was trying to get out.

Flashbacks of the Twin Towers once again entered Empire State Building's mind as he wept, forcing him to recall how he initially hadn't thought much of them, and how he had griped when they took his "world's tallest" title away. Such superficial thoughts, in light of what transpired on this deadly day, only encouraged more tears to be shed. Empire State Building then began to speculate that had he still been the tallest, perhaps the Twin Towers' lives would have been spared, and his life taken, which only compounded his guilt.

"I couldn't save them," the tower said softly.

"None of us could have," Lady Liberty replied.

Moments later, Chrysler Building, Citicorp Center, and several others appeared from out of the smoky haze and the orange glow, looking on with solemnity and rushing to comfort the two weeping giants. More of the city's skyline followed suit, emerging from all directions to pay their respects and begin the long, arduous task of looking for survivors. Buildings short and tall, circular and orthogonal, young and old. Buildings constructed for every conceivable purpose, gathered now for just one. There they stood for a long while in mourning, without words and powerless to change anything.

Since the number of survivors was small, several towers began to turn away from the scene, choosing instead to help those who had escaped uptown.

While remaining buildings and emergency personnel desperately continued their search for survivors, a cold breeze permeated the air, and many of the flames were put out by fire trucks. The smoke seemed to lessen in an unnatural way, however.

"What could be happening?" Empire State Building pondered, as Lady Liberty looked up in similar bewilderment.

"I don't believe what I'm seeing," Chrysler Building said.

Alarmed at her tone, the other buildings turned toward the remains to witness a sight each of them would never forget. The captivated audience watched with caution as the ground came alive with a soft rumble, and hovering against a backdrop of near-blinding light, the specter of the Twin Towers appeared before them, seemingly intact and alive, each lit in a brilliant orange radiance. Perched beside them were the other unlucky buildings who had succumbed to the attack as well. Empire State Building, transfixed by the sight, called out to the spirits.

"Don't leave us!" he begged, before realizing that his friends had already crossed over. The Twin Towers hovered in silence for just a moment longer, taking one last look at the panorama of buildings who had been their friends for nearly three decades. To witnesses, their final gaze upon the city seemed to be a resolute one, and after a collective nod, the spirits began their gradual ascent upward and out of sight.

Lady Liberty, moved by the spectacle, tried her best to fly up and follow them into the sky. But the green lady soon realized that the towers were now beyond even her reach.

Soaring above any traces of smoke and ash, the Twin Towers and their departed neighbors were seen from a great distance in every direction. Their journey on this planet was complete, but their time beyond the horizon was infinite.

"Now they are at peace," Lady Liberty acknowledged as she settled back down to the ground.

It was time to accept that the Twin Towers were gone, and that life had to continue for those left behind. Following their departure, the optimistic tones of the sky again surrendered to dark, brooding hues, as if foreshadowing the city's uncertain future. A collective sense of responsibility now bore into everyone present as the events of that morning—that eleventh day of September—ushered in a new and mature Manhattan, one that had come to grips with the fact that not everyone out there was on its side.

The aftermath of the attack brought unrest, fear, and vulnerability to the island. Thousands of Manhattanites were dead or missing. Numerous buildings, forever lost. There were also dangerous toxins in the air from incinerated office supplies, furniture, concrete, steel, and gas lines, which threatened to bathe the rest of the city with contaminants. It was clear that Manhattan needed to prepare any way it could for such growing aftereffects. Decisions had to be made fast.

The next day was a blur. While firefighters battled overnight against various blazes, multitudes of Manhattanites and buildings took on the recovery effort with full force. Empire State Building's mind grew weary as he continued to assess the devastation, even as he joined the effort in surveying the wreckage for any signs of life amid mountains of rubble. Nearby, Chrysler Building, Rockefeller Slab, and many others scanned the ruins in a similar state of bewilderment, for nothing around them seemed to display any kind of movement.

Manhattan became an unfamiliar place for the towering giants who long called it home. The skies above them were dotted with jets deployed by the Manhattan Military, and they were constantly heard whirring overhead. The streets below them stewed with agitation and chaos, as press conferences offered frequent updates, including listing any victims who went from being classified as *missing* to *deceased*. Looking beyond the devastation for some kind of relief from the proceedings, Lady Liberty felt a storm brewing regardless, and whether anyone else saw it or not was inconsequential. The skies over Manhattan were grim, indeed.

TWIN TOWERS MURDERED!
THOUSANDS MORE PERISH IN BRAZEN TERROR ATTACK.

Global headlines screamed with words like this, sending shock-waves across the continents and sparking a panic unlike anything in recent memory. Millions across the planet mourned. Financial markets plummeted, as did humanity's faith in the safety of buildings everywhere, and the most prominent architectural icons were placed on high alert across the planet.

"Initial findings of the investigation have just been released by Manhattan Military personnel," UN Building relayed as calmly as he could to an astute audience that included Lady Liberty, Empire State Building, and Rockefeller Slab. "Discoveries at the site reveal the remains of two commercial-grade aircraft that were confirmed to have been hijacked mid-flight and forced to redirect toward Manhattan Island. Each plane was deliberately steered full speed into Towers One and Two, killing all on board and triggering the resulting destruction."

"My God," Empire State Building said, recalling his own brush with death with a plane all those years ago, while the rest of the group remained stunned by the calculated nature of the assault.

"But I thought humans scrapped air travel a while back," Rockefeller Slab pondered, alluding to the fact that the industry was a globally declining one, given its harsh environmental impact and poor safety standards. As such, larger cities like Manhattan had repurposed their airports due to their low attendance and growing public disfavor of flying.

"Apparently some smaller cities and towns still rely on it, but it's not as common as other forms of ground and sea transportation, which could be why these perpetrators chose it in the first place. I mean, who could have expected such a particular scenario to transpire. Planes deliberately targeting buildings?" UN Building said in a grim tone.

"Well, be that as it may, thanks for the solid report, UN Building. I will relay this info to the other buildings. Meanwhile, let's urge human authorities to shut down airspace across the entire nation, before this scenario repeats itself," Empire State Building said.

"It's already done. The President's House just confirmed an indefinite, nationwide grounding of all public aircraft this morning," UN Building confirmed.

"And above all else," Lady Liberty said, "we will need to operate calmly and with great proficiency, for many could quickly give into panic over this."

In the immediate aftermath of the event, the atmosphere in the city grew increasingly hostile as its perceived safety net eroded. Soon, Manhattanites were evacuating to far-off settlements in droves, fearing that the island had become a sitting duck for future attackers. Across the spectrum of civic services, a lack of faith dominated the city's actions. Fear and mistrust were rampant.

Far away, the TERROR Group welcomed news of the devastation with glee. The first goal of its ravenous mission had been carried out in such a way that it successfully shook Manhattan to its core. Intent on following up in rapid fashion, the TERROR Commander readied his team for the next piece of the puzzle, in what he saw as a demonstration of force for the ages.

During his immediate appeal to Chieftains, the TERROR Commander used the attack as leverage for requesting remarkable new levels of power. "The enemy city is low on morale right now. Therefore, we must strike them again in no more than a month or two, hitting them while they're down before they regain any trace of stamina! Manhattan would never expect something so brash and so quickly, and our takeover will gain momentous respect and fear from the global media. This would be a win-win for us all."

That last selling point tickled the Chieftains. After all, publicity was something the TERROR Group had grown to crave since it was a way for its messages to spread without taking much action.

"As Manhattan still smolders," the Commander continued, "we will strike with a second blow far more spectacular than the first, and their nation will forever know the Order of Righteousness."

Granted a unanimous wave of approval by the Chieftains, the TERROR Commander knew he had gotten what he wanted, and from that point forward, virtually all hands were now under his authority. Blinded by the personality and actions of their ambitious disciple, the Chieftains failed to realize that their own powers were eroding in the process. Soon enough, the TERROR Commander would answer to no one, including those he deemed to be tired old leaders who'd perched themselves atop the organization's food chain for too long. They were yesterday's news, and he was today's and tomorrow's. Of that he was sure.

Eager to act, the TERROR Commander began his fateful call to arms in a live-streamed message that was disseminated across the entirety of the order.

"Brothers of our great and mighty legion, the time is now upon us. Let us act more brazenly and more forcefully than ever before, for when we strike the enemy city with this next blow, the *planet* will know it at a rate far greater than that September victory. The Order of Righteousness shall be feared without a trace of dissolution! And as for their so-called Manhattan Military, fear not, for it will be overwhelmed by our wave of demolition. Pegmatite has imposed a historical revision of a unique scale upon us, for neither force of arms nor time will defeat us!"

Across territories far and wide, the TERROR Commander's speech was met with resounding howls from his bloodthirsty fanbase, and the effective leader had once again garnished his words with conviction and believability. To his followers, he could do no wrong, and to the Chieftains who backed him, such abilities made the Commander's standings within the organization invaluable.

To those seeking to bring the TERROR Commander to justice for his atrocities, his deified persona only confirmed their concerns. His words, after all, provided fuel for the order's continued growth. So even as Manhattan was licking its wounds, the TERROR Group was preparing for its Second Coming.

"Give me some updates, UN Building. Where are we on population figures?" Empire State Building asked his trusted diplomat, anxious to know just how many were leaving Manhattan Island per day.

"Well, I've got bad news and better news, Empire State. Which one do you want to hear first?" his friend replied.

"You know me."

"Fine, bad news first," UN Building said. "Manhattanite authorities are telling me that large numbers of people, mostly those who can afford to or who have connections elsewhere, have already left Manhattan Island in the past twenty-four hours, with many more expected to follow. They estimate that, by week's end, we could have as much as seventy-three percent of our buildings walking around without anyone inside them. They just don't feel safe here."

"That *is* bad," Empire State Building remarked. "Now, what about our buildings? How many have expressed a desire to leave?"

"Well, there's your better news. Most of them have decided to stay, though I've got a lot of hospital buildings complaining about levels of toxicity being found in the patients within them. It's a valid point and one we should discuss further. They'd rather the patients be treated in a safer region away from the city, but where that should be is anyone's guess. We also have a few dozen apartment buildings looking to relocate to towns north of the Manhattan Forest."

"Yes, I heard. This issue should be a key point of discussion during our next conference. I'd like you to invite some hospitals and apartments to the meeting so we can come up with some sort of solution. I know they're all overworked right now."

"That's putting it lightly, my friend," UN Building said. "There's been talk among Manhattanites to separate the toxic area from the rest of the island so that fewer people are inhaling whatever chemicals are still spewing into the air."

"Yeah, but what about any potential survivors who are still buried? I can't see that happening," Empire State Building presumed.

"Well, they're still debating it, from what I've been told."

"Okay, in the meantime, we've got most buildings staying on. Even Wall Street Tower?"

"Yep, him too."

"That's surprising."

"I share your sentiment," UN Building quipped. "So, aside from the buildings I mentioned, the rest of the towering giants are choosing to remain. I just spoke with a few buildings of Times Square, as well as Rockefeller Slab, and they said they'll be coordinating to deliver breaking news as it comes in. I guess this begins our twenty-four-hour news cycle of speculation and fear," he admitted.

"And misinformation. Tell Rockefeller Slab to be on extra-high alert in that regard. I want to make sure all news stories have been vetted by Manhattanite fact-checkers before we start disseminating information among buildings," Empire State Building said.

"You got it," UN Building agreed.

Are they planning to hit more targets?

Who is claiming responsibility for this devastation?

What is the nation at large doing to protect its most populous city?

What is Manhattan doing to protect itself?

Just as Empire State and UN Buildings anticipated, these were just some of the questions dominating news feeds as towers and people alike hung onto every new development or "breaking news" headline, no matter how speculative it could have been.

One issue that was a unanimous point of focus was whether normal life would be forever altered by security measures. While most tried their best to get back to some form of routine existence, Manhattanite authorities declared an emergency mandate to fortify the island, meaning that a constant military presence was established, and the city was closed off to visitors for the foreseeable future.

Far more controversial, but as UN Building had warned, the area marking the final resting place of the Twin Towers— labeled as "Ground Zero" by the press—was set to be splintered off from the rest of Manhattan proper. In spite of pleas from still hopeful families of victims and staunch requests from others to preserve it as a memorial, environmental experts deemed the land far too volatile from a safety standpoint. The relentless spewing of toxic fumes into the air, they argued, endangered the lives of any Manhattanite within a three-mile radius.

Overworked hospital buildings were being filled to capacity by patients needing treatment for lung infections in the days following the attack, and their protests made the option of detonation all the more understandable. In the end, Manhattanite leadership—Empire State Building reluctantly included—approved the decision to break off the toxic acreage.

To be sure this was executed without a hitch, however, the responsibility of excavating and removing millions of tons of bedrock, toxic soil, and debris fell to skilled detonators from the city's leading construction union, with supervision from the Manhattan Military. So that they could perform a controlled removal of the island's southernmost tip, the area was blocked off, downtown subway tunnels were closed and sealed off, and detonators were placed at key locations deep within the island's core. After a final unsuccessful search-and-rescue attempt for any last survivors, the time came to press the button.

With crowds of buildings and people watching from a safe distance, detonation was set to occur on a breezy morning of the last day of September. Given the staggering number of attendees who came to Ground Zero to pay their final respects, the event evoked a funeral-like deference from the island's inhabitants.

Empire State and Chrysler Buildings were in attendance, as were UN Building, Lady Liberty, and Rockefeller Slab. Also present were many of the city's houses of worship—Trinity Church, Central Synagogue, St. Patrick's Cathedral, and Masjid Malcolm Shabazz among them. Each provided solemn prayers in their own way, and each struck a chord with the crowd. As the memorial was underway, security was understandably tight, and the Manhattan Military's fleet dotted the harbor all around them.

Following a final moment of silence, the area was cleared, and crews began the process of separation. The sound from the blast produced a gasp from the crowd, and a soft rumble from the shearing earth was felt on many streets and beneath the buildings' bases. Spectators watched in solemn wonder as waves from their mighty harbor rushed into the newly formed cracks of the separating landform.

While he watched, Empire State Building took one last glance at the twisted skeletal remains of his deceased friends, which gently drifted away from the island. "How could it end like this?" he whispered, no doubt reliving the horrors of that September morning in his mind.

Chrysler Building glanced up at him and saw a building physically drained by the month's onslaught of events. Based on his body language, she sensed that Empire State Building, long the buildings' steadfast mayor, was wearing his title more wearily than ever. He was hunched over, she observed, likely from a dangerous mix of grief and responsibility. He also developed an emptiness in his voice, she felt, especially when the press questioned him about policy or ongoing safety guarantees. Truly, Chrysler Building's companion was crushed with expectations and unable to answer many questions with confidence.

But the towers needed a leader, she reminded herself, and Empire State Building filled that role, even if he was in uncharted waters almost as much as they were. Chrysler Building continued to study her partner's shaky demeanor, knowing she could do little else at the moment but draw nearer to him as they buried the remains of their twin friends.

The event lasted another half hour, as they watched the contaminated site drift to its final resting spot far out in the harbor, past a distance deemed safe enough not to pose a health threat to the island. Long after the last toxic fumes had been exhausted off from the site, the severed land and its remains were expected to gradually sink into the sea. When that happened, the last physical evidence of the Twin Towers having ever existed would be given back to the waves of time.

PART 2 **THE RISING WAR**

PRIOR TO THE MURDER of the Twin Towers, Manhattan had been a largely euphoric place of infinite splendor, offering its inhabitants a dazzling menu rich in opportunity and inclination. Freedom to come to Manhattan and remake oneself was not only possible but encouraged, and once someone took a bite of the apple, it was as if nothing else beyond their little island mattered. Call it urban naiveté, but such was the power of its promise, which was probably what helped the city overcome previous calamities like slavery, global war, and economic depression.

In light of the murders, however, Manhattanites and buildings awoke to a place that was much more fearful of its own shadow. Security defined most aspects of daily life, and as the TERROR Group had anticipated, *trepidation* dictated the city's behavior from that point forward.

On a global scale, cities, towns, and villages struggled to come to terms with the meaning of Manhattan's recent tragedy, for that city, in a strange way, still belonged to everyone. For instance, as soon as news of the attack spread, governments far and wide donated blood of all types that was shipped to Manhattan. Letters from foreign dignitaries professing love and well wishes for the city's buildings and people followed, and vigils by the hundreds of thousands sprouted up across the planet, with portraits of the Twin Towers displayed alongside a sea of candles that commemorated the many human lives lost. Such incredible gestures of kindness reinforced the city's unshakable cultural influence and ran counter to any forces trying to crush it. As this mourning continued, songs were sung in earnest, prayers were recited in a thousand tongues, and each night, many regions of the planet cried themselves to sleep. Many regions ... but not all regions.

Out of everyone on the list of suspects, the TERROR Group was the obvious frontrunner. But exactly where it was headquartered remained a thorn in the sides of UN Building and his human constituents.

From the Modern Global War to just prior to the assault on the Twin Towers, the order was all but nonexistent on anyone's radar, managing to stay largely absent in the press. Reports of deadly activity were few and far between, and this absence was most evident during fruitless Manhattan Building Conferences.

But that was then. With the planet no longer sleeping, the search for the TERROR Group's whereabouts intensified, and while smoke from Ground Zero still fumed, security forces revved up their engines for what became 24/7 surveillance of the island and its surroundings. City officials signed orders that sought full protection by way of the Manhattan Military, giving the defense force the job of deflecting another possible attack by the TERROR Group or any affiliates. Armed with a dazzling fleet of streamlined vehicles, from state-of-the-art warships and jets to cutting-edge helicopters and tanks, the Manhattan Military also boasted an impressive army of soldiers dispersed throughout the city.

Almost overnight, Manhattan switched to a wartime economy for the first time in generations. Factory buildings were again put to work as venues for the production of new equipment and supplies that fed the city's defenses, and the Manhattan Military vigorously checked the cargo of every ship that went in and out of the harbor. Food rationing was in effect on a citywide scale, and a mandatory evening curfew was enforced for all Manhattanites. As was decided by both humans and buildings, such military activity became the dominating hustle and bustle filling Manhattan's streets.

"You believe what's going on around here?" Puglia Ristorante asked his equally short-in-stature and reactionary companion, Guggenheim Museum, during their evening walk.

"I can't even fathom the transformation," Guggenheim Museum replied, while numerous tanks drove past them.

"It seems *everyone* is swept up in the growing fear," Puglia Ristorante said as he gazed at a domineering portrait of Uncle Sam that dangled off of a nearby tower.

"Tell me about it," the museum said. "My lead curator just redirected all textile artists to produce uniforms for the Manhattan Military. They were just about to be featured in an upcoming exhibit about peace symbols! Even our graphic design team was taken off previous jobs to focus on creating these large-scale banners instead."

As they spoke, the image burned through their collective conscience, a frightening symbol for whatever challenges might lie ahead. Always a national folk-hero, Uncle Sam was used here to instill a "can-do" spirit in the streets below. *I WANT YOU*, the towering posters of the man with the furrowed brow demanded, his sharp finger pointing with an urgency equaled only by his distinct, piercing gaze.

Produced in droves, the ominous posters were draped onto buildings across the entire city, from the most pronounced towers in Times Square to those nestled near the narrowest of side streets. As a result, Uncle Sam dotted the cityscape in relentless, arresting fashion. The image—evoking war, fortification, and the feeling that another attack could happen at any moment—was unavoidable.

Though the buildings could remember Uncle Sam from the Modern Global War's heyday, a sense of visual intrusion was more apparent this time around. Back then, he was just another symbol of national unity, his image worn by buildings and people with casual pride as the war was being fought overseas. Lately, though, his presence forced itself into the view of the two friends who were just trying to forget their woes for a bit, to no avail.

"We may just have to get comfortable seeing him for the time being," the famously couth Guggenheim Museum conceded.

"Hey, whatever we gotta do, we gotta do," Puglia Ristorante said.

Given the high stakes climate, the city's precautionary measures didn't end with posters. High above the streets, for instance, many other towers of Manhattan had been pressed into service. At the insistence of the Manhattan Military, Empire State Building urged all buildings higher than fifty stories to keep watch for suspicious activity beyond the city's borders, such as in the sand dunes and forests surrounding the island. Come nightfall, tall buildings were also required to rest along the outer edges of the island, to form protective blockades for smaller buildings and Manhattanites sheltered farther inland. And any building designed with floodlighting capabilities was instructed to stay lit up for the entire night.

The Manhattan Military also insisted on mandatory practice drills for the buildings. In the event of an incoming missile attack, for instance, buildings were trained to bend downward or huddle themselves into groups for protection—a kind of "duck and cover" on a grand scale. Of course, Manhattanites within would be warned via loudspeaker to grab hold of anything fixed or secured to the building before these measures took place. While some questioned the effectiveness of these tactics, the training seemed to calm the city's nerves.

As a result of these precautions, buildings everywhere were outfitted with sirens in the event of mass evacuation or evasive action. Lady Liberty was to keep constant watch from her perch on Liberty Island, and Empire State and UN Buildings received daily security briefings from the Manhattan Military's top officials.

Gone were flagrant notions that Manhattan was still a safe harbor. Change was, once again, the only absolute, and the island's fortification was complete in a short amount of time. Its former self a memory, the city became a transformed symbol of sheltered living amid a rising war.

The grieving process could've gone on forever for some, but not for Empire State Building. Given the preponderance of moving parts involved in running a city during wartime, it was never an option for him. In fact, the tower felt more compelled than ever to turn his grief and angst into action, which was why he became involved in everything from search and recovery efforts to security measures, even as the press dogged him with questions concerning everything from safety protocols, to ethical violations, to Manhattan's financial losses from the attack. As much as the questions stung, he knew that they were a reflection of justified concerns. Manhattan was hurting badly by that time, and on a daily basis, Empire State Building could see how angry and lost his colleagues were. Towers once so proud and dignified were now hunched over as they walked about, often muttering something derogatory or mean-spirited along the way. Other buildings squabbled over the slightest inconveniences. Things like radiators that suddenly made too much noise, or lights that were either too dim or too bright, became popular complaints. In short, these buildings needed a calm leader to get them through this rough patch.

If he sometimes wanted to stop and mourn the haunting images of his slain friends when they entered his mind, Empire State Building instead used all his angst to lead anew. Gone were any lingering self-doubts, because that represented weakness. Henceforth, whenever any critics questioned his strategies, even the voices in his own head, he put those questions aside for a later date and pressed on. There was no time for debate, he resolved, for this was *real*, and real decisions required a reliance on instinct.

While certainly not flawless, his intuition was unquestionably seasoned, and Empire State Building saw no reason why he couldn't rely on it. This clarity of vision renewed his love for all that he held dear, including his beloved island and its inhabitants.

"I'll defend this place to my last breath," he swore to himself, knowing that somewhere within him resided a fully emancipated leader, and that Lady Liberty must have been proud to sense it.

Given the fractured state of the times, Empire State Building also knew that his decisions ran the risk of sparking controversy at every turn. His full-fledged cooperation with the Manhattan Military, for instance, forged a wartime identity onto the city, one that happened literally (and uncomfortably) overnight. This meant that strict new protocols—curfews and regular basement-to-rooftop searches among them—stripped away certain levels of freedom for the buildings, all in the name of Manhattan's security. But after receiving exhaustive advice from various experts, Empire State Building saw no other way for the city to carry on in the wake of the Twin Towers' murder, and the memory of his callously slain friends was all the justification he needed, anyway.

Ironically, the first hurdle that Empire State Building's emboldened mindset faced came not from another terror attack, but from an old friend and part-time rival. Rockefeller Slab, ever media savvy and intent on breaking stories, often fed Manhattan's news outlets headline-worthy updates from the city's most prominent towering giants. He was never one to publicly chastise Empire State Building's policies like Wall Street Tower was often inclined to, but

Rockefeller Slab was aware of his rocky history with the mayor, especially when matters regarding Chrysler Building were concerned. But given the diverse reactions confronting Empire State Building's policies of late, Rockefeller Slab offered his contemporary a chance to share his point of view in an upcoming interview. After all, he felt a journalistic responsibility to let viewers in on their chosen mayor's rationale regarding those controversial policies.

Empire State Building, in turn, sought to keep the city on his side, and welcomed the challenge. They arranged to have the interview at the end of yet another exhausting day by the eastern edge of the island. While Chrysler Building looked on eagerly, Rockefeller Slab activated his journalistic instincts, seizing the moment to hit the mayor with real hardballs.

"Thanks for taking the time to chat with me," he began as the interview streamed into homes all across the anxious city.

"It's good to be here," Empire State Building replied, though with a bit of apprehension in his tone.

"Now, wherever I seem to go, both buildings and Manhattanites are asking me this question, Empire State Building: Is there anything you'd like to say to your detractors? To some very vocal critics like Wall Street Tower, for instance, who complain about the risks associated with Manhattan becoming a police state? What I mean to say is, considering all that the city's been through lately, do you think this is the right direction for us to go?"

It was a tough punch to block, and Rockefeller Slab delivered it with a mixture of panache and determination, even if it rubbed his interviewee the wrong way. Normally, Empire State Building would have charmed his way through a minefield of such questions with answers satisfying enough to make the opposition dissipate, but not this time. Perhaps it was how Rockefeller Slab had posed the question that incited Empire State Building's sudden agitation, or maybe the tower was just sick and tired of the smell of burnt metal and charred remains, which still lingered over the island so stubbornly. Whatever the case, he went off the rails, and the frustration he'd been suppressing for the past few weeks culminated in a reprisal unlike anything he'd unleashed on camera before.

"First of all, you're bringing up Wall Street Tower to me? Seriously? I shouldn't have to explain much to him. Can you imagine how he'd handle this crisis right now? I certainly can't," Empire State Building let out sharply as he moved in closer to Rockefeller Slab's upper stories, as if engaged in a stare down.

"Well, that's fair, but what about other critical buildings, or those of the Manhattanites watching this from their homes right now?" Rockefeller Slab countered. "What do you say to them?"

"To all of them, yes, I will always provide details when I can, because I strive to level with them," Empire State Building said before pivoting a bit. "Look, something out there will attack us again if we let our guard down. I'll tell you this, Rockefeller Slab, and anyone watching right now. So long as I am mayor to my fellow towering giants, I will not sit back and accept a sitting-duck approach to this phantom threat! I was both designed and elected to serve Manhattan to the fullest extent of my abilities, and that's what I plan to keep doing."

Appreciating his subject's candor, Rockefeller Slab kept the momentum going. "Okay, and what is the extent to which buildings will work with the Manhattan Military? Are you expecting this to be a permanent relationship?"

"For now, yes, it will have to be ongoing, according to Manhattanite authorities. But it wasn't a decision taken lightly, Rockefeller Slab. Rather, it was one that involved intense consideration from a variety of constituents."

"And this is all to guarantee our protection, I presume?"

"Of course! Nothing's guaranteed, but that's the goal, yes. I believe that full cooperation with the Manhattan Military is essential in ensuring that *we* buildings stay focused on our wartime tasks, thereby allowing us to remain vigilant protectors of the Manhattanites we serve." After a long exhale, Empire State Building glanced over at Chrysler Building as she watched with approval. "Now, what else do you have for me?"

For the first time in all the years that he'd known his great rival, Rockefeller Slab struggled to come up with a pithy follow-up. It had taken a swift tragedy for Empire State Building to sharpen his decision-making skills, and Rockefeller Slab saw in his subject few signs of a shaky leader. At that moment, both buildings welcomed a liberating newfound mutual respect.

Replacing his final question with a simple observation, Rockefeller Slab conceded. "Well, on that note, let's stop there for now, for I see why you're doing what you're doing, Empire State Building. Based on our talk, I would say to everyone watching at home that I feel a little safer, and I think that many of my fellow buildings would agree. I appreciate you taking the time to entertain these questions tonight," he uncharacteristically conceded.

*AGAINST A BACKDROP OF UNSPEAKABLE TRAGEDY
AND LINGERING CRITICS, MAYOR REBRANDS
HIS IMAGE AND REDISCOVERS HIS VOICE.*

Such was the press' post-game analysis of the interview, which landed with a feeling of welcome support for Empire State Building, and his approval ratings climbed steadily. Even though Manhattan had momentous challenges to face, its buildings still had a mayor that they could count on, and he would never again be labeled as an unsure policymaker. From that point forward, Empire State Building always told himself to lead with his instincts, a practice that came to matter more in the days ahead.

Motivated by his newfound catharsis, Empire State Building seemed to accept any new challenge with panache, especially meetings requested by Lady Liberty. During her latest emergency session, featuring a roster that included UN Building and top defense strategists from the Manhattan Military residing within him, the buildings expected a range of topics to be debated by a spirited panel. Wall Street Tower was also invited to attend for tradition's sake, even as he famously remained a detriment to Empire State Building's leadership—especially in light of the recent Rockefeller Slab interview.

Such partisan division was set to be on full display, even if the true reasoning behind the session remained a mystery. As the buildings gathered on the heavily fortified Liberty Island, Empire State Building seemed emboldened and primed for a proactive session, and upon being given the green light from Lady Liberty to handle opening remarks, he began in earnest.

"I understand that the green lady called us here to discuss certain classified topics, but as long as we're all present, I hope to discuss ways that we buildings can remain vigilant protectors of the Manhattanites we serve. With that, I'm open to any topics to start." He gestured to his fellow buildings.

Following the tower's introduction, Lady Liberty remained idle in the background, even as she sensed the mood of the session shifting because of the conflicting interests and egos. Wall Street

Tower, fearing primarily for his own safety as a potential target, immediately emerged as the loudest voice.

"Let me just get some thoughts out there. Now, I've had some very long and, frankly, perfectly executed discussions with some of my constituency, and we're already planning a motion to pay off the attackers," he proudly announced.

"Excuse me?" UN Building said, shocked.

"Just hear me out. It's obvious we can't measure the perpetrator's destructive potential, and thanks to Empire State Building's incompetent leadership, we absolutely have *no idea* what else they're capable of. But money talks, as they say, and I can prepare an enticing monetary offer in a matter of hours that will sweep our problems under the rug. Our enemies will have no choice but to agree to spare us from any future attack." Fiscally driven even in the darkest of times—this was Wall Street Tower's approach to things big and small.

"So, your solution is to simply throw money at the problem? It's unbelievable to even suggest this," UN Building remarked with disdain.

Empire State Building stepped in firmly, as Lady Liberty continued to watch in silence. "I agree, that's *not* going to happen. Period. You can't buy off enemies."

Shocked that the rest of the group wasn't embracing his proposal with open arms, Wall Street Tower doubled down. "Correct me if I'm wrong, but whose fault is it that we're in this position in the first place? The fact that you, Empire State Building, couldn't prevent what happened shows a certain degree of incompetence on your part!"

Before Empire State Building had a chance to defend himself, UN Building beat him to the punch. "Wait, wait, wait. Just what are you saying?"

"What I'm saying," Wall Street Tower continued, "is that if I were still mayor, we would not be having this conflict and the Twin Towers would still be here today!"

"And you believe that, do you?" Empire State Building asked.

"Not only do I believe it, but I can almost guarantee it. And if we had been attacked under my watch, I guarantee you I could have ended it within probably twenty-four hours."

"I see," Empire State Building said in a mocking fashion.

"It's ridiculous to get into such a blame game," UN Building objected. "We've much more pressing matters to discuss than these petty notions!"

His façade pulsating with disgust, Wall Street Tower amped up his ire against the diplomat. "I suppose you're gearing up for yet another peace-pipe talk then, UN Building?" he challenged.

"Hey, at least I'm not proposing to buy my way out of this problem like some," the diplomat retorted with further agitation.

"Oh please, you're just focused on kissing the world's ass and making everyone love you. I got news—not everyone loves you!" Wall Street Tower shot back.

For all watching, it was an unpleasant exchange of slights, slurs, and slanders, indicative of how the city was gradually turning on itself.

Lady Liberty had seen enough. "This stops now!" she shouted mightily. "Infighting is *exactly* what our opponent expects us to do. Besides, we have a greater matter to focus on now, so put your ego aside and listen. The reason why I called this meeting is that something was revealed to me in a vision earlier today. Another impending threat, far more grand and hellish than the first, is likely coming to our shores. This is classified, so please refrain from telling anyone else until a plan is forged."

All arguments and accusations came to a crashing halt in light of the statue's disturbing announcement.

"A plan for what?" Empire State Building asked.

"If my visions are true," the green lady continued, "we must be ready to leave Manhattan at a moment's notice if necessary."

"You've gotta be kidding me!" Wall Street Tower gasped, his columns weakening from under him and forcing the building to rest against the island's pedestal.

UN Building, equally floored by the revelation, shook his upper stories in frustration and stared out toward the harbor, while Lady Liberty, her expression ripe with fear, turned her attention to Empire State Building.

"This is the second time I'm seeing you like this as of late," Empire State Building admitted as he took in the green lady's grim demeanor. "Here you stand before us, our stoic purveyor of peace, telling us we're about to be attacked again. Are you positive about this?"

A cloud of anxiety seemed to hover over everyone present as they waited for Lady Liberty's final prognosis.

"If history is any guide, then yes, I have no doubt these Schistian visions warn of Pegmatite's further malice," she confirmed, her voice fragile as glass.

"I understand," Empire State Building said in a regretful tone, as crashing waves struck more violently against Liberty Island's shores. The resulting mist felt unpleasant against each building's façade.

"Winds are picking up," UN Building said. "We better continue this *wonderful* session first thing tomorrow."

"Yeah, whatever. Fine," Wall Street Tower agreed before swimming back to Manhattan Island.

As the others dispersed one by one, Empire State Building took a moment to collect his thoughts, ruminating on all the necessary precautions, since it appeared that no other option existed than to trust in Lady Liberty's visions. "Where would we go?" he whispered to the statue.

"Wherever Schist guides us. But exactly where that might be is yet to be known," the green lady said. "Let us rest on it for tonight. Come dawn's first light, we will think of something tangible."

Following his restless evening, during which a thousand possible scenarios seemed to play out in his mind, Empire State Building's morning commenced in earnest.

"I've just been informed that the Manhattan Military has completed its investigation and confirmed that the TERROR Group is the sole perpetrator of the attack that killed our friends," he announced during the reconvened session.

"Our worst fears are true then," UN Building said, "and Lady Liberty's premonitions are on the mark."

"Yes," Empire State Building continued. "Which means we must confront the uncomfortable task of deciding just when Manhattan stops being a place worth holding down."

"Oh! So you want an exit strategy?" Wall Street Tower scoffed.

"It may be the only way to save everyone should things accelerate," Lady Liberty said. "We must be open to any and all scenarios."

"It's a possibility right now. Not anticipated, but a possibility nonetheless," Empire State Building replied, a bit calmer in his demeanor than he'd been the night before.

But Wall Street Tower continued to throw a fit, and UN Building became more acclimated to the notion.

Whatever their reactions, however, all involved agreed that such an existential conundrum rattled the strategy session with fervor. As the morality of the topic was dissected and discussed further, the buildings finally agreed on something—Manhattan could be anyplace, so long as its citizens were around to carry the torch.

"It's settled then," Empire State Building said after much back and forth. "If Lady Liberty's visions become real, we will indeed leave this island and relocate, but as no less *Manhattanites* than we are right now."

By the end of the session, a concrete plan was forged. Working directly with the Manhattan Military, the buildings outlined exit procedures, referred to as *Code One* and *Code Two*. The first code called for a "local evacuation," where Manhattanites would flee from danger zones by heading into adjacent districts still within the island's bounds. If this strategy occurred, all buildings were mandated to house their maximum capacity of people for an indefinite period.

By contrast, *Code Two* was the unpopular backup plan, albeit one more in line with accounting for Lady Liberty's grim premonitions. In the event that *Code One* was taken off the table, *Code Two* involved a mass exodus of the island's entire population of buildings and people. While several sanctuary sites across a wide area beyond Manhattan's borders were discussed, exact destinations remained murky given the fact that nobody knew where the enemy would come from. As a result, *Code Two* allowed for the possibility that Manhattan's population might flee into even the notoriously vast, mysterious, and unforgiving sand dunes beyond the island's mapped out scope.

The strategy triggered a sequence of events in which Manhattan Military representatives drafted up documents to push the agreed-upon directives into official procedure. It was a process that was considerably easier to discuss than to enforce. Nevertheless, *Code*

One and *Code Two* became legitimate options, despite the frightening prospect of having to actually carry them out someday.

The next week marked two months following the attack that claimed the Twin Towers' lives, and Empire State Building gazed upon a wintry city in lockdown. As the winds crashed with an icy chill against his sides, the building's hope that Lady Liberty's premonitions were misread grew stronger by the day.

It was a bewildering time for Manhattan's leadership, with one public relations headache after another. The TERROR Group remained elusive on a global front, and the passage of time began to downplay the city's sense of urgency in having such high-level security measures as *Code One* and *Code Two*. Rumors even began to circulate around the idea that the order had dissolved, in light of what many experts classified to be its accomplished mission, namely, the murder of the Twin Towers and the resulting impact it had on Manhattan's economic standing. To average Manhattanites watching their city go from a vibrant gateway to an isolated bunker, the idea that the TERROR Group had gotten all that it wanted seemed very plausible.

Empire State Building's mind roiled and replayed many such concerns as he continued to breathe in the city's air. He shook his upper stories in frustration when reminded of the conspiracy theory suggesting the Twin Towers' murders had been an inside job, as certain media outlets entertained. It was a charge he vehemently denied publicly, knowing full well how such claims angered much of Manhattan's building population, and added another public obstacle in the way of the Manhattan Military's safety measures.

However unfounded the claim had been, the past several days did involve Empire State Building spending extra time justifying each new decision in an increasingly frustrating public fashion, while the growing backlash against wartime restrictions forced the Manhattan Military to compromise by lifting several minor rules.

But for many, these reparations weren't enough, and Manhattan's human population had plummeted to only thirty percent of what it had been before the Twin Towers' deaths. To add insult to injury, many of the towering giants who'd hoped to stick it out on the island wound up departing for the nearest northern towns and sanctuary cities that existed beyond the Manhattan Forest. As a result, the streets looked and felt bleak to Empire State Building as he patrolled them that night, their cavernous stretches of asphalt and sidewalk devoid of that most precious component—activity.

The city, to him, was beating with only half its heart in the game, as buildings performed their daily tasks with apathy, hardly speaking to one another, and obviously on edge—a direct reflection of what Manhattanites were also feeling. It seemed everyone remained shellshocked in the face of such bleak proceedings.

Empire State Building's mind continued to flood with these dreary observations. But after another tough day of contention, the building decided to rest it all off, and he perched himself just south of the park before Chrysler Building was set to join him. Night was the time to recharge, he reminded himself as he continued to admire Central Park's leafless groves of willow trees that poked up from the grass like needles from a carpet; a landscape lifeless at first glance but very much alive up close.

"When will our once-teeming city be able to awaken from this long slumber?" he whispered against the howling November winds.

As he waited for his partner, Empire State Building played out the next morning's Manhattan Building Conference, knowing that any grimness in his body language could raise concern if detected.

I must continue to keep my composure, now more than ever, the tower reminded himself.

Like most great leaders, he had the unfair responsibility of maintaining his countenance in times of grave concern—a task easier said than done. But despite lingering challenges to his leadership, it remained clear to him that all roads still led to this. There *was no* conspiracy, he believed, and little chance of a sudden "dissolution" of the TERROR Group. Still, what did the future hold?

Remembering his own surveillance policy, he switched on his floodlights, which lit up his top floors that night with a patriotic display of red, white, and blue. It was his go-to lighting combination ever since the Twin Towers had been killed—a display of permanence in an otherwise fragile time.

Then, *she* appeared.

Chrysler Building, careful in her steps to not disturb any streets below, moved in to join him for the evening. As he gazed upon her with sentimental, boyish reverence, Empire State Building maintained an unnatural obligation to this glowing ember—his devotion to her a microcosm of his devotion to the city at large.

Together, the two had experienced the best and worst over the years, each often drawn into the heart of the city's endless episodes, heartbreaks, successes, and scandals. Through stories of triumph and trepidation, the two had been there to experience Manhattan in all its emotional shades.

"Red, white, and blue look mighty fine on you tonight," Chrysler Building whispered as she drew nearer, before seeing in Empire State Building's demeanor a need for more than flirty interaction. "What's wrong?" she asked upon sensing his dejection.

Empire State Building quivered slightly, grateful after all these years that a building like Chrysler Building would even give him the time of day. She ran one of her eagle gargoyles across his side, anxious to hear what was on his mind.

Empire State Building unburdened his long-controlled insecurities. "After all this, I'm not sure that I can lead for much longer, Chrysler Building. The city's getting increasingly frustrated by my direction. Hell, *I'm* frustrated by my direction," he admitted. "And I'm not sure if I'm thinking with my instincts anymore. I thought I was. But perhaps things are getting beyond my control. Maybe the city needs a fresh perspective."

Chrysler Building was startled by her lover's admission. "Hey, you know as much as anyone that this is what I've been wanting to hear for a while now, but guess what? This is *no* time to be thinking that way," she cautioned, reminding herself that Empire State Building was a building who always prided himself on being a thoroughbred. Now, the complexities that ran amok in his mind—that certain obsession he harbored of trying to solve every problem— were chipping away at his character.

"What do you mean?" he asked.

"I know you're working at full capacity," she continued as another cool breeze grazed the two buildings, "and I can see signs of fatigue in your body language, in the way you've been carrying yourself as of late. I see it right now. The loss of the Twin Towers was a blow to us all, but especially to you. I know what they meant to you, ever since you took them under your wing. But that's exactly why you can't step down just yet."

Empire State Building turned away in quiet shame.

"Let me help you more along the way," Chrysler Building insisted, as she veered back into his view.

"You just might have to," he said. "If the buildings turn against me at tomorrow's conference, it's a sign that they want someone better."

Chrysler Building shook her crown in disapproval. "Why think along those lines?" she challenged.

"Because my instincts say one thing, but the voices inside me say something else. Day and night, I hear Manhattanites talking away, saying that I should give up my position, or change my approach, or do this or do that. And it's even worse with buildings, because I can read their discontent just by how they greet me. I'm trying to keep everyone safe, my love, while staying true to my convictions. But if I feel the buildings have turned against me tomorrow, I'll relinquish my mayoral responsibilities then and there, and ask you, Lady Liberty, and the rest to select a new nominee."

Chrysler Building gave thought to the prospect of Empire State Building trading his political life in favor of something more normal. Nearly as quickly, however, she felt taken aback by the idea. Over the last few months, Manhattan had shifted on such a seismic level that all precepts and desires had come into question. What was in store for the city of tomorrow? Better yet, would there even *be* a tomorrow? In many ways, Chrysler Building recognized that such normality no longer existed.

"Well, if that's truly the way things turn out tomorrow, then I'll think about it, but that's not what I had in mind when I said I'd help you," she said.

Empire State Building looked at her in a state of bewilderment. "Why are you fighting me on this?"

Chrysler Building, glancing out at the windswept park, clarified as only she could. "Why? Just look around, my love. What do you see? The buildings are scared. We lost two of our brightest along with countless others, and we've been asked to step up to the plate and pretend that none of this hinders us. We're all in pain, and the only way we will forge ahead is with you at the helm, despite any objections. We need a leader, and that leader is you! You're the right one at the right time, whether or not you can see it."

Chrysler Building then leaned in closer, her gleaming crown gazing with candor into Empire State Building's highest floors. "When the Twin Towers collapsed into a billow of smoke and dust, you told me that it felt like you had stared death in the face, remember that? They can't replicate that kind of experience. Believe me, I'd love to run away from all this and start a new life with you, someplace far off where the monsters won't ever come. But no such place exists, and that's not what we were designed for. The buildings who took off to other places have gotten it all wrong. We're built to defend what we love, not run from it."

The right one at the right time, indeed.

As he processed Chrysler Building's argument, Empire State Building looked around at the seemingly infinite perimeter of the island, its remaining buildings keeping watch for the night, their upper stories washed by floodlights like lighthouses in a sea of darkness. *Vigilant and dedicated are these towering giants*, he thought.

"Well," he finally replied, "maybe all I've worked for is indeed ripping at the seams, or maybe it isn't. I may never be able to single-handedly heal the city like I want to, or remain as emotionally resonant as Lady Liberty is on a daily basis. But if you say that I'm the right one at the right time, then I'll try harder, my love. I'll try harder."

In a sign of approval, Chrysler Building's neon windows glowed brightly before dimming back down again to their usual intensity. "I'm proud of you," she said warmly, and the two icons drew in closer to prepare for another night's repose.

PART 3 **THE WRATH OF TERROR**

WAKING TO CATCH the first rays of light striking the morning sky, Empire State Building was relieved to have gotten any sleep at all. His upcoming itinerary was set to be chock-full of strategy sessions, defense talks, and policy hearings—a day where victory at one gathering didn't necessarily mean the same at another. At least Chrysler Building's welcome and motivating words would linger in his mind throughout the day.

Per his usual routine, UN Building approached the waking couple, no doubt eager to go over the day's busy schedule, if a bit more anxious in his strut than usual.

"Top of the morning, everyone, top of the morning!" he let out boisterously as other towers big and small perked up from the sudden wake-up call.

"I'll, uh, catch you later, my love," Chrysler Building said, seeking her chance to remove herself from the policy-heavy proceedings to come, choosing rather to spend most of her day cheering up buildings who were out guarding the island's perimeter. But it wasn't exactly cut and run on her part, for public relations was an artform she excelled at. Given that this was an island where building morale had been declining for quite some time, a simple "how are you doing" from Chrysler Building was enough to lift any tower's spirits. The press, meanwhile, loved every second of her behavior, for her gestures often attracted the attention and support of donors looking to aid in the city's upkeep. *If only Empire State Building were lucky enough to inspire such gestures of approval with his procedures*, Chrysler Building mused as the two icons parted ways.

Shortly thereafter, UN Building plowed through various tasks with Empire State Building—each a more important action item than the previous. As soon as he read off his last checklist topic, the overburdened ambassador let out a sudden sigh of relief. From one overworked tower to the other, Empire State Building could read fatigue all over the façade of his Modernist friend.

"You look tired, champ," Empire State Building observed. "How are you holding up?"

UN Building slouched a bit, as if weighed down by the question. "Oh well, you know how it is … lukewarm these days, I suppose," the diplomat replied, his glass-curtain wall reflecting a sky now fully aglow with morning light. "Sometimes it's hard to believe such beautiful rays can still touch down on this place, am I right?" he added with a degree of fatigue in his voice.

It was Empire State Building's turn to slouch as UN Building continued his train of thought. "I just can't believe how things could fall apart like they did. And I tried, do not get me wrong, Empire State. I tried hard, but they gave us nothing, this TERROR Group, not a crumb, despite all this time, all our efforts to create a global watchdog, all those attempts at diplomacy, years of trying to come to some kind of accord with this invisible presence. And look at the result. We've faced conflict before, sure, but not like this. Not like this at all. Maybe I just don't have it anymore. Maybe I oughta retire!"

Empire State Building looked around to notice more towers beginning to wake. "You and me both, my friend," he said. "But let's not retire just yet, eh? Besides, your commitment to this city is something I treasure, and your calls for world peace are still the right ones, despite what the circumstances are giving us."

"If you say so," UN Building obliged. "Now, how do you want to open today's conference?"

A look of determination came over Empire State Building as he straightened his posture. "We open," he said, "by restating my position that under *no* circumstance shall we bow to the TERROR Group's ominous silence. From there, I'll double down on my stance that buildings should remain in the city, and that we're doing every-thing possible to keep this island intact."

Though he tried his best to stay attentive, UN Building appeared preoccupied by other concerns.

"What am I missing?" Empire State Building asked.

"There's one more thing I should mention," his friend added. "Mind you, this is highly classified and the only towering giants who have clearance to know are you, me, and Lady Liberty for now. Manhattan Military intelligence ran a few more suspect profiles to identify who could possibly be leading this TERROR Group."

"And?" Empire State Building inquired anxiously.

"And they support our theories that the so-called Chieftains probably rule the upper brackets of the network with an iron fist. They also can confirm that many of the human remains found in various pillaged towns and villages around the world were of defec-tors, meaning most of those kidnapped were either recruited or killed off during training."

"I see. That's how their forces are able to grow in number, then," Empire State Building noted as he took in a long, deep breath. "What else?"

"There's also early information coming in about some so-called Commander figure, a separate entity, it seems, from the Chieftains, and one who our intelligence indicates may be the one carrying out the latest global attacks. He could very well be the mastermind behind the Twin Towers' assault, if that's the case."

"What else do we know about this Commander?"

"Not much, Empire State, but there's talk about this guy being a poster boy for the movement, thanks to newly recovered propa-ganda. Still, there's little rhyme or reason to his methods. That's what frightens me most about him," UN Building said.

"Why's that?" Empire State Building pressed.

"Because nothing seems sacred to this guy, this Commander, who just so happens to be leading a sympathetic organization with no other purpose than to decimate; no logic or motivation other than power over whoever's in his way, be they friends or foes. If that's accurate, Empire State, we could have a real problem here," UN Building admitted. "There would likely be no reasoning or diplomacy with this guy. A killer without loyalty is the most unpredictable and dangerous of them all."

***

Elsewhere that morning, near Manhattan's dramatically altered southern tip, Trinity Church's clanging clock plucked him from yet another "on and off" sleeping episode. Despite many of his colleagues preferring otherwise, the church found a strange comfort in hanging about so near to where the recent tragedy had taken place. But the aging structure awakened at a slower pace than usual, his Schistian-infused steel framework creaking and moaning noticeably from the changing seasons. Not every building had that ageless dexterity that Lady Liberty possessed.

Must be this chill in the air, he thought as such arthritic reminders made the church long for his earlier days of unlimited vitality. Still, he managed a short walk under the calming morning rays, hoping to ease his ailments. Pacing carefully along the shore, the church reflected upon his many sermons of the past that connected suffering with reward, for instance. *Is this another such example?* he wondered, like so many of his colleagues who were simply trying to make sense of their new normal.

While older icons like Trinity Church—and Lady Liberty before him—had a staunch belief in Manhattan's capacity to learn from calamity, it seemed no amount of morning light could make the church forget the city's latest grievances for too long. His aches and pains remained a stubborn, nagging presence for the remainder of his walk, even as he surveyed the sullen city all around, and took a quick glance out at the lifeless, half-sunken skeletal remains of his twin friends that jutted up from the harbor beyond.

"So gentle-hearted and larger-than-life were they," he whispered solemnly, all the while recalling times when he'd given them each a quick "hello" before tackling whatever tasks his own day had in store. Alas, never again.

The Manhattan Building Conference was just about to start along the island's eastern edge, and as droves of fully occupied buildings made their way to the event, Guggenheim Museum, the drafted master of ceremonies for the morning, did his best to help direct the flow.

"Single file! Yes, thank you. Mind the street, please ... Much obliged! Sorry, excuse me. Single file, single file, thank you. Good day, move along, please."

The museum's nervousness was a microcosm of the collective angst that loomed large over the proceedings. It was a hotly anticipated event, after all, to be broadcast by many more media outlets than usual. And given the fact that it was the first official Manhattan Building Conference since the formation of the *Code One* and *Code Two* protocols, there was every reason for the buildings to be wary. Security remained on high alert for the occasion, with Manhattan Military helicopters and airships patrolling the air and seas at a maximum radius, fervently keeping an eye out for anything unusual.

Organized as usual by UN Building, the goal for the day was to provide the city's inhabitants with updates on the state of the island, as well as to answer any pressing questions. Aside from UN and Empire State Buildings, others scheduled to speak included Lady Liberty, as well as senior officers from the Manhattan Military. Central Synagogue, Trinity Church, Masjid Malcolm Shabazz, and St. Patrick's Cathedral were on hand to lead an interfaith closing prayer, while a number of Times Square towers, under the watchful direction of Rockefeller Slab, were present to live-stream the session to millions tuning in from cities, towns, and villages across the nation.

Given the circumstances, one aspect *not* present was a sense of good cheer that usually came about whenever these conferences had happened in the past. Gone, for instance, were fun-loving greetings between buildings as they settled in, while in their place a palpable sense of suspicion hung ominously over the proceedings. It was as if everyone present had the same question on their minds: what *exactly* was the state of their city?

Just before the conference commenced, Lady Liberty pulled aside Empire State Building as he was getting ready. "Is everything okay?" she prodded.

His concerns, recently shared with both Chrysler and UN Buildings, still lingered in the back of his mind, and he paused for a second before replying. "I hoped my demeanor wouldn't be too obvious, Lady Liberty, but seeing as you're the third one to ask me that today, maybe you can say a few words before I'm up, just so I can get my bearings. I don't know what's wrong with me this morning."

"I understand, for we are all a little on edge," the green lady added before agreeing to the tower's suggestion. "Let me open with a few remarks and then hand it off to you. But do not worry, it will go fine," she reassured him.

Moments later, Guggenheim Museum prepared the crowd with what became an off-the-cuff monologue that was contrary to what he'd previously rehearsed the night before with Puglia Ristorante, since his ever-jovial confidante had suggested opening up with a joke or two, in order to alleviate what was sure to be a dire session.

"Good morning, everyone. Let us begin. As you have probably gathered, there will be no opening remarks today like we've done in times past, no light-hearted words to keep up appearances. In truth, my anxiousness to receive updates about our fair city mirrors yours, so without further ado, let us welcome our very own UN Building to the fore."

After thanking the emcee, UN Building began in earnest. "Buildings and Manhattanites, good morning. We're here today to not only remember our beloved friends who were taken from us, but also to look ahead. Concerns are great, so let us share how we feel, in the hope of forging onward with a strategy that will renew us. And to echo the sentiments of Lady Liberty, Empire State Building, as well as numerous Manhattanite leaders, it's crucial that we band together and look after each other." Letting his words sink in, UN Building then invited Empire State Building to elaborate, unaware of the last-minute switch between his forthcoming speakers.

Lady Liberty ascended abruptly, hoping to avoid any grumbling among the crowd. "Thank you UN Building, and good morning everyone," she began. "I want to just share a few words before we hear from our mayor. As we know, something sinister came to our shores two months ago. And though I sensed its impending danger in visions as real as any, I too lacked foresight to prevent the inevitable. I am sorry that I could not do more to stop it."

Following restrained applause, Lady Liberty continued. "In spite of all the struggles we have faced since, however, I want you to know that the spirits of our great twin brothers, as well as all those taken with them, from our firefighters to our fellow buildings, are now at peace. We will pr—" Suddenly overcome with emotion herself, Lady Liberty stumbled to conclude her sentence, and Empire

State Building approached to whisper a few words of encouragement to her.

As the crowd's enthusiasm grew encouraging, the emboldened statue pressed on. "Sorry, what I meant to say is that we will *prevail*, through thick and thin. Manhattan *will not* bow to those who did this!"

The applause subsided after a few more moments, and Empire State Building couldn't help but be reminded of the raw sincerity Lady Liberty exuded, wanting nothing more than to follow her words with deference and action. Taking a deep breath, Empire State Building gazed out at a skyline ready to hang onto every word he was about to utter, and now was the time to regain his composure yet again.

"Thank you, Lady Liberty, for everything you do," the tower said as a gesture of personal reflection before segueing into his prepared remarks. "Let me just start off by reaffirming to you that we're doing everything in our power to combat this looming threat. For example, *Code One* and *Code Two* were initiated in order to..."

Suddenly, Empire State Building stopped mid-sentence, realizing just how empty his explanation would seem to the ears of the wary audience, who in his mind let out a collective groan as if to say, "These are the words of a tired politician who's just convoluting a problem with endless commentary." So, after pausing to collect his thoughts and remember why he was there in the first place, he started over.

"Look," he continued, "my friendship with the Twin Towers happened gradually, and only after I was able to get past my own pride and ego. Thinking of all that now, I see that I owe plenty to them and never had the chance to let them know it. They carried a youthful spirit I *used* to know, that I'm sure a lot of us used to know but may have lost along the way. This is one thing out of many that I won't forget about them."

He paused again to survey his surroundings, noticing Chrysler Building, who had turned up after all, hoping to lend some moral support for her companion.

"Now," Empire State Building went on, "regarding the security of our city, I know that there were great concerns with my support of quarantining Ground Zero, but trust me when I say that it wasn't an easy decision to make. Only when informed of the toxins that the site would continue to release into the air, I listened to the science which said that separating the site was the most logical answer to keeping us safe. So serious was the danger, in fact, that if given that same choice today, I would still support such a measure."

Gaining sway with the crowd, Empire State Building segued smoothly into his next point. "Now, the difficult decision of maintaining a temporary police state, if we want to call it that, is something that I have to support, as long as its singular goal is to ensure our protection. You've asked why I'm putting more buildings at risk, and why I'd like every building, including myself, to stand tall and keep watch. As unwelcome as this strategy may seem, we simply *cannot* look past our Schistian building codes, which call for diligence in protecting those we house, no matter what. If you recall, the Twin Towers complied with this principle until the very end, as they heroically demonstrated by standing upright for as long as possible to ensure that those within them had a better chance of escape. I witnessed this gallant act firsthand when I rushed to try and get to them. I imagine they must have endured *unimaginable* pain by that point."

Empire State Building paused to take a breath as he thought of his lost friends. "We can't downplay the suffering they endured, or live it down, or take it for granted, for we buildings have a strong bond with the people we serve. Manhattanites are our lifeblood, and we are their great protectors. It's really that simple. Nothing should ever run counter to that, despite what critics say. For that reason alone, I trust the Manhattan Military's dedication to our safety, and I ask each building to join me in trusting it as well. I also implore you to come to terms with *Code One* and *Code Two* as necessary precautions, because that's what they are. Like you, I hope we never have to activate either one of them, but that remains to be seen as we continue to navigate through this nightmare together. I'll close by asking for your renewed patience in this time of relentless challenges. With that, let's take some questions."

He couldn't have possibly stated his case any better, but Empire State Building's public duties always invited some kind of criticism, and like clockwork, as the hard-earned applause began to wane, an ever-skeptical Wall Street Tower rose to cast the first stone at his longtime rival.

"If I may just jump in here, Empire State Building. Your administrative buildings are all doing a fine job of nicely sugarcoating the situation for us, but I think we need to get past all the heroic schmaltz and talk more about dollars and cents. Lift the ban! Pay the man! That's what I say anyway. It's the only way to make this problem go away. You know it, I know it, *everybody* here knows it!" he declared. "As it stands, we're living in a freedom-less state because of your decisions!"

The accusation was enough to provoke heated debate from out the windows of many buildings, as Manhattanites within argued their views on the matter, and buildings soon joined in the commotion.

"There, there, let's not reduce ourselves to shouting!" Guggenheim Museum uselessly scolded from the street below.

"Hey, let's have some order here!" said UN Building with a bit more bite, as Lady Liberty and Empire State Building stood by silently, each taken aback by the hoopla but also expecting it to a degree. Like most traditions as of late, it was obvious that the conference was unraveling by the second, and the shouting began to intensify.

Amid the ongoing outbursts, Chrysler Building approached her lover in an attempt to shield him from the mayhem. "You said what you should have. He's way out of line for accusing you like that," she said vehemently.

"No, he's just angry. They all are," Empire State Building acknowledged. A renewed sense of failure began to nip away at any thoughts of progress he had felt only a few minutes prior.

UN Building tried once again to contain the situation as best he could. "Please, everybody, let's not reduce ourselves to this. Let's talk things out. That's why we're here!" he pleaded to no avail, as the streets below rumbled from the upheaval of the agitated towers. Clearly, the dignity of previous Manhattan Building Conferences had no place in a post-September 11th climate, and UN Building, for one, needed to accept this.

But in the thick of the commotion and mounting frustration, there came a faint hissing sound from several Times Square buildings' feeds, and unexpected interference appeared on their projection screens soon after. One by one, images of news coverage and advertisements faded, replaced by an obscure, twisted figure set against a bright-red backdrop.

Rockefeller Slab was the first to notice the disturbance. "Quiet, everybody, quiet! Look at the screens!" he shouted.

Chrysler and Empire State Buildings turned their attention to the image with a knowing gaze, and the rest of the buildings paused to watch the shadowy creature as well. In no time, the crowd's behavior shifted from showings of anger to one of stillness.

"There he is," Lady Liberty said to UN Building as she stared at the menacing presence.

The TERROR Commander's deafening voice reverberated through the crowd as he made his public debut. "Good morning, one and all. Nice to find my animals feasting so early in the day! And how predictable it is to see this behavior," the figure on the screen mused, as onlookers remained motionless. The TERROR Commander's glowing red eyes burned brighter, and he grinned while he continued. "Firstly, I hope that you appreciated our little gift two months ago, for we certainly worked extra hard in making it memorable."

"Where's this coming from?" Empire State Building asked the Manhattan Military personnel within his upper floors, who tried to pinpoint the signal's origin as fast as they could.

"No indication so far, sir. There's too much interference. He's using some kind of scrambler," one technician responded.

"Well, unscramble it before we lose him!" the tower urged as the TERROR Commander continued his verbal tirade.

"Secondly, I've got breaking news, and it's that we're planning a follow-up for you all very soon, one that will be bigger, bolder, and more memorable than before."

Aside from several gasps, the crowd remained numb with disbelief while the ominous presence on the screen kept spewing his poison. "But enough with my teasers. I put myself before you to proclaim what I know so far, which is that your city is an outdated, outmoded cesspool of ideals. The time has come to purge your unclean pursuits and replace them with a more applicable recipe for righteousness, one fit for Pegmatite. So just sit back and enjoy the show. I look forward to meeting you soon."

At that instant, the screens turned static, and the crowd became restless again.

"And just like that, he's gone? Did we manage to trace it?" UN Building asked anxiously.

"Nothing," Empire State Building relayed.

"It doesn't matter. I have a feeling we'll be hearing from him again," Rockefeller Slab surmised with trepidation in his tone.

With his bold and declarative introduction, the TERROR Commander's words sparked emotional shockwaves across the entire city and into the homes of the millions of Manhattanites watching, who in turn flung open their windows to shout words of panic at the buildings all around.

"This is a warning not to take lightly," Lady Liberty said in a stern voice.

The intently focused Empire State Building soon formulated a strategy. Upon being informed that the TERROR Commander's whereabouts were still unknown, he gathered UN Building, Lady Liberty, and several others for an emergency session with the Manhattan Military.

"All other buildings are to return to their designated areas until further notice," Empire State Building announced. "Rockefeller Slab, relay this message across all platforms, please."

"I'm on it," his peer complied, and he scrambled the Times Square buildings.

Among a growing list of unknowns, one thing was clear to everyone: the Manhattan Building Conference, for all its drama, was adjourned.

Empire State Building moved at a frantic pace during the impromptu strategy session, barking orders left and right while barely taking a breath.

"Captain, we need all craft to prepare for possible attack. Gather the fleet along every border of the city, and ready our aerial crews. I'll make sure all perimeter buildings maintain a keen watch, but we need long-range defenses activated. Also, put a call in for all Manhattanites to stay indoors. And we need emergency personnel to remain on high alert and ready for anything, especially our hospital buildings. UN Building, please coordinate with them. Rockefeller Slab, I need you to contact nearby regions and ask for reports on any suspicious behavior. Officer, is there any news on the signal's origin? If not, keep trying to pinpoint it."

In the meantime, frenzied buildings struggled to disperse in an orderly fashion. Aware of the confusion, Chrysler Building felt compelled to take initiative, and started guiding buildings away from the island's eastern edge.

"Gently now, this way, that's it," she offered calmly, rerouting their path. But despite her best efforts, towers large and small still grappled with logistics, and the severity of the situation escalated by the minute.

Soon, the ground trembled at an increasingly alarming rate, not just from the restless crowd, but from something else entirely. Empire State Building felt the tremors radiating through his structural frame and glanced over at UN Building, who seemed distracted by something off in the distance.

"What is it?" he asked anxiously, trying to pinpoint what UN Building was gazing at. It didn't take long for Empire State Building to share in his friend's disposition, for some thirty miles south of Liberty Island was an incoming fleet of several hundred high-flying objects, each in silhouette against the hellish-colored sky beyond.

"I ... don't think that's the Manhattan Military," UN Building warned.

As they made their way uptown at a frantic pace, more buildings turned to notice the looming threat coming in from the skies to the south. Lady Liberty levitated in order to get a better view for herself, spotting the telltale dome-like profiles of the incoming aerial fleet. The green lady's heart raced faster as she processed what her eyes were taking in. Once she saw and heard enough, the statue dropped back down to the ground and reported to Empire State Building and Manhattan Military personnel within him, as each awaited updates.

"Notify those within you of this message, Empire State—the incoming presence brings nothing but fire and destruction. It is also stacked deep; I counted about fifty vehicles so far. I will ensure that remaining Manhattanites get indoors at once, but the rest is up to you," she said.

"Understood," Empire State Building replied as he scrambled his team within to begin their aerial counteroffensive. "And one more thing, Captain," the tower added with regret. "Prepare to issue a *Code One* vertical evacuation for the entire island."

"We will proceed as noted," the Captain confirmed.

The incoming objects reached airspace over Breuckelen much faster than expected, and remaining Manhattanites darted inside the nearest buildings. Amid more noticeable tremors, sirens began to wail all across the city. In an instant, huge explosions could be seen riddling the skies just above Breuckelen and the harbor beyond, as the streamlined silhouettes of Manhattan Airships engaged head-on with their stealthy opponents in an intense dogfight.

The battle over Manhattan had begun.

As the aerial assault intensified, buildings below had little to do but watch, each hoping that the Manhattan Military would win out. Empire State and Chrysler Buildings were among the throng of towers congregating closer to the southern tip of the city, held motionless by the unfolding events in the distance, even as thunderous bursts from above haunted their ears.

"What do you think? Does it look like the military's staving them off?" Chrysler Building asked.

"I don't know yet, it's so hard to tell," Empire State Building admitted. He heard the tumultuous sounds growing in ferocity, but another resonance began to fill the tower's head.

Emanating from deep within his structure, he thought it at first to be low whispering, but the message grew clearer as he tuned in more keenly. It was, he realized, the sound of hundreds of different voices engaged in prayers. Empire State Building took it in and thought about how the very Manhattanites he was responsible for protecting were now fearing the worst. This reminded the tower that his steel frame could only do so much to defend them, which agitated him further, even as the continued pleas from desperate Manhattanites went on, and were soon joined by a chorus of other voices from inside neighboring buildings.

Chrysler Building, feeling her own occupants' desperation, drew closer to her lover by brushing her façade up against his.

Empire State Building could feel his partner trembling quite noticeably. "It's gonna be alright," he whispered reassuringly.

"I know it is," she replied, sounding unconvinced.

While the city and its skyline continued to watch, the aerial battle reached feverish proportions. Squadrons of Manhattan Airships showered their opponents with ammunition, and TERROR Cruisers lashed back with their own mighty weapons. As the conflict continued, the glow of battle seemed almost beautiful to some spectators, like a thousand fireflies magically appearing and disappearing. The city's youngest residents peered out their windows and smiled as they mistook the glows in the distance for fireworks—unaware that each new explosion meant the end of someone's life.

To those tracking the Manhattan Military's progress, it was clear that its fighting capabilities were top-notch. But while the city's defense forces demonstrated a spectacular array of tactical maneuvers against their opponents, the question of whether this would be enough lingered. Manhattan Military Airships inflicted much damage, but the fleet of TERROR Cruisers seemed to replenish itself.

From his undisclosed position, the TERROR Commander took note of the Manhattan Military's efforts, admiring the fleet's sleek aerial choreography.

"They're eager to keep the fight going. Wonderful!" he enthused to his aides via intercom. "But I bet we can exhaust their ambitions. Get every TERROR Cruiser to cease fire but increase evasive maneuvers. Let the enemy throw a tantrum trying to chase us before they burn themselves out. The old rope-a-dope trick," he said, sounding like a kid in a candy shop.

Thanks to his enviable scrambling system, which allowed him virtual anonymity whenever he disrupted an enemy's frequency, the TERROR Commander was only a few short miles east of Manhattan's coast, a fact unbeknownst to the Manhattan Military, which remained desperate to pinpoint his whereabouts. Accompanying the brazen ruler was the TERROR Group's planned second wave of assault—a full phalanx of Cyclops Bots, undetectable in the dense forests that blanketed the regions north of Breuckelen, that was waiting patiently for the leader's go-ahead to pummel Manhattan Island.

Empire State Building's frustrations mounted as the air battle continued.

"We've got to be weakening them by now!" he exclaimed to Manhattan Military personnel within his uppermost floors. "Captain, do we know the latest count? How many of their cruisers are left?"

The Captain relayed results with trepidation. "It's not looking good, sir. I'm getting readings of *three* of their cruisers to every *one* of our airships, but we're doing everything we can to cut off the enemy's pace."

With that less-than-enthusiastic update, Empire State Building's tone shifted noticeably. "Well, can't we increase our fighters up there? Send our whole fleet if you have to! We've *got* to cut off their assault before they move past the harbor and end up right on top of us. And I want to know how many troops we've got on the ground in case that happens. We need to stay one step ahead of them."

There were times when Empire State Building's instincts reached levels that matched those of the finest four-star generals, and when that happened, any division between buildings and people once again waned. Undoubtedly, this was one such time for the great tower.

To everyone's astonishment, the air battle reached the two-hour mark with no signs of abating, inclining more buildings to pile up along the southern tip of the island, fearful yet eager to take in the spectacle firsthand. And as the battle unfolded, witnesses were privy to what felt like a hellish tennis match between two warring forces, each opponent granted or denied the upper hand at various stages in the game.

By day's end, the curtain was closing on what felt like the longest day in the island's history. Dusk's rays hung low over the city, their glowing embers causing Central Park's leafless willows to glimmer like icicles. And even after the sky surrendered to darkness, it remained punctuated by violent bursts of light as the hours ticked by. Deep into the night, a wondrous blue moon, big and bright, emerged as if to take part in watching the ongoing spectacle. And why not, since any attempt at catching a few winks was moot against the far-off booms that rang in everyone's ears? Whether human or building, nary a soul was able to sleep that night.

Speculation, meanwhile, grew among the nighttime crowd which was riddled with delirium and fear. From his perch, St. Patrick's Cathedral pointed out something dire to a half-awake Ladder Tower, who was standing nearby.

"Our sea carriers head out loaded with airships, only to return badly damaged and without any trace of their cargo, while each successive wave of our vessels, mind you, sends out fewer and fewer airships," the cathedral observed. "I fear we're doling out our resources too quickly while the TERROR Group seems to be doing the opposite."

Staving off his own insanity, Ladder Tower struggled to grasp the cathedral's observations at first.

"What the hell are you talking about?" he asked brashly. "That's not what's happening! It can't be. We've got more troops lying in wait. I mean, I just saw a whole brigade over by Liberty Island, didn't you? Here, see for yourself." But as Ladder Tower gestured for his friend to look out at the harbor, he felt foolish and perplexed, for neither troops nor brigades could be seen.

A sympathetic spirit overcame St. Patrick's Cathedral as he watched his friend come to terms with reality. "Trust me, I thought the same thing." He motioned to Ladder Tower while leniently patting him with one of his steeples.

The worsening situation compelled Ladder Tower to confront the notion of a suddenly defenseless city and the ramifications that might bring. This, coupled with his growing paranoia, sent the structure spiraling into a deeper panic.

"There's got to be more ships ... there just has to be! Why is this happening, St. Patrick's? Why are they doing this to us?" he moaned, which sent shivers through the human crowds huddled inside him. More buildings all around also began to pick up on signs of a depleting fleet.

"We're almost six hours into this now, and I'm getting impatient. Tell me what I want to hear, Captain," the TERROR Commander cautioned as the latest reports poured in.

"Thirteen additional enemy airships taken out, fifty-seven in total. Two enemy carriers sunk so far ... Estimated enemy casualties as a result are 350 and counting. Advancing our air fleet northbound now ... Clear to proceed over Manhattan's airspace in T-minus thirty minutes," the voice on the intercom listed off.

"That's music to my ears!" the TERROR Commander relished. Grinning, he then issued his next directive, undoubtedly intent on maintaining the order's hard-fought gains. "Now we shall prepare for our second wave. Awaken the beasts!" he exclaimed.

Immediately following the TERROR Commander's order, shearing sounds of moving metal parts began to emanate throughout the dense foliage of the Manhattan Forest, with towering Cyclops Bots emerging from their underground catacombs and hideouts like unfolding, mechanized spiders. As they rose high above the trees, the TERROR Commander gazed upon them with the same awe-struck reverence he'd first displayed when they torched his village, plucked him out of his birthplace, and placed him into his destiny, all those years ago.

"From out of the earth they came," the vile ruler recited to himself with amusement, alluding to the fact that his robotic armies had tunneled a great distance—even traveling beneath large bodies of water and endless landforms—to reach their destination virtually unnoticed. "The time to claim the city is upon us, so go and do my bidding, for it's the will of Pegmatite."

In moments, the Cyclops Bots prepared their march to Manhattan Island.

With the clock ticking, Empire State Building sensed escalated activity within his upper floors, as Manhattan Military personnel shuffled and strategized amid worsening news from the front.

"Captain! We're picking up faint traces of new activity in the Manhattan Forest. No indication of its identity from the encryption, but whatever it is, it's only two miles away and closing in fast," one officer reported with alarm.

Standing nearby, Lady Liberty overheard the latest reports, which propelled her to nudge Empire State Building's side. "There must be more of them," she warned. "And two miles away is nothing. We need to act. I could fly over there and attempt to distract them while you prepare for the evacuation."

Empire State Building's mind was flooded by a thousand thoughts at once. "How could they have sprung up on us so quickly like this? No, Lady Liberty, I can't have you do that, since flying there will be too risky even for you. We won't know what'll be waiting for you once you land. There's gotta be another way," he determined before summoning the Manhattan Military again. "Captain, every move counts now. I urge you to put all remaining zones on high alert and get ground forces to assume positions along the island's perimeter. Focus every tank we have on the Manhattan Forest while I move all buildings and civilians closer to the center of the island. Whatever emerges from those trees, we'll be ready to strike with fury," the tower directed.

Lady Liberty began to levitate above the ground again, intent on relaying Empire State Building's directives as fast as she could.

"Hold this zone," she told Empire State Building, "I will alert units on Liberty Island to do the same."

"Good idea, but be careful down there!" he cautioned. Lady Liberty nodded and flew off.

Buoyed by Empire State Building's urgency, the Manhattan Military recalibrated its defense positions to form a tight line of tanks that stretched along the island's entire eastern rim, and the group anticipated just about anything as it waited. Moments later, relocated buildings noticed the Manhattan Forest shuffle and sway violently, and shifting and snapping sounds grew louder within its dense topography. Surely, such unnatural noises were indicative of something horrible just beyond Manhattan Island's bounds.

Staring out at the landscape anxiously, UN Building was among the first to notice pairs of glowing red lights that hovered in the dense and dark wilderness. Sharpening his gaze, he realized that the lights were the eyes of mechanical beasts. "Looks like they're upon us," the tower observed wearily, and neighboring buildings became transfixed by the growing number of red eyes that emerged from the woods. "They're upon us!" he repeated, provoking tanks to lock onto their targets.

Assembling in the clear with nothing but broken trees in their wake, the Cyclops Bots stood high above their surroundings, instilling new levels of fear in the hearts of the buildings. As they gathered en masse opposite Manhattan just across the river, the spiked, demonic-looking giants let out deep mechanical moans as if to announce their arrival. Then, they proceeded to cross the river, their torsos barely clearing the water as they advanced. Manhattan Military tanks quickly aimed their barrels at their moving targets and opened fire with a deafening barrage.

As the commotion continued, all Empire State Building could hear happening within him was a situation fast becoming undone.

"We won't last long with these numbers ... Enemy stretches the entire length of the river ... Reinforcements needed ... Cannot hold them off forever ... Prepare to issue *Code Two* protocol."

Empire State Building's antenna lowered down to his sides as he gazed hopelessly toward Chrysler and UN Buildings.

By all accounts, the situation worsened by the minute, and Cyclops Bots were soon less than a river's width away from their intended target. Desperate to regain the upper hand, buildings noticed a handful of Manhattan Military Airships swooping in and attempting to divert the Cyclops Bots.

"Everyone lay low!" Empire State Building ordered as missiles pierced the skies just above the city's highest towers on their way toward the mechanical beasts, while tanks continued to fire from below.

But despite the Manhattan Military's last-ditch efforts, TER-ROR ground forces were more than prepared, and they continued to inch closer toward the island. The buildings watched in horror as the glowing, bluish-white arms of each Cyclops Bot morphed into powerful weapons of concentrated energy that they directed at their aerial opponents. As a result, Manhattan Airships were blasted out of the skies with ease, their fiery remnants raining down and barely missing the terrified towers below.

Senior Manhattan Military officials tracked the unfolding horrors from their base at Liberty Island and demanded news from the frontlines. As soon as she touched down, Lady Liberty listened in from her perch above, sensing a new kind of panic among the officials.

"I want updates, Pilot! What is your status? Repeat, what is your status?" demanded one official over the airwaves.

As with Empire State Building's reports moments earlier, each new response came in more distressing than the last. "We're under heavy fire here … Enemy not under control. I repeat, the enemy is *not* yet under control … Missiles having little effect on target … Squadrons getting hit hard … Need more backup … I repeat, squadrons under heavy fire! Possible evasive action … Tell the mainland to take cover."

The voices grew fainter, and officers looked up at Lady Liberty with emptiness in their expressions.

While she took in the dire situation, it soon dawned upon the statue that only one option remained as she turned to her officers below.

"The time is now," she declared to her human counterparts, with a defeated expression on her face.

The senior captain took the green lady's cue and turned to his team. "Prepare to announce a *Code Two* evacuation for the entire island," he ordered.

Lady Liberty then took it one step further. "*Code Two* preparation alone will not help us, Captain, for there is no time. We will all perish if we stay here any longer."

"Understood," the Captain noted with disdain in his tone. "Correction, everyone. Implement the protocol effective immediately."

Nothing will stop it now, Lady Liberty thought morbidly as the alternate evacuation measure was officially relayed across the entire city.

As the fighting uptown continued, Empire State Building received the new directive from his topmost floors. "I understand," the tower confirmed.

"You understand *what?*" Chrysler Building inquired with agitation in her voice.

"It's okay," Empire State Building replied with unusual calm. "There's nothing else the Manhattan Military can do."

Chrysler Building, horrified, then watched in earnest as her lover directed his gaze to the crowd, took a deep breath, and delivered the fateful news to nearby buildings.

"*Code Two* was just put into effect," he reported, "which means we must take evasive action *now* by heading to the northern perimeter of the island. Total evacuation will commence from there. All Manhattanites must stay indoors until further notice."

The towers were shocked by the sternness in Empire State Building's delivery, and despite the growing danger, they were also hesitant to move. Losing whatever was left of her patience, Chrysler Building came to her lover's aid.

"You heard him, everybody needs to move uptown, calmly and carefully! It's no longer safe to stay where we are," she said.

UN Building and Rockefeller Slab followed her lead, and a host of others began their journey as well.

As the buildings undertook their escape from Manhattan, the shadows of terror drew closer with each passing moment. Of course, an orderly evacuation was preferred, but it became increasingly clear to Empire State Building that it wasn't in the cards for long.

"They're advancing on us too rapidly. We don't have much time," he admitted. Fearing a lack of Manhattan Military activity, he looked up at a sky devoid of most Manhattan Airships, yet still plentiful with enemy aircraft.

Indeed, TERROR ground forces continued to advance, and touchdown on Manhattan was imminent. While Manhattanites hid in relative safety within their walls, the majority of buildings worked their way uptown toward Inwood Hill, stopping just short of the river that divided them from the cliffs and sand dunes beyond.

Ladder Tower panicked. "What do we do now?" he asked, and others around him repeated the same question.

Moments later, high-flying TERROR Cruisers reached their target, entering the airspace over Manhattan with pent-up fury. As they soared overhead, the ships attempted to blast anything that came into view, from straggling buildings to clusters of tanks along the streets. Following this rain of fire from above, Cyclops Bots finally stepped foot on the island for the first time, taking over the assault.

Manhattan's historic acreage had become an unruly battle-field, with remaining Manhattan Military tanks firing everything they had against the Cyclops Bots, but to little avail. The towering mechanical beasts continued to unleash incredible destruction onto the streets below, wiping out droves of tanks and troops in the process. Buildings continued to navigate away from the horror and toward Inwood Hill, with blinding explosions, choking smoke, and abrupt crashing sounds coming at them from every direction.

Despite their increasingly vulnerable location out in the harbor, Lady Liberty and Manhattan Military personnel coordinated with feverish intent from their base atop Liberty Island.

Hoping to act as a diversion for any advancing foes, Empire State and Chrysler Buildings chose to stay behind while most other towers continued uptown. While they waited just northwest of Central Park, the two noticed that a majority of the island was being claimed by TERROR forces, with no sign of slowing up.

"I don't believe what I'm seeing," Chrysler Building said, horrified.

As both towers surveyed their vicinity for survivors, smoldering remains of several unlucky structures nearby put their grim situation into sharper focus.

"Do you see any others? I've got nothing so far," Empire State Building said.

Sharpening her focus, Chrysler Building called out the situation facing Lady Liberty and her team just south of the island. "No one's up here, but look over at the harbor. Fighters are closing in on Lady Liberty. She needs to leave that area at once! We should tell her," Chrysler Building warned, and her companion nodded in agreement. The two towers rushed as far south on Manhattan Island as they could, dodging enemy fire along the way.

Wasting little time, they then flashed their lights sporadically, and Empire State Building called out to the green lady. "They're closing in on you fast! Get your team and get out of there now!" He motioned to her anxiously.

Sure enough, Cyclops Bots came within a few thousand feet of Liberty Island, forcing the statue to act.

She signaled to the people down below. "Captain, there is nothing more we can do here. Leave everything and get everybody inside me," she said.

The Captain turned to his crew. "Prepare for immediate evacuation," he ordered.

But just as Lady Liberty stretched her hands down to scoop some of them up, a rapid blast from a Cyclops Bot's weaponized arm hurtled toward Liberty Island and eviscerated the fort where the Manhattan Military was stationed. All occupants were killed instantly from the explosion. A second blast followed, hitting Lady Liberty's base and causing enough of an impact to rock her off her platform and into the waters below.

"Oh no! She's fallen in the harbor," Chrysler Building cried out.

"I'm on it, but hang on a second," Empire State Building said before addressing the Manhattanites still sheltered within him. "I need everybody to close all my windows and get as far away from them as possible. Then, grab onto something anchored to the floor or wall!" The tower's deafening voice circulated throughout the pipes, corridors, and rooms of his interior for all inside to hear.

After waiting a few moments more, he took in a deep breath and leaped base-first into the river to swim toward Lady Liberty, causing a towering splash in his wake. Minutes later, he found the statue struggling to regain her footing against the powerful currents, and quickly latched onto her with his antenna, eventually pulling Lady Liberty onto Manhattan's shores after much effort.

"What about the captain and crew? We must go back," she said as enemy ships closed in on them.

"They're gone, Lady Liberty! We've gotta catch up with the others, or we'll be dead too," Empire State Building urged.

Realizing that their only means of escape was up, the aggrieved statue wrapped her arms around both Chrysler and Empire State Buildings and flew away from the immediate danger. As they surveyed the number of Cyclops Bots distributed across the island from high above, it was clear that the TERROR Group had achieved almost full control over Manhattan, and they watched as numerous bridges in the distance succumbed to dark plumes of smoke before collapsing into the water.

Adding to their rage, they then spotted several cornered apartment buildings along the far eastern rim of the island, watching helplessly as the frightened structures were surrounded and dispatched by a horde of Cyclops Bots. The screams of victims inside them permeated the air as the buildings were burned alive by a torrent of concentrated energy.

Following the swift execution, the Cyclops Bots advanced westward without remorse, trampling a once-serene portion of Central Park and blasting anything that moved along the way. Like clockwork, a horde of lava-spewing Death Rays soon advanced in the Cyclops Bots' wake and began transforming the island's terrain into a crisscrossed array of fiery lake beds and volcanic ash mounds. Manhattan's new status as an occupied territory was becoming more obvious by the second.

"I need to set us down," the statue said, the sheer weight from the towers finally catching up to her. The three touched down as softly as Lady Liberty could manage on Manhattan's northwestern rim. But being the two tallest towers and most prominent statue around meant they had to take drastic measures, and each began to cover themselves with thick globs of mud from the nearby shoreline in an effort to garner as little notice as possible from enemy eyes. While Empire State Building rolled on all sides across the loose soil, covering nearly every square foot of his limestone body, Chrysler Building muttered to herself as her gargoyles delicately applied the murky muck to her once gleaming crown.

"Don't ever tell anyone I did this," she groaned to her peers.

Minutes later, both towers were camouflaged from base to spire, and Lady Liberty appeared a muddy but disguised mess herself.

"Good for the skin," Empire State Building quipped in a moment of light relief, before the three of them needed to plan their next move. "Now, how are we gonna get outta here?"

"We lay low as we head north. This mud should help us avoid being seen for a while, although who knows what other tracking systems they have. And I need time to recharge my energy before I can fly again, meaning we walk from here," Lady Liberty cautioned.

With that, the three buildings began their treacherous journey up the island's rim.

As his Death Ray touched down on Manhattan's lower east perimeter, the TERROR Commander surveyed the map on his console with seasoned acuity.

"What are those slowly moving objects up there?" he asked a field soldier via intercom. "You told me the entire island was swept. Are those moving targets?"

Following a telling silence, the befuddled Soldier's voice came back on. "My apologies, Excellency. Yes, they're in some sort of advanced camouflage, but we're locked onto them now. They appear to be the escapees from the harbor, including the statue. Shall we take them out?"

"Advanced camouflage? Moron, it's just mud!" the TERROR Commander snapped. He took a breath and stroked his chin pensively. The vile leader knew value when he saw it, and he undoubtedly saw it there. "You will fetch this slippery trio, but *do not* kill them!" he ordered sternly. "Use any desired method of capture, but I want Lady Liberty and her friends breathing when I meet them."

"*Meet* them, my Excellency? I thought we were to purge the entire isl—"

"I'm *modifying* your directives, Soldier! And since you missed these three the first time, what difference does it make?" the TERROR Commander cut in. "Besides, this could be a morale defeat for the ages on Manhattan's part, for when the Chieftains learn that even Lady Liberty herself couldn't escape us, my victory here will be etched in stone. The statue and her friends shall become fitting trophies," he added.

"Understood, my Excellency."

Time continued to work against them, but the exhausted and muddy trio finally reached the northernmost shores of the island just beyond Inwood Hill, only to discover the entire vicinity empty.

"Where is everyone? I thought they were supposed to be at this spot," Chrysler Building said with alarm.

"I told UN Building to head farther out if we didn't make it back in time. I guess he took me up on that," Empire State Building conceded.

"Wonderful," grumbled Chrysler Building.

"I hear them uphill. They must still be close!" Lady Liberty said.

But with Cyclops Bots rapidly gaining on them, Empire State Building suggested a detour. "We should head for that embankment ... Looks like it's the easiest route up."

The three crossed a narrow riverway to reach an area just below the towering cliff, while from high atop the same rock formation, the rest of the escaped buildings waited to make their next move.

From his position by the tail end of the group, Rockefeller Slab glanced down below the cliff to spot Lady Liberty, Chrysler, and Empire State Buildings.

"Survivors are down below! What do we do?" He motioned to UN Building, who rushed to the edge of the cliff to get a better view for himself.

"They barely made it. Okay, let's do this," UN Building strategized. "You and I will climb back down to help them up the path of least resistance. Lady Liberty looks really low on energy, so I think they could use our support. In the meantime, everyone else here should head deeper into the dunes, following Ladder Tower's lead since he's the tallest and has his orb to light the way. It shouldn't take us long to catch up later."

Most agreed with UN Building's plan, with the exception of Wall Street Tower, who was always contrary. "You're kidding me, right? We made it out of there by the length of an antenna, and now you want to go back and leave us out here to rust? Preposterous!" the tower griped.

But UN Building's patience was as thin as single-pane glass, and he immediately snapped back at his constant critic. "Don't be so dramatic. I'm tired of arguing with you, so you either follow the plan or get left behind. It's that simple. Which do you prefer?"

Wall Street Tower reluctantly backed off.

"Good choice," UN Building said. He turned back to Rockefeller Slab. "Now, let's get going."

From his location below the cliff, meanwhile, Empire State Building caught a glimpse of his friends above as they mobilized their rescue effort. While at first encouraged by what he was seeing given how exhausted he was, the tower quickly calculated the worst, considering that the TERROR Group wasn't far behind.

"We need to tell them *not* to come back down here, for if they do, nobody will make it back up and out of here in time," he explained to Lady Liberty and Chrysler Building. "The TERROR Group will be here any minute. I'll hold them off, but you two need to climb up there and tell them to go back. Then ... I need you both to go with them."

Lady Liberty and Chrysler Building were taken aback by the idea of leaving Empire State Building behind. "No, no. We go together," Chrysler Building countered as the statue nodded in agreement.

"This is the best possible option," Empire State Building said quietly, knowing full well what such a plan would mean for him.

"Maybe so, but when have I ever abandoned you before?" Chrysler Building asked before turning her attention to Lady Liberty. "I'm staying with you, but Lady Liberty, he's right."

Empire State Building wanted none of it. "I'm right about what? No, you *both* need to—"

Chrysler Building interrupted him. "I *said* I'm staying with you. But Lady Liberty, you have to go and help the others through those treacherous dunes. They won't need us for that, but they will *certainly* need you."

Chrysler Building's admission troubled the statue further, since she still lacked the strength to fly and grew hesitant as she assessed the height of the cliff. "I cannot leave you both behind," the green lady announced.

There was another brief pause until Empire State Building decided he was at peace with Chrysler Building's decision to stay behind, and he doubled down. "Who knows what dangers await them all, Lady Liberty. Please, you need to do this for us."

As their friends began to descend the cliff, Lady Liberty could see that despite their best intent, by the time UN Building and Rockefeller Slab came down to rescue them, there wouldn't be enough time to make it back up. Undoubtedly, more mass casualties would occur. It was a calculable certainty.

"Okay, I will do what needs to be done," the statue agreed with regret.

"Wait! One more thing," Empire State Building said. "Chrysler Building and I are filled with precious cargo. We'll need you to take in as many Manhattanites as you can."

In short order, civilians were instructed to exit from each tower and board Lady Liberty as rapidly as possible. As they poured out of the buildings, most entered Lady Liberty through a series of hatches in her sandals. But space was filling up quickly within the statue, causing others to strap themselves onto her exterior bolts by tying clothing together into makeshift ropes.

Manhattan Military personnel still stationed in Empire State Building's top stories, meanwhile, insisted on staying behind to leave more room for civilians within Lady Liberty.

"We'll go with you, Empire State Building, and we'll fight with you," their Captain said.

As the last civilian boarded Lady Liberty, the ground around the structures began to tremor and shake. The TERROR Group loomed just over the other side of Inwood Hill by that point, causing the three buildings to say their goodbyes.

"I regret I cannot get us all out of here," Lady Liberty said.

"You've done all you can for us. Just get these people to safety," Empire State Building insisted, while he and Chrysler Building prepared for whatever punishments lay ahead.

"Manhattanites, I need all of you to hold on for dear life," Lady Liberty instructed as she held back tears. Moments later, Chrysler and Empire State Buildings witnessed their copper friend motioning UN Building to head back, and she made her way up the cliff with every ounce of her strength.

Watching the action from above, St. Patrick's Cathedral and others soon noticed Lady Liberty advancing while the other two buildings stayed behind.

"Why aren't they all making a run for it?" the cathedral asked as UN Building and Rockefeller Slab came back up the cliff.

"I think those three just saved our bricks!" Rockefeller Slab said.

UN Building addressed the crowd. "They're going to divert the TERROR Group away from here so that we can escape," he announced.

Many buildings gasped in astonishment.

Shocked like everyone else, St. Patrick's Cathedral took one last glance down the steep cliff. "Godspeed, my friends," he uttered grimly.

Following much struggle and strain, Lady Liberty joined the other survivors at the top of the cliff, and just as she nearly lost her footing and risked tumbling back down, Ladder Tower came out of nowhere to cast out his slender body and allow the statue to grab hold.

While that disaster was averted, Chrysler and Empire State Buildings remained idle below the cliff, watching with heavy hearts as their friends disappeared from view. Moments later, shadows began to loom over the defenseless pair.

"Whatever happens to us, know that I love you," Chrysler Building stated softly.

Her partner strove to keep his composure. "It shouldn't hurt for long," he replied. The two towers then huddled together closely, prepared for any torment they were about to face but at relative peace in knowing they'd face it together.

"Stay where you are or be destroyed!" a deep and intimidating voice ordered from behind them. The towers did as they were told while a hungry horde of machines surrounded them from all sides.

"Prepare for capture," another voice said.

The frightened towers remained motionless as the Death Rays opened to release a small brigade of TERROR Soldiers from within their bodies. Weapons drawn, the troops encircled the pair with calculated choreography.

Chrysler and Empire State Buildings saw just how tall and formidable these beings were up close—undoubtedly agents of destruction with no indication of fragility. The towers realized what a miracle it was that the Manhattan Military had lasted for as long as it did against such an intimidating force.

The prisoners were smothered by the angry brigade, who mercilessly poked and jabbed their weapons through the buildings' bodies. Each tower screamed in agony as pain pulsed through their nerve sensors with sharp and unadulterated force, causing a variety of damaging interior malfunctions in the process. It was a raw shock unlike anything else they had ever known, but the towering giants fought hard to sustain the pain, standing their ground for as long as possible.

"Seems like they can't get enough!" mocked a TERROR Soldier.

"Get some grappling hooks in 'em then," suggested another.

Amid the escalating assault, large gashes in their outer walls exposed the buildings' interior floors to the elements. Empire State Building was the first to succumb to his injuries, collapsing to the ground and crushing several of his lower levels. With his calamitous fall, countless Manhattan Military personnel tumbled out of the building's upper stories and onto the exposed ground. Many of them, including the Captain, died instantly from the impact, but others valiantly stood back up in defense against the seething TERROR Soldiers many times their height.

"Leave 'em alone!" Empire State Building pleaded to the perpetrators, before his wounds stung more sharply and made him slip in and out of consciousness.

While her lover lay defenseless, Chrysler Building succumbed to the pain from the harpoon-like grappling hooks, which knocked her down shortly thereafter, awash in seawater and wet sand.

TERROR Soldiers piled atop her structure like ants, and just like that, the once-indomitable towering giants found themselves reduced to beached captives.

As the two icons foundered, the remaining Manhattan Military personnel were rounded up along the beach for inspection.

"These are not ground troops," one TERROR Soldier pointed out. "We were told to eliminate ground troops. Most of these are office personnel and admin."

"Just call it in and see what *he* wants us to do," suggested his colleague.

The human prisoners waited silently for their fates to be determined. After several agonizing minutes, one of the encircling TERROR Soldiers pointed to the readout from his Death Ray.

"Kill any and *all* humans," the Soldier said. "But bring the buildings to him."

Then, without so much as a single plea for mercy, the brave Manhattan Military personnel accepted their fates as the TERROR Soldiers obediently went to work, using their weapons to butcher each one of them until the sands of the beach were stained with blood.

"All in a day's catch," one Soldier said once the massacre was complete. "Throw the bodies in the river and alert His Excellency that he'll soon have his prize."

MIGHTY MANHATTAN, HER HEART BEATING NO MORE.
THOUSANDS OF YEARS OF LIFE AT EVERY LEVEL,
ALL BUT ERASED IN JUST ONE DAY,
HER MEMORY THRUST UPON THE SHOULDERS
OF A FEW WEARY AND WORN SURVIVORS.
SUCH WAS HOW THE PENDULUM OF POWER
SWUNG, FROM THIS DAY HENCE.

From his Death Ray's position along Manhattan's southern edge, everything and everyone seemed to stop as the TERROR Commander prepared to emerge out of his ship's cocoon. His soldiers looked on eagerly for a glimpse of their ruler, and the top hatch of the Death Ray slowly rose and unfolded along the side of the vehicle. After a few moments more, any dust that had been kicked up had settled, and out crawled the TERROR Commander on all fours, like some kind of overgrown spider coming out of a container half its size. Straightening out his spindly form, the formidable ruler took a giant step onto the island's surface, which felt welcomingly hot when he bent down to touch it.

Upon his landing, hundreds of memories had flooded the TERROR Commander's mind. Now as he surveyed his surroundings in silence, he inhaled the conquered air with a deep breath and noticed his followers clinging to his every move.

"To be back on this island is to feel at peace with a destiny fulfilled," he said as he knelt down again to pick up a handful of charred dirt. The vile ruler studied the darkened matter for a while, and grinned as it escaped his grip to fall back onto the earth.

"Like what happened to me," he told his observant troops, "this pile of dirt will soon undergo a physical transformation unlike anything it's ever known. Let's blanket every speck of it with lava and ash, freeing it from its past and securing its future as the royal ground for our new kingdom! Such is our destiny, and the will of Pegmatite."

With that, the TERROR Group worked in overdrive, unleashing Death Rays all across the island and its surroundings. He relished the sight of his low-lying machines spewing lava trails atop every surface, knowing his wishes to reshape Manhattan into a new kind of promised land were being fulfilled before his very eyes.

But while the atmosphere was thick with the blood of his conquest, the TERROR Commander soon realized that something was amiss.

"Alas, I stand only partially fulfilled," he said before gesturing to his crew. "Where are my captives? Bring them to me."

Within moments, giddy TERROR Soldiers dragged the battered, entangled towers into his view, like poachers touting their latest catch.

"Wonderful! And where is Lady Liberty?" he asked with a chilling calmness, to which his troops had no response. Agitated by their silence, the vile ruler redirected his focus to the two captive towers whose futures were now in his hands, though their near-lifeless conditions only irked the ruler further as he inspected them.

"So, um, what shall we do with them, Excellency?" asked one Soldier brave enough to speak up.

"What do we do with any heaping pile of trash? We incinerate it," the TERROR Commander shot back. He turned from the prisoners and headed back to his transport. "I asked for trophies, not these sad, pathetic remains! Start by removing those hooks from them, and then clean them up. Report back to me when you think they're worthy of being in my sight."

The door to the TERROR Commander's Death Ray sealed shut, separating the ruler from his imperfect catch, while his troops scurried to fulfill his wishes.

With Manhattan's transformation underway, the surviving buildings beyond its borders pondered their looming exodus from the familiar to the unknown. For UN Building, Rockefeller Slab, and the others lucky enough to have escaped this wrath of terror, an uncertain road awaited them.

"Who knows what kinds of secrets this place holds," UN Building speculated with anxiety, remembering countless legends and myths about the vast sand dunes beyond Manhattan's shores. The journey ahead was bound to be an unexpected one, and however true those legends were, the dunes were sure to be formidable.

Although situated west of both Manhattan Island and the well-trod Manhattan Forest, the dunes could have been a world apart in terms of familiarity, since none of the buildings had ever traversed through them. There were several roads that connected the dunes to Manhattan proper, but for most buildings and Manhattanites, this landscape meant danger at every turn. However, now was not the time to ruminate on that aspect. The dunes were the lesser of two evils, and any preconceived fears about them had to be put to rest.

Just as soon as the cruel desert winds began to pick up, so too did protests from survivors. Naturally, the most outspoken was Wall Street Tower.

"Why are we out here? There's nothing in every direction. I must be a fool to follow you all!" he ranted.

"Keep your voices down, all of you!" Rockefeller Slab snapped.

"Oh, so you're in charge?" Wall Street Tower said. "Or are you just a dim-witted sheep following orders?"

"I'm no sheep. If this is what *Code Two* calls for then this is what we should adhere to," Rockefeller Slab replied.

"Oh, is that so? Sounds pretty dim-witted to me," his opponent said.

Rockefeller Slab grew more heated than ever. "Why, you no-good—"

"Alright, that's enough from everyone!" UN Building broke in. "Look, there's nothing back there for us anymore. Only what's ahead matters now."

As the commotion died down, UN Building took a quick glance back at Lady Liberty, who trailed the others with a limp in her step and a blank expression on her face. Like many at that moment, he wished Lady Liberty would say something, *anything*, to calm their nerves. But the statue could barely walk, much less utter a rousing speech, he realized.

"Whatever happens," UN Building said, "we will keep pressing north until we arrive at the nearest town. And that's that."

It had been a painful process to remove the grappling hooks from their outer walls, but once the process was complete, the prepped and polished Empire State and Chrysler Buildings were presented to the TERROR Commander once again.

"Now *this* is a far more worthy display," the vile ruler said, admiring his captives with a sheepish grin.

The TERROR Soldiers cackled with excitement, knowing they had pleased their leader.

"Now, where to display them?" the TERROR Commander pondered.

"I got it, Excellency," shouted one Soldier. "Let's strip 'em down and scatter their parts all across the island!"

"No, no, let's burn 'em alive, and then bury 'em in a pool of lava!" suggested another without restraint.

"Oh dear," the TERROR Commander said, his expression growing cold. "Is that the best you can think of? Listen to my words, for here before us stands an important symbolic catch. One that begs us to make a *shining* example out of it. So, we must first propagate the image of their captivity across our entire network, to inspire others. Ultimately, these buildings will die *when* I say and *how* I say, but not before we've squeezed every last drop of potential from them. In the meantime, I want them to be our token prisoners at the center of our new island, like two trophies on a mantle for all to see. From this point onward, my friends, anyone who *dares* try to challenge us will look upon these two towers and ask themselves, *'Do we want to wind up like they did?'* Am I clear?"

Following their leader's calls for a newfound triumphalism in what they'd achieved, the TERROR Soldiers' obnoxious howls of celebration grew louder throughout the island, as if Hell had suddenly unleashed a party like no other.

That night, the sky grew animated with shapes of a foreboding new world order, and the atmosphere over Manhattan Island teemed with an unfamiliar energy. But unlike the more optimistic skies of yore, the environment turned harsh, volatile, disturbed even, mirroring the misshapen landscape that now existed below.

At the TERROR Commander's behest, Manhattan Island continued to transform into something unrecognizable, as the lava-spewing Death Rays were close to completing their task of blanketing every piece of the island's surface in the fiery liquid. While the hours passed, layers of magma exposed to air had soon hardened into Pegmatite-rich rock, and their inner layers smoldered as they formed subterranean channels of hot streams and fiery lake beds.

"All within view is now mine," the equally fiery leader observed as he took in the progress all around. While the TERROR Commander knew that Lady Liberty and others had escaped the slaughter, his concern was futile at best. When asked by his troops that night if a search party should be created, the satisfied leader hesitated.

"What a wonderful situation to be in, when the only worry is looking for a few frail survivors! And I understand they fled into the sand dunes. Well, those are relentless and unforgiving anyway, are they not? If that's the case, my answer's simple. Why waste too many resources on something that's bound to fail on its own? Sure, send out a search party, but Lady Liberty and her friends are as good as dead out there," he said.

Against all expectations, Manhattan's survivors pressed deeper into the barren and windswept dunes. The journey behind them had already been a long and arduous one, but with unforgiving sand-storms ahead, the next few days would be more trying still.

Lady Liberty struggled to keep up, and displayed more signs of wear. She breathed heavily as her pace continued to decline. Puglia Ristorante, roaming not too far behind the sorrow-stricken statue, searched deep for the right words that might cheer her up. To the diminutive restaurant, the green lady represented everything that was so special about the city he once called home. Such feelings were not uncommon among the buildings, for Lady Liberty's confident demeanor and elegant ways long brought inspiration and hope to all around her. Given his feelings, the restaurant could no longer stomach the sight of his hero languishing in such a sullen state.

"I'm gonna go talk to her," he announced.

Overhearing his friend's intention, Guggenheim Museum stepped in, for he, too, sensed Lady Liberty's fragility yet knew of nothing they could do to placate it.

"Just let her be," the museum said. "She needs to be left alone for now."

But Puglia Ristorante disagreed, his heart set on the possibility that he had the right words to bring Lady Liberty alleviation, good cheer, or something different than the current mood.

"I know what I'm doing," the little restaurant insisted.

Guggenheim Museum's patience wore out. "Hey, have you gone deaf or something? Forget it, I tell you!"

Other buildings took notice of the souring verbal exchange.

"Well, what about those stories she used to tell us about the Spring Sprite?" Puglia Ristorante asked.

"Spring Sprite? Whatever are you talking about?" Guggenheim Museum said.

"You know," the restaurant continued. "About how the Sprite could rise out of rain drops to turn ashes into trees and such? Or her tales about Schist, and how life can be created from basic elements. Why can't a miracle like that help us here and now?"

The very idea only further amplified Guggenheim Museum's misdirected angst. "Do you see any rain out here? Those are stories, you naïve moron, stories! They probably never happened in the first place, so quit dreaming and face reality. We're all alone right now."

As the museum's hurtful remarks sunk in, Puglia Ristorante broke from his usual jovial demeanor and lunged at his friend, sending both buildings into a pointless melee of juvenile frustration as they toppled and rolled about in the sand. Onlookers tried to break them up, but it only heightened the dense air of frustration that had been building. In no time, throngs of towers were shouting at one another for no other reason than to let out steam.

Even with her frailties, Lady Liberty was alarmed by the commotion and belted out a sudden and commanding order. "Stop this! All of you!" she howled despite her weak voice and sandy joints.

Given her untarnished influence, the buildings ceased their ruckus and the green lady approached them wearing a stern expression. "You could be right, Guggenheim Museum. Maybe those are naïve and insignificant tales that I once told, tales from which there are no takeaways. But I still like to think otherwise. No, I *hope* otherwise, because miracles can transpire in the unlikeliest of places," she said with a renewed sense of purpose.

A sudden sense of guilt came over both Puglia Ristorante and Guggenheim Museum, provoking them to apologize to Lady Liberty even though she wanted to hear none of it.

"Listen to me," the green lady said. "Not one of you is at fault for the tribulations that have plagued us, so all we can do right now is be calm and stay focused on forging ahead. Infighting is just what our enemy expects of us. The important thing is that we never succumb to such desires." She took a deep, clarifying breath and surveyed the crowd with a subtle smile on her face—a gesture that invited calm to an otherwise dreadful setting. "Now, let us venture onward."

With that, the statue pressed northward and the lingering buildings faced one another, realizing that there really was no other feasible option after all. Still reeling from their squabble, they took a moment to embrace each other before moving along as well.

Through it all, and despite her emotional and physical anguish, Lady Liberty once again demonstrated her mastery at mending the mood of her city and its inhabitants, a critical skill during a highly charged time, indeed.

Such encouragement became invaluable, for many trying days and nights among the volatile dunes confronted the survivors as they marched on against the unsteady ripples of sand. Led by the last few remaining tanks and ground forces of the Manhattan Military, most buildings sought to keep in tight groups as they walked. Others were gradually losing ground and falling behind in the pack, their creaking walls and cracked façades wreaking all kinds of havoc on their own structures and for Manhattanites who did their best to keep shelter inside them.

Seldomly did any of the human survivors go near their building's windows, for one unexpected move could send someone careening out of their building and down onto the treacherous sands below. Weary Manhattanites also had to ration their limited supplies of food and water to make sure there was enough to go around for the long and grueling days.

Thoughts of buildings large and small were accompanied by a growing chorus of misery and heartbreak from the people inside them, or hopeful sounds of chanting, meditation, mantras, and prayers. The struggles facing everyone were relentless, and Lady Liberty tried her best to offer words of comfort to as many as she could, despite the disturbing amount of injuries on all fronts. As the march became less coordinated over time, the statue often moved to the back of the group to help steer those who had trouble against the ceaseless dust and winds. The laggards included a number of weary travelers, such as St. Patrick's Cathedral, Times Square Tower Two, Metropolitan Baptist Church, and Puglia Ristorante.

Closer to the front of the ever-lengthening line marched a weary Rockefeller Slab. Although one of the tallest buildings to escape, his hunched demeanor and damaged appearance seemed a far cry from the media-savvy, newsmaker image he once so freely exuded. Injuries he had sustained during the TERROR Group's invasion were bothering him more each day, as Rockefeller Slab's pace began to slow over time.

UN Building was technically the "acting" mayor in light of Empire State Building's absence, per protocol. But aside from that circumstantial boost in leadership, the diplomat's once-evocative curtain wall of turquoise brilliance was cracking rapidly from each harsh step in the unforgiving sand. Steadfast and determined, though, UN Building remained driven by a desire to make it through their nightmare, and as he pressed on, he motivated others like the nearby Ladder Tower and Guggenheim Museum to do the same.

But just how long any of them could last was anyone's guess, for every mile gained presented new reasons to become unhinged. At one point, Ladder Tower stopped in his tracks and swiveled his glowing red orb to face his neighbors.

"What the hell are we still marching on for?" he moaned, aiming his frustration at Rockefeller Slab, whose only crime was that he had managed to head past him. "And why am I following you, Rockefeller Slab? Your guess at where to go can't be any worse than mine! I mean, just *what* do you expect to find out here? Tell me, I wanna know!" Ladder Tower demanded as others looked at him with empathy.

Staying calm, Rockefeller Slab glanced back at Ladder Tower with an apathetic expression, and continued forward without so much as a rebuttal. It was just enough for Ladder Tower to realize the absurdity of it all, and to eventually rejoin the moving circus like nothing had happened. Hope for the future was all that mattered now, since none of the survivors, including Lady Liberty, knew exactly *where* they were going. But keep going, they did.

As the evening sun again reached a steep angle over the horizon, the surrounding sand dunes evolved from bright and peachy forms to objects of stark, contrasting studies of light and shadow. This caused the landscape around the survivors to take on an increasing level of mystery in their minds as the days went on. Guggenheim Museum was particularly startled by the shifting dunes that appeared once again, and he picked up his pace to situate himself directly behind frontline towers. Moving with paranoia in his step, the museum no longer seemed to care about any delicate artwork that was still mounted to his interior walls. His once beautiful glass dome enclosure now sported a gaping hole, and it seemed protecting his art was a moot concern anyway. But before the museum could ruminate too much over the consequences of his haste, a loud voice blared from a tank's speakers near the frontlines.

"Radar is picking up something directly ahead. Repeat, unknown object directly in our path. Everybody, slow your pace. All troops, prepare to engage!"

"Oh, what now?" Wall Street Tower said.

The warning provoked subtle gasps from throughout the crowd, with many buildings slowing to a crawl as they looked around in an effort to pinpoint the cause for alarm.

"Over there!" Ladder Tower said as he directed his orb's glow toward something in the wind-swept distance. In short order, they each noticed a large, sculpted, triangular object looming in and out of focus as they approached.

"What could it possibly be?" Rockefeller Slab asked, mirroring the thoughts of many others.

The tanks rolled on ahead of the cautious group to encircle the mysterious object, their gun barrels primed and ready for any surprises that might transpire. After the vehicles thoroughly surveyed the vicinity, one of the Manhattan Military's Tank Commanders opened up her cockpit hatch and motioned at them.

"You're all clear to proceed. This area's been scoped out, and no signs of life have been found," she said through her loudspeaker. "It's just a giant stone of some kind."

"Thank you, Commander," UN Building said, eager to inspect the object for himself. As he did so, several curious Manhattanites began to exit from their buildings, hoping to brave the winds and take in the sight firsthand. High above them, Rockefeller Slab approached the object with trepidation.

"So, what do you make of it?" he asked as he turned to UN Building.

"Not sure, but I want Lady Liberty to take a look. *That's* for sure."

While the towers continued to assess the matter, a few Manhattanites approached the monolith with a bit more ease. One daring human observer started tapping the surface of the object with his knuckle, as if attempting to awaken a sleeping giant.

"How tall would you say this thing is?" UN Building asked as he assessed the difference in scale between the man and the monolith.

"About thirty-five, forty feet high, I think. Just over three stories above the surface of the sand," Rockefeller Slab estimated.

"Makes sense," UN Building continued. "What about below the sand, though?"

"Good point," Rockefeller Slab acknowledged. "Looks are deceiving here, for there's no way to tell just how deep this thing is buried. For all we know, it could go on forever!"

The buildings continued to pour over the mystifying object, with far more questions than there were answers.

"How long do you think it's been out here?" UN Building asked.

"Who's to say? Such a barren and strange place for a monolithic object of this kind. Who could have put it out here?"

"Beats me," UN Building admitted. "You think it's animated, like we are?"

"Well, I don't see it moving at all," Rockefeller Slab said upon closer inspection. "But it can't be naturally carved either; it looks too perfect in its sculpting."

"Agreed," said UN Building. He surveyed the vast desert area all around the mysterious stone, undoubtedly remembering the various stories and legends associated with this unfamiliar place.

"What should we do?" Rockefeller Slab asked.

"Let's keep an eye on it for the time be—"

Before UN Building finished his instruction, the strange object let out a sudden, soft rumble followed by a faint scratching noise, like chalk on a stone surface. It was enough to entice Guggenheim Museum to inch in closer, and he spotted large letters being carved onto its exterior in real-time.

"Oh dear," the museum said almost breathlessly as the inscription on the triangulated surface soon completed itself. "Is everyone seeing this?"

He signaled to other buildings and after stepping back a bit farther, the museum inspected the carved inscription in earnest. "Ring for freedom," he read to the crowd.

"That's so ... patriotic?" Rockefeller Slab quipped in puzzled bemusement.

"What should we use to ring it with, a Salvation Army bell?" Wall Street Tower added sarcastically as he pushed through the crowd.

"Oh, I think we'll find out soon enough. Take a look!" Guggenheim Museum said as his ribbon windows gestured toward the ground nearby.

Weapons drawn, remaining Manhattan Military troops exited their vehicles for a better view of the action, and the captivated audience turned its attention to a formation that was rapidly rising from out the sand and resembled an anthill. A tall, brass-colored pole, with a twenty-four-inch diameter bell of similar finish hanging from it, popped up from the center of the mound. Many questions arose. Just *who* was sending this message, and *how* had it appeared literally out of thin air? Most importantly, perhaps, the survivors wondered what to make of this mysterious object in general. Was it *for* or *against* them?

"This could be the end of us all," Wall Street Tower speculated.

UN Building tried to appease the worried crowd. "Let's not get ahead of ourselves over this," he said. "Whatever this thing is, we're all still alive right now."

Rockefeller Slab said, "I think someone should ring it."

UN Building, figuring there wasn't much else to lose, concurred. "Yes, the fact that we have time to decipher this already gives me a feeling of hope. Why would we stumble upon this now? Why was it put *here* of all places?"

He looked around the crowd and noticed three sacred buildings, namely St. Patrick's Cathedral, Masjid Malcolm Shabazz, and Central Synagogue, inspecting the monument for themselves. While the debate continued as to whether or not to ring the bell, UN Building admired how each house of worship meandered slowly around the object to look at its stark message.

"I need some enlightened viewpoints on this," UN Building said as he called the sacred buildings over to him. "Is this message something we can trust?"

The sacred structures looked at one another for a moment while they processed UN Building's question.

"Well, since you ask, the object before us reminds me of a certain passage," St. Patrick's Cathedral said. "*Look to the rock from which you were cut, and to the quarry from which you were hewn.*" The cathedral then turned to Masjid Malcolm Shabazz, who had his own take on the matter.

"From where I stand," the mosque advised, "*there are some rocks from which streams burst forth*, or so it is written. Since we're in the middle of a desert, my friends, I believe this monument could very well hold some promise for us."

Central Synagogue put it most bluntly. "Just ring the damn thing, and we'll see what happens," she suggested. Her no-nonsense demeanor won chuckles from the otherwise weary crowd.

Satisfied by their interpretations, UN Building put to rest any further debate. "Well, I'm sold. Let's ring it then. However, this task requires human hands. Manhattanites, is there one among you willing to perform this duty?"

Soon enough, a volunteer emerged from Ladder Tower's lobby to heed the call. "I'm a retired baseball player, UN Building. I'll ring this bell proudly and with all my might," the Manhattanite announced. "But I need something to strike it with."

Guggenheim Museum gestured to the volunteer. "Head inside me, lad," he offered, "and walk up to my second floor, or whatever's left of it, where you should find an instrument, a mallet in fact, on display. I *do* hope it has survived this perilous journey."

Sure enough, the former ballplayer exited Guggenheim Museum a few minutes later, mallet in hand.

"No going back now," UN Building whispered as the group stood by anxiously, hoping they had made the right decision.

The volunteer approached the gleaming brass bell and admired the towering triangular monolith perched just behind it, its words looming over his diminutive frame. With the buildings watching and waiting, the ex-ballplayer took several deep breaths, drew his arms back, and prepared to swing away. His expression was one of deference, for trying to awaken a bell of such magnitude would be no easy task. Ready and willing, the man released his swing, striking his target several times and causing new reverberations with each blow.

For a long while, it seemed the effort was for naught.

"This is suicide—somebody's gonna hear us!" Wall Street Tower shouted as he hid behind another tower.

"Never mind that, just keep swinging away, son!" UN Building encouraged, realizing it was all or nothing at that point. The man continued swinging for several minutes more, but yielded nothing other than loud, jarring clangs that rattled everyone's auditory senses.

"What a big, loud waste this is!" muttered Wall Street Tower.

But the determined Manhattanite had no plans to give up, and keen listeners started to notice a definite change in the sound. With each new strike of the bell, deeper tones were being released.

"Listen to that. Something's definitely happening," UN Building said with anxious excitement in his voice. "Keep ringing it, you're doing great!"

The ex-ballplayer's efforts seemed to be paying off, and the ground suddenly came alive with even more momentous rumbles. Alarmed by this development, Rockefeller Slab, Ladder Tower, and others beckoned Manhattanites to head back inside. The rumbling just under the buildings' bases grew exponentially.

"All civilians, seek cover in the nearest building," the Tank Commander yelled as she guided Manhattanites away from the commotion. The rest of the soldiers did their best to direct the crowds, but it became a tall order as sand began to stir up into a spiraling upward vortex both blinding and awe-inspiring.

"I hope this wasn't a huge mistake," Rockefeller Slab said while other towering giants looked on with equal apprehension.

As when the brass bell appeared, they soon noticed another mound that was whirling into formation. Low to the ground at first, it rose to a height of fifty feet in no time. Even the three-story tall Guggenheim Museum found himself being dwarfed by the growing presence, and the sand continued to swish about in a tornado of mystery. While the air swirled into clouds of dust, onlookers were paralyzed by the phenomenon, as if having made some kind of nonverbal agreement to simply face the storm head on. Or perhaps they just grew tired of being fearful by that point, but in any event, there they all stood.

In the seconds that followed, conditions worsened as visibility surrendered to a swirling sandstorm that rose higher still. Just when it seemed the survivors would be swallowed up forever, the whirling dervish was eviscerated by a sudden burst of white light. It wasn't an explosion, but something else entirely; a new kind of light that seemed luminous but never blinding, emitting a warmth that the onlookers had never felt before.

The ground then reached a violent, rumbling crescendo and a strange, white object began to emerge from the lit mound. Witnesses struggled to maintain their footing as they watched the spectacle, its illumination intensifying. After a few moments of trepidation, the rumbling ceased, everyone's balance returned, and the glow softened. Once the dust had settled, everyone—from the shortest Manhattanites to the tallest buildings—looked up at a towering giant that hovered high overhead.

After much struggle, Lady Liberty and the other survivors had finally caught up with the pack, having only caught glimpses of the disturbance from farther down the sand dune. Like everyone else, the green lady cranked her neck to look up at the new building, trading glances between it and the nearby rock's inscription.

"Ring for freedom ... Ring for *freedom*," she repeated to herself in an attempt to unravel the meaning of it all. Remembering the parting words of her dying sculptor, Bartholdi, all those years ago, her eyes widened in sudden amazement. "This Freedom Tower could be Schist's doing!"

"Oh, please," Wall Street Tower snapped. "With all due respect, why would Schist decide to step in now, after all the godforsaken times of the past when he could have but didn't?"

The other towers awaited clarity, and Lady Liberty ignored Wall Street Tower's derisive tone to further reflect on the coincidence. "We are in need now more than ever. Schist goes where we go, and perhaps we can go no farther without help."

Despite her critic's scoffs at the idea of late-inning divine intervention, Lady Liberty knew better. Foreseeing possible deliverance from their woes, the statue looked upon the glowing giant with hope in her heart, feeling that what mattered most was that this so-called Freedom Tower was even present at all—her glowing silhouette bringing a very real prospect of renewal for the statue and her friends.

PART 4 **EMANCIPATION**

EMPIRE STATE AND CHRYSLER BUILDINGS awoke to a dark and dismal scene. Astonished to even be breathing at all, they were otherwise trapped inside some kind of vertical encasement that had covered them to their topmost floors with hardened lava. Trying to wiggle out of their adjacent cocoon-like confinements, each tower soon realized that movement was impossible, and escape was out of the question. To make matters worse, surrounding them were a half dozen guards and three fully armed and alert Cyclops Bots.

Empire State Building turned to face his lover as best he could. "Are you hurt?"

"Nothing too damaging," she said.

"Good. Don't look now, honey, but we're officially POWs," he quietly pointed out.

"At least we get to spend some quality time together," she replied with aplomb, demonstrating that the TERROR Group couldn't hinder their banter.

But such wit only lasted a short time against their grim new reality, and as the towers surveyed the changed world around them, they were startled by Manhattan Island's transformation. Its once vertical landscape of rich, vibrant colors that defied the spectrum was now buried under thick fogs of monotonous grays and blacks. Gone was any trace of its former vivaciousness.

Staring off in the distance, Chrysler Building knew that such a polar change wasn't just a local phenomenon. She took in the streams of glowing lava that burned brightly across the landscape, like rivers from Hell. Her agitation only grew as she saw that Central Park had all but vanished, its trees, bridges, and grassy hills buried beneath hardened layers of lava. All around them were pockets of ravaged, mangled earth and newly formed caves and cliffs.

And something far more sinister lurked beneath the surface of where they were perched, for every few minutes, the captive towers were disturbed by a soft rumble in the earth that traveled up their lava encasements and deep into their structural frames. This ringing sensation was followed by a low, resonant bellow that came from somewhere behind them. Anxious and exposed, the prisoners looked at each other with alarm, unable to pinpoint the source of such quaking tremors.

Straining to catch a glimpse of whatever was behind him, Empire State Building noticed some cave-like outcroppings that probably led to subterranean depths of the island's core, or so he suspected. Some, he saw, were as tall as he was, while others were hollow channels that dug deep into the island's fiery innards.

Chrysler Building turned to see for herself, focusing on the cavity-like punctures in the surfaces of the caves. While the punctures lent eerie, anthropomorphic features to the rocky formations, they also alluded to some kind of fiery activity occurring within. The buildings remained both transfixed and terrified by the strong, smoldering embers of bright orange that originated from inside the outcroppings, indicative of whatever hellish activity was causing the earth-shaking tremors below them. Whatever their purpose, the beastly-looking caves stood as symbols of Manhattan's new ownership.

"So this is our grim new world," Chrysler Building said with newfound bleakness. She turned to look the other way, hoping for some relief while a landscape layered with the same dark tones continued to remind her of their reality.

Empire State Building could find no words to help alleviate the situation. He was aware that nothing he could do or say would change their present danger, for they were now staring doom directly in the face. The only thing clear to both towers was that Manhattan's skyline had been utterly transformed.

The buildings' attention focused back on their immediate surroundings as sounds of approaching voices could be heard coming from the thick smoke nearby. Soon enough, the TERROR Commander, flanked by several armed guards, came into view and looked up at his prisoners with gleeful satisfaction.

"Ah! The legendary Empire State Building ... and the iconic Chrysler Building. What a pair, and what an honor to finally have this chance to meet you both," he remarked, circling the captive towers. "I *do* apologize for the less-than-ideal accommodations, but I trust you understand why we need to utilize such a strict form of bondage. You two being so *rebellious* and all."

The two towers stood silently.

"But not to worry," the vile ruler continued. "You can rest assured that more of your friends will soon be joining you. They have no other choice, after all."

Empire State Building resisted the taunts no longer. "Well, you're right about one thing, Commander. Our friends *will* come back for us, and with help. In fact, the whole planet will seek retribution for what you and your cronies have done here."

Chrysler Building feared repercussions from her lover's remark, and her gargoyles began to tremble at the thought of the TERROR Commander's capabilities if tested. "What are you doing?" she whispered to her companion.

Empire State Building's defiant tone was enough to make the TERROR Commander to halt his pacing. "Careful, my friend. *Retribution* is a strong word for the uninitiated," he warned, and paused to reflect on the situation. "You know, I don't think you have any idea how much I once admired you and your kind, back when I was so young and unrealistic. Anyway, I suppose your statements will be tested, barring the possibility that those pesky sand dunes haven't already buried your friends by now, which is more than likely considering that my scouts haven't found a trace of them. And like I said, if your friends *are* foolish enough to return here, I'll have a few surprises that I'm simply dying to show them."

"I guess we'll just have to wait and see," Empire State Building said.

The TERROR Commander scurried up the prisoners' hardened cages like a spider, his menacing red eyes coming within a few feet of their topmost floors as he fixated upon them. "You know something?" he observed. "As I look at you two now, I sense a great unlikelihood that your friends could ever make it without you, even with Lady Liberty at their side."

The captive towers remained silent despite the TERROR Commander's continued probing.

"And you know what else? I find you two to be the absolute, how shall I say it, *top* of the heap, indeed. They need you. But again, so do I, since you're the reason for Manhattan's supreme decadence, basking in glory as the rest of us suffered! Rest assured, my dear friends, the planet is not coming to save you," he predicted.

Empire State Building continued his stern resistance. "You must have missed the memo, Commander," he said. "Chrysler Building and I were just two members in a very *long* line of equals in our society. I was a representative voice in the crowd, nothing more. If there exists such a decadence as you describe, then I'd argue your regime hit closer to that mark that we did."

The TERROR Commander leapt back to the ground, startled by his opponent's proposal. "What a bold repudiation. But I guess I shouldn't be surprised that you're giving me the ol' blame game. You are a politician, after all!"

Gazing out at the wreckage of the once impenetrable city, he challenged the buildings' preconceptions once more. "Who *dares* to consider that this place was a bastion for equality before I arrived?

No one! Yours is, or *was*, a society of hierarchy, privilege, gaudy wealth, and useless democracy. It was a false profit of safety that turned a blind eye toward a planet in despair. Such poisons naturally breed resentment and class warfare, and you're telling me that your streets did *not* have people who slipped through the cracks; homeless undesirables and wretched refuse who would just as soon be stepped over, while your so-called 'civilized' inhabitants went to fetch another designer handbag? Don't be naïve, Empire State Building. Your society was *indeed* decadent, a failed study of a warped lifestyle now reduced to ashes, thanks to me. The TERROR Group is the *equalizing* voice of this city. Accept that, I beg you."

Fed up with the Commander's speech, it was Chrysler Building who sharply interjected this time. "Well, at least we don't solve our problems by committing mass murder, Commander!"

"My dear Art Deco princess," the TERROR Commander replied, "you left us little choice in that regard. Would you have changed your ways otherwise? I think not. If mass murder was the only way of injecting righteousness into this obsolete system, then we did what was necessary."

Chrysler Building held her composure with all her strength, even as the TERROR Commander doubled down. "Whether or not you agree, my dear, is irrelevant anyway," the vile ruler continued. "You are nothing more than a cockroach to be squashed, and everything dies in the end, even cockroaches. Look around, and you'll see what I mean! Pegmatite is on *my* side, not yours."

Mindful of the TERROR Commander's poisonous words, Chrysler Building had no other choice than to stare at the ground in defeat, and an emboldened Empire State Building tried once again to break free from his rocky prison.

Alarmed by this, the TERROR Commander signaled his guards to send volts of electricity surging into Chrysler Building's upper floors. She let out a painful cry—a clear message for Empire State Building to stop struggling.

"Leave her alone, you cowards!" the tower yelled as Chrysler Building slipped into unconsciousness from the paralyzing shock.

With a casual wave of his hand, the TERROR Commander motioned his guards to stop before Chrysler Building's injuries became fatal.

"Violence, violence, violence. Must this be our only way to get through to you?" the composed Commander asked. His eyes traveled across Chrysler Building's limp body with the same apathy he had afforded to Empire State Building moments earlier. "You must believe me when I say that I don't *want* to torture you, Empire State Building. But know that *every time* you provoke me, *every time* you resist what's going on here, I am unhappy. And when I'm unhappy, so will it be with you and yours. If you learn nothing else, learn that."

Empire State Building looked on helplessly at the situation facing him. "You *better* just leave her alone," he threatened, as TERROR Soldiers cackled. And though his anger grew, Empire State Building reassessed his predicament at hand, realizing that no amount of self-determination could overcome his opponent, at least not at that moment. As such, the tower was forced to change his tune. "Just ... *please* ... punish me instead, not Chrysler Building. I'm the one resisting," he said in a faint voice.

Sensing Empire State Building's submission, the amused leader toyed with him further. "Oh boy! Chrysler Building must treat you *very* well, indeed. Very well. Anyway, just sit tight for now and take in some air. If we locate your friends, you'll be the first to know, this I guarantee!" His dominance on full display, the vile ruler walked off, leaving the captive towers to acclimate to their new reality.

Hour after hour, a grim scene unfolded before Empire State Building. All around him, billowing skies of gray continued to engulf the island and its surroundings. Seeking some kind of solace, he stared at the Hudson River in the distance, still mighty but murky. Popping sounds made by fresh, flowing lava could be heard coming from every direction, offering little comfort to the troubled tower. For temporary relief, he found himself often gazing upon Chrysler Building's sleeping form, feeling somewhat comforted by the fact that his lover wasn't awake to see such devastation. Unfortunately for him, however, Empire State Building *was* awake, and forced to bear the agony of the situation at hand. All the while, the sequence of events leading up to that moment played out in his mind, reminding him of all the times he could have been more privy to the planet's ills, or more aware of the threats Manhattan had attracted.

Such thoughts only disgusted him further, causing him to hypothesize what he'd do if ever given the chance to go head-to-head with the TERROR Commander. The possibilities consumed the tower to the point that he began to mumble his dark fantasies to his unconscious companion.

"There's no reasoning with this monster," he muttered. "And the first chance I get, I'll end him. Mark my words, my love. Of that I'm sure."

Being stuck in such a dark place for too long and in an attempt to calm his agitation, Empire State Building focused once again on Chrysler Building's seeming tranquility. "You're still beautiful, no matter what they've done to you," he whispered, even though her once gleaming crown of triangulated windows had violently dented and dulled, and her chrome eagle gargoyles hung helplessly down the building's sides.

Seeing her signs of distress, he tried to recall memories of when they first met, their budding romance, and other happier times. As he revisited those moments, he was reminded of the eternal pleasure and power of unbridled love, but left to wonder if such a feeling would ever be his again. After yearning for a little while longer, he noticed Chrysler Building's triangular lights start to burn more brightly as she began to regain consciousness.

"Welcome back."

"Wish I could say I'm happy to be here."

Banter restored.

The prisoners endured long periods of isolation from there, and the opportunity allowed them to quietly conspire possible escape scenarios. But each plan seemed to reach a dead end, and the buildings faced a fact that could no longer go without saying.

"I don't think that TERROR Commander's bluffing. He probably *is* using us as bait," Chrysler Building said as she turned to her partner. "I hope Lady Liberty's not thinking about coming back for us."

Empire State Building sighed. He understood the measure of her words, but he also realized an inevitable truth. "You and I both know they're a brave group that just might try it, regardless of what we fear," he replied.

"That's exactly what scares me, because I don't know what else this guy has up his sleeve," Chrysler Building said.

Surely, the days ahead tested their growing worries.

Back atop the desert dunes, Freedom Tower sensed a world of chaos and apprehension from the moment she arrived. While the crowd continued to wonder what the tower's dramatic debut meant for them, she scanned her surroundings with similar unease.

"This place we are in," she said in a deep and resonant voice, "is barren and menacing, prone to dust and stale air."

"Well, it's only temporary!" UN Building yelled. "I hope, any-way," he said in a softer voice.

Still, despite some initial misgivings about the world around her, Freedom Tower felt grateful for being alive. Acclimating herself, the tower twisted gently from side to side to free any stubborn grains of sand that lingered in her floors and windows from the long journey. While she stretched and swayed gracefully, the transfixed crowd studied her glowing and radiant design, which included a 200-foot square base, a main structural shaft with tapered corners that spi-raled upward, and a roof capped off by an equally radiant, needled spire that rose higher than any tower giant they'd ever known.

Freedom Tower focused her attention back on the ragged and weary figures staring up at her. Surveying them carefully, she took in concrete marred by giant gashes, missing bricks, exposed inte-rior floors, and shattered windows across many of the buildings' façades. All of their scars were indicative of some ravaged and vio-lent recent past.

Tired of speculating the purpose of this strange new visitor, Lady Liberty stepped forward to confront her. "We stand before you desperate for help, as our way of life and all we have known was taken from us. The buildings you see here are all that remain of a once thriving place. I feel your presence to be a Schistian gift. Have you come to help us?"

Freedom Tower straightened her posture before speaking. "Your insight is strong, Lady Liberty, and the answer to your question is yes, I have come to help," she replied, understanding that the statue's wisdom reaffirmed why she'd been chosen to interact with them. "Your situation is what I was told to expect. Allow me to explain."

She summoned her next words with care for the anxious crowd. "Survivors of strife, the bells sound from nation to nation to announce that a warrior for peace and *free will* stands beside you.

May tears soon be shed not only for the fallen, but also out of joy for the future. Despite your past anguish, fear not, for you, too, are warriors imbued with the spirit of Schist. Let us share our burdens, then, and *embolden* one another to resist and overcome Pegmatite's destructive ways, so that we can claim emancipation. Together, we shall fight on and forge ahead until new life is breathed back into Manhattan, that island you call home."

Freedom Tower took in a deep breath while the power of her words ran through the weary crowd. Lady Liberty's growing grin was indicative of a steady reawakening all around. From inside their buildings, cheers erupted from Manhattanites young and old, as everyone expressed their excitement. Buildings large and small stood by with similar stimulation. Among this buffet of emotion, one thing was clear: Freedom Tower's call for rebellion had fallen on receptive ears.

Surviving buildings gathered in a circle around the stone-like monolith where Freedom Tower was first discovered to come to terms with their situation. The desert winds had picked up more ferociously by that point, and Manhattanites and members of the Manhattan Military were instructed to listen in from behind closed doors.

As she actively participated, Lady Liberty looked around the circle to take in the historic moment, reminded that the small band of survivors—just under thirty towering giants in total—was all that remained of Manhattan's former glory. Surely, the green lady was well aware of the risks that lay ahead.

Once the group was assembled and emotionally primed to entertain a certain "strength in numbers" mindset, thanks to their strange new visitor, Freedom Tower went to work articulating a workable strategy.

As the hours passed over the windswept desert sands, a bold proposal to reclaim what remained of Manhattan was formulated, and if accepted, it was a proposal sure to be the riskiest and most daring counteroffensive the city had ever engaged in.

"I know this has been a trying journey for all of you," she began, "and that you seek rest, so I will be brief. In the next twenty-four hours, we will harness every *ounce* of our collective strength in order to reclaim Manhattan Island." Her words carried through the crowd with both invigorating charge and daunting gravity. "Now, this TERROR Group would never expect a coordinated offensive against them because it is both brash and difficult, given our small numbers. More than likely, they would see it as a suicide mission on our part, which is why we must defy those expectations and move fast. The longer we wait, the more they will begin to think we were summoning other national forces for help."

While the crowd kept silent in light of Freedom Tower's weighty proposal, Wall Street Tower spoke up. "So, let me see if I understand this. Are you proposing that we simply head back through those god-awful sand dunes, to an island we no longer control, in order to go head-to-head against an enemy with triple our force and firepower, and do so with the aid of no other military force?"

With a patient tone, Freedom Tower said, "In a word, yes. Now, I know it is a tall order, but I ask only for your trust. My preset instructions are all we will need."

Wall Street Tower fired back in his usual fashion. "*Trust*, you say? How can I *trust* you when I don't even know you? None of us know you! This whole thing has to be the most ramshackle excuse for retaliation that I've heard in a good long while! In fact, I'd be surprised if you even get one of us to go along with this bombastic idea."

"He'd be surprised by his own shadow," Guggenheim Museum whispered to Puglia Ristorante.

"Those who trust in it will join in it," Freedom Tower said to her critic, calmly. "But you are right, trust is a matter of believing in something to the point that your preconceived notions are cast aside."

The former mayor scoffed for likely his millionth time, and Guggenheim Museum had heard just about enough from him. "Are you about finished with your latest adolescent rant, Wall Street Tower?"

Puglia Ristorante did his best to calm his companion by caressing his curved upper floors, to no avail.

"I can stand your skepticism no longer!" said the museum. "Were it not for Freedom Tower's arrival, we'd still be wandering aimlessly in the damn desert! Is that what you want? At least with her help we have a fighting chance."

Wall Street Tower quickly shot back, "Wait a second, Guggenheim, are you actually *considering* this idea? Forgive me, I guess I'm just not as eager to be blown to bricks as you are!"

Soon enough, bickering clogged the air as emotions ran high and the crowd once again turned on itself.

Freedom Tower persisted. "Listen," she said, "I know the trials you endured were miserable. But if you consider my strategy and take note of my words, we can rest easy soon. If we work together, the Manhattan that we all recall will not be gone for long."

Wall Street Tower seemed startled, and he redirected his ire back at Freedom Tower. "What do you mean, the Manhattan *we* all recall? You weren't there."

Freedom Tower knew the only way to present a clear case was to reveal her deepest truth in a more relatable way. "Ask me a question, Wall Street Tower. Anything," she said.

"A question? What question?" he replied.

"Never answer a question with a question. Seriously, just ask me something you never told anyone else besides, say, the Twin Towers," Freedom Tower challenged.

Enticed, Wall Street Tower took the bait. "Fine," he said. "Let's see. I want you to tell me *exactly* how heavy the entry cylinder that leads to my gold vault is. I'll wait."

"May I guess and say … ninety tons?"

Wall Street Tower's columns buckled as surprise took hold of his façade. He'd never revealed that number to anyone except the Twin Towers, given their often confidential dealings in trade and finance. "How the hell did you know that?" he asked.

"Because I was part of Manhattan once. *Twice*, actually. You see, your friends who were lost now reside in me. If we work together, then their plight, their sacrifice, will not have been in vain. You can believe me when I say that I know where you all come from."

The enigmatic tower paused for a moment before leaping back into her argument. "Wall Street Tower, your concerns do not fall upon deaf ears, but if we agree to come together, know that you will have nothing to fear. This army of terror would never expect such a unified resurgence from us. It is our spirit they hope to crush, because it is this spirit that can stop them. Pegmatite is strong, yes, but Schist is stronger. The choice is yours."

Lady Liberty observed the crowd as they patiently absorbed Freedom Tower's proposal, and to her delight, several buildings came forth to voice their position, starting with UN Building.

"I'll follow you in battle, my bold new friend!" the diplomatic tower announced.

"*We* will follow you in battle, you mean," Rockefeller Slab added.

"I'm in as well," a brittle-looking Trinity Church chimed in.

"Ha! You're far too old, my friend. I think you should sit this one out. In fact, I think *any* of us over a certain age should sit this out, and that includes me," Wall Street Tower rudely proposed, as if insulted by the church's sudden vigor.

Egged on by his critic's remarks, Trinity Church directed his thoughts right at the crowd. "You know, except for this one old building, and I don't mean myself," he said, "I have not heard anything to make me believe we should *not* engage in this plan. And that other old building, mind you, is just a cantankerous, stubborn one anyway. I do *not* intend to spend my few final years thinking that everything I knew is gone. I want in, not only because this is a chance to reclaim our home, but also to prove our only skeptic wrong!"

Trinity Church's spry retort delighted and swayed the crowd, which was obvious from the jubilant laughter all around. Soon enough, most other towers pledged their support to partake in Freedom Tower's proposal, regardless of their age or doubt.

"Mi compadre, I am at your service!" offered a buoyant Puglia Ristorante.

"I suppose that includes me, too," Guggenheim Museum said.

"And me," added a hopeful Ladder Tower.

It didn't stop with the buildings. Loud shouts from within each of them, a rallying cry from Manhattanites of all ages, kicked their plan into high gear.

Clearly outnumbered, Wall Street Tower gave in to the growing show of support. Whether they were buildings to live or work in, places of worship, dining, or meant for some other purpose, the skeptical tower detected an unprecedented unity among them all. He was truly the lone voice of dissent, but given the tenacity of Freedom Tower's nature, Wall Street Tower saw no other option than to listen to popular opinion for the first time in his life.

After Freedom Tower's fearless disposition won over her detractor, the prospect of overcoming a monstrous obstacle was boosted by a sense of collective and regenerated morale, and it was then that Lady Liberty saw fit to speak her mind.

"Freedom Tower," the green lady said, "you are asking us to believe that the resilient spirit of Manhattan is not bound by its geography, but rather, that its spirit resides deep within us, no matter where we are. I trust in this promise, and I trust in your desire to help us through this most uncertain hour."

It was clear that Freedom Tower had awakened a sense of urgency in the survivors' minds, a kind of spiritual revival that inspired them to act courageously despite the barriers that plagued them.

That was the easy part, for the next steps entailed putting the tower's words into swift action. A few hours later, their bold new strategy was sketched out. With the aid of the Manhattan Military, the plan charted the group's journey *back* to Manhattan Island, including where to camp on the night before their surprise retaliation. Given the serious risk of the whole endeavor, fighting would have to be managed by the most able-bodied buildings in the group, along with Manhattan Military forces. Many civilians volunteered to take part in the fight, but it was obvious that they were far too vulnerable for such a full-scale assault, and nobody wanted to sustain collateral damage that could have been avoided. As a result, a compromise was reached where Manhattanites would remain inside the buildings as they fought—close to the action but safer from imminent danger.

"Our course of action is set, then," Freedom Tower informed an alert crowd. "Lady Liberty and I will lead the first stampede from the shores to the mainland, followed closely by Rockefeller Slab, St. Patrick's Cathedral, and Ladder Tower. Alongside us will be all Manhattan Military units. Once we break through any weak spots in the TERROR Group's defenses, UN Building and Trinity Church will lead the rest of you for that crucial second charge." Freedom Tower paused for a moment to let her words sink in.

"Nervous yet?" Guggenheim Museum asked Puglia Ristorante in a gesture of much-needed relief.

"Are you kidding? Me? Nah," his companion replied, as his rooftop water tower trembled ever so slightly to indicate that Puglia Ristorante was hiding his nervousness.

"I guess I believe you," Guggenheim Museum said.

"Our next stage is critical," Freedom Tower continued, "so we must perform it flawlessly. I expect the area to be swarming with troops, forcing us to fight through whatever is in our way to gain as much ground as possible in a short amount of time, using all our weight and might to do so. As that happens, keep an eye out for any prisoners, including Chrysler and Empire State Buildings."

Freedom Tower turned to Lady Liberty, who seemed reinvigorated by the proceedings, and UN Building, Ladder Tower, and others couldn't help but notice a brighter, fuller coloring of the green lady's copper exterior, as she appeared to be more full of life than she had been for the past few days. To some, the statue even seemed like her old flying self, though time would tell if they were correct.

"Nightfall is fast upon us and incoming winds are picking up from the south," Freedom Tower observed from her high elevation. "Nothing more to do right now, but at first light, we will start our journey back. In the meantime, let us try to clear our minds and recharge."

But the buildings, most of whom had hung onto the glowing tower's every word, looked around aimlessly at the thought of catching a few winks. Surely Freedom Tower knew that *sleeping* would be a tough sell for a crew so battle-weary, given that such a luxury was for those with clear minds in a safe place, and these survivors had neither. However, *resting* was something she knew to be within reach if everyone tried.

To achieve such lofty aspirations meant that buildings first needed to protect themselves from the relentless desert winds. They decided the best way to achieve this was to contort their structural frames in such a way that they could form temporary building clusters close to the ground, so drafts passed over them as easily as possible. There were four of these groupings planned in all, with the tallest towers concentrated along the perimeter and shorter buildings huddled in the center of each makeshift cluster. Once everyone was in position, the tallest buildings bent over to cover the shorter ones, forming a protective dome shape with their bodies.

The process took about thirty minutes to coordinate, but once that happened, aided by camouflaging sands that blew in the breeze, it was almost as if the survivors weren't there at all; a perfect cover against anyone seeking to find them.

While buildings sought rest despite constant howling winds that brushed across their sides like sandpaper, concerns both large and small added further fuel to keep them awake.

Did this plan of theirs stand any chance? Was it wise to put their trust in Freedom Tower, or wiser to die in the desert? Were Empire State and Chrysler Buildings still alive? How much of Manhattan remained? How many TERROR forces would they need to fight through? And what kinds of surprises could the TERROR Commander have waiting for them?

Such questions were in bountiful supply in a place with little else to offer, as the buildings attempted to slumber.

Deep in the middle of the night, Lady Liberty grew tired from outstretching her arms as she clung onto her neighbors, doing her best to keep their temporary shelter intact. While she tried to clear her thoughts and rest at the same time, faint yet familiar voices entered her subconscious mind, imploring the statue to untangle herself from the grouping of half-awake buildings.

"Come to us, Lady Liberty," the voices whispered. She made her way on unsteady feet across the moonlit sand, and the voices only grew more distinct, until Lady Liberty found herself within reach of Freedom Tower, whose blinding light was instead muted for the evening. Fully awake and standing in silent watch over the rest of the buildings, the vigilant tower turned to notice the approaching statue. Lady Liberty indulged her own curiosity.

"I need to know for sure," the green lady said with determination, beckoning the towering giant to lean down to her height. Once within reach, Lady Liberty outstretched her hands and clasped Freedom Tower's upper floors, hoping to feel her steady pulse. Closing her copper eyelids, Lady Liberty focused on the whispering voices again, which now felt as if they were transmitting their presence directly between Freedom Tower's upper floors and the statue's own fingers.

"She is us and we are her now," the voices said, cryptically.

"Is this *truly* so?" Lady Liberty asked, her eyes remaining closed.

"It is," they stated in unison.

Over the next several minutes, the spirits of the Twin Towers continued to communicate with Lady Liberty, asking her to embrace Freedom Tower as not only a Schistian gift from beyond, but also to see her as a messenger of hope according to their dying wishes. Upon learning of this insight, Lady Liberty opened her eyes and released her hands from Freedom Tower's frame. The glowing figure and the copper statue stared deeply into each other's souls, while saying nothing and everything all at once.

Freedom Tower diverted her attention to look past Lady Liberty's right shoulder, as if to sense something coming near. Curious, the statue turned, peered downward, and noticed the vision of a familiar human form approaching them.

"Frédéric-Auguste Bartholdi," Lady Liberty said with long-lost yearning in her tone, while Freedom Tower straightened back up to her full height.

"Hello, my dear," the spectral figure said as he greeted them with glee. "It's been a long time, hasn't it?" He knew that his presence was shocking yet welcome to Lady Liberty's eyes.

"Are you a mirage? Are you really here?" the green lady asked.

"Now, I don't think that matters at this point, do you?"

"Well, no."

"Exactly. No, what really matters is that you heed the words of Towers One and Two, for what they're saying is true."

"About Freedom Tower?" Lady Liberty asked as she stared up at the gleaming giant.

"About all of it. Manhattan's fate should never be determined by Pegmatite's destructive doings. That would take us backwards. You remember that, don't you?"

Seeking a moment of reprieve, Lady Liberty rested her hand upon Freedom Tower's base for support. "Yes, but this is a challenge greater than any that has come before, Bartholdi," the statue admitted.

"I know it is! That's why you need to trust in the Schistian gifts that have been granted to you. You're gonna need all the help you can get for whatever's coming next.``

Upon hearing the Sculptor's advice, Freedom Tower looked back at the statue and nodded, who in turn began to choke back emotion resulting from the combination of hope and fear.

"Remember what I told you all those years back, my dear," the Sculptor said. "Respect Schist, the ancient one who begot you. Indeed, there's no greater time to do so than now."

An anxious expression took hold of Lady Liberty as she came to terms with Bartholdi's advice. "I understand," she replied, "but…"

"But what?"

"But how do you know all this? How are you able to relay this to me from, well, wherever you have been all these years?"

Bartholdi paused for a moment, and a knowing smile overcame his face. "Let's just say my services were requested one last time to design something for a good cause." He grinned as he directed his gaze up at Freedom Tower. "But keep in mind that this is a one-time thing, so should you choose *not* to go along with Freedom Tower's proposal, however brazen it may sound, understand that the Twin Towers' gift will have been for naught. So, I guess it's just a matter of *believing* then, right?"

With that, the two buildings witnessed Bartholdi's image disappear against an incoming wave of moonlit dust, washed away by the sands of time.

Following a moment of soul-searching reflection about what they had just experienced, Freedom Tower broke her silence. "Well, tomorrow is a new day for us," she noted softly.

"Yes … Yes," Lady Liberty agreed, and the two went their separate ways.

Upon returning to her post, the statue rested a little easier with the knowledge that Freedom Tower truly was an otherworldly addition to their cause. And as early morning greeted the survivors, the statue's thoughts held tightly to those revelations made by her departed friends the night before.

Once the sun had fully risen, the desert winds subsided and visibility cleared up all around them. The buildings unfolded from their makeshift domes and returned to their natural structural shapes. Watching this, Lady Liberty was reminded that the time was near to begin carrying out Freedom Tower's plan. Once they started out, there would be no going back, because simply *considering* that the tide could turn in Manhattan's favor was no longer enough. This was, as the specter of Bartholdi had so dutifully noted, the time to *believe*. So, as the morning rays turned the landscape to bright tones of tan and beige, the statue and her friends began their long march back toward whatever devastation and destiny awaited them.

Deep in the bowels of his conquered Manhattan, the TERROR Commander sat alone in his specially created chamber. Much like the army that he controlled, the chamber was a seamless blend of state-of-the-art technology with old-world craftsmanship in line with the order's traditions. Walls were an artful study of contrasts, composed of a charcoal-colored mix of Manhattan's natural bedrock with recently poured hardened lava, and accented by thin, fresh, streams of glowing fire that seemed to flow infinitely from ceiling to floor. Sprinkled throughout the chamber were various technological amenities—everything from projected infographics and moving images that displayed and mapped out every aspect of the order's global territories, to heart rate monitors and diagnostics for each individual TERROR Soldier. The chamber was the product of a highly strategic and successful rule, and it represented just how far the TERROR Group had come under the Commander's watch.

Yet from this enviable fortress deep within his reimagined Manhattan, something bothered the TERROR Commander. While he hadn't admitted it to anyone, the source of his ire was the fact that Lady Liberty and others had evaded his masterful assault. He fervently awaited the latest reports from the scouting crew ordered to find the escapees, but the searches continued to come up empty even though most of the known regions around Manhattan had been swept. Nevertheless, the TERROR Commander kept his eyes trained on the monitors, hoping for the best, when a new report streamed in.

"This is Scouting Crew One to Base. We've finished surveying remaining unmapped regions of the northernmost dunes, and no targets have been located. I repeat, targets *not* located along the northern dune perimeter. Awaiting further orders to proceed."

The results irked the TERROR Commander further, as they were indicative of a flaw in his perfect strategic planning. Perhaps it was his own hubris that had allowed such a mistake to occur, given that the meticulous military leader never once considered the possibility that anyone could escape the TERROR Group's calculated advance, much less manage to flee far enough into those unforgiving dunes without having to answer to him. A true misstep, indeed, and despite aggressive efforts to locate this small band of fugitives, not even a trace was to be found. Add to that the relentless desert winds, meaning that neither the TERROR Commander nor his scouts could find a single track in the sand. No tracks, and therefore no trace. Nothing.

But even as he ruminated on his failures, the TERROR Commander remained confident that he and his army had both a statistical and moral advantage over any enemy. Based on his estimation, should Lady Liberty and her crew somehow survive the dunes and return to the island with guns blazing, it would be an inconvenience at best. In the grand scheme of things, he figured, none of it mattered anyway; the final steps of his top-secret plans for "Manhattan's Salvation" were already underway. In the past twenty-four hours, the TERROR Commander received unanimous approval by the Chieftains to activate a network of missile stations that had been quickly constructed within a one-mile radius of Manhattan Island. To the Chieftains, this "next-gen" defense system seemed like a logical step in securing Manhattan's stronghold against any force brazen enough to swoop in and retaliate.

Earlier versions of this system traced back to previous TERROR campaigns, but Manhattan's was the largest and most sophisticated by far. With its implementation, the TERROR Group sat on its newfound spoils with unchallenged ownership. For his part, the TERROR Commander knew his proposal was music to the Chieftains' ears—a logical distraction from something far more sinister that would come their way.

Faithful to his ulterior master plan, the TERROR Commander remained patient and gave his scouting crew some new directives.

"Never mind the northern perimeter for now," he ordered through his intercom. "I want you to rescan all remaining areas within a 200-mile radius of the island. Report to me when you have something. In the meantime, I'll get more information out of the prisoners."

The TERROR Commander emerged from his insulated private chamber to press his towering captives still imprisoned atop the island's barren surface. As he approached them, the vile leader took a moment to find out just how frail Chrysler and Empire State Buildings were getting. Not expecting them to admit much, the TERROR Commander prodded his prisoners regardless.

"I want you two to indulge me now," he said. "Let's say your friends are still alive. Now, where would they be going? Who might be helping them? Anything you care to share? I know that you know something, and if I don't get an answer soon, I'll have little choice but to compound your miseries. You don't want me to do that, do you?" The TERROR Commander feigned urgency in his tone as he signaled his guards to prepare for whatever torture he had in mind.

"You're wasting your time, Commander," Empire State Building quietly said. "You and I both know that they're likely dead out there. The dunes are an unforgiving place, after all."

Wise to Empire State Building's game, the vile ruler took a moment to process the tower's suggestion. "My friend," he countered, "how uncharacteristic of you to suggest such a thing! You and I both know there's a chance they could have survived, especially given Lady Liberty's cunning talents. So, I'll ask again. Where would they go?"

Following stubborn silence from Empire State Building, the TERROR Commander fixed his attention upon the tower's lover. "Where are they hiding, my dear? Tell me and I'll make things easier for you," he whispered into Chrysler Building's crown.

"As you were just informed, Commander, you're wasting your time," she said with calm defiance.

"I see. Well, we can't say I didn't try." The TERROR Commander grinned as he motioned for his guards. "But unfortunately, those were not the answers I was looking for. Before I have my men teach you a lesson in honesty, I want you both to bear witness to my future plans for Manhattan."

The vile ruler directed the buildings' attention to a nearby Death Ray's projection screen which broadcasted the sight of three shadowy figures, each waiting attentively on their thrones from within a bunker. It quickly dawned upon the two towers that the figures were high-ranking Chieftains who had tuned in to receive updates on their latest territorial claim.

The prisoners stood by in disgust as the TERROR Commander filled the Chieftains' heads with a mix of groveling adulation and detailed data on casualties, security developments, and acreage gained.

"Now, before I have the honor of giving you all a virtual tour of this entire island and presenting you with several noteworthy prisoners, I'd like to thank each of you, my most high mentors of *Righteousness*, for all that I've learned from you over the years," the TERROR Commander added.

Minute by minute, the pace of the Commander's voice grew more hurried as he glossed over remaining details about the TERROR Group's progress. Wise to this change in behavior, Chrysler and Empire State Buildings began to sense deceit in the way he was playing to his audience.

"With each new victory that Pegmatite grants us," he continued, "I in turn have striven to please you, dear Chieftains, and to respect the will of Pegmatite while also dutifully carrying out the order's mission. You've never once gone against me doing so, and I'm most grateful for that."

"We remain delighted, Commander, for we've enjoyed shaping you into a more righteous version of what you used to be," the middle Chieftain replied with ostentation.

"And indeed you have," their sly protégé confirmed as he remembered the powerless young man he once was. "Now, to return the favor to my three wise rulers, I wish to offer you a gift for allowing me to carry out *Manhattan's Salvation*."

A sudden stillness permeated the air and the TERROR Commander's expression changed from welcoming to ominous in a heartbeat. Chrysler and Empire State Buildings watched with alarm as the "Manhattan's Salvation" code words triggered something sinister, while the three Chieftains clasped their throats and thrashed violently, as if to signal a loss of oxygen. Voices from their guards were heard off camera, shouting in obvious panic about the unexpected event.

Even though there must have been ample security all around the Chieftains, the buildings realized that no one was able to save the men from whatever was hindering them.

As their struggles continued to unfold, the TERROR Commander grinned even wider. He watched his mentors enter their final throes of suffocation, their bodies contorting and eyes bulging as they succumbed to the inevitable. Each revered Chieftain then collapsed in rapid succession, taking their last gasps for air off-screen, the cause still unclear.

"From the ashes of three, there shall be *one*," the TERROR Commander proclaimed, and he motioned for his Death Ray to turn off its projection screen. Focusing back on his captive towers, each shaken by what they had just watched, the vile ruler pulled out a microscopic object, about the size of an ant, and showed it to them. "I owe it all to this," he said.

The buildings studied the tiny, orb-shaped capsule in his claw-like fingers, which, they then learned, was a small but deadly asphyxiating agent so powerful that it could kill any lifeform if swallowed.

"My latest creation," the TERROR Commander gloated, "and one I've kept dear to me for quite some time. It works just like any implant. It can, for instance, be swallowed quite easily for a timed release that then is activated by certain code words. It's really quite brilliant if you think about it!"

"Absolutely inventive," Empire State Building remarked with obvious insincerity.

Accepting the fact that they had nothing left to lose, the towers became curious about the TERROR Commander's next-gen weapon of terror.

"Just so we understand, Commander," Chrysler Building said. "I take it that the final piece to 'Manhattan's Salvation' was to simply knock off your superiors?"

The TERROR Commander cackled in the face of Chrysler Building's sardonic question. "Precisely, my dear, precisely! Except you're downplaying the most significant part. They are my *superiors* no more. Which reminds me."

The TERROR Commander then instructed his media team to live-stream his new global message across all TERROR-controlled territories.

"Followers, from this day onward," he proclaimed into the cameras, "I shall be hailed not as your Commander, but as your one and only *Supreme Chieftain* for the Order of Righteousness, a title to benefit all and be usurped by none. The old guard has been swept away. Nothing will come between us and our future, and what a glorious future it shall be. Follow me, my brethren, and I promise you that we'll be closer to Pegmatite than ever before!"

The buildings stood by helplessly as the new Supreme Chieftain went on to declare that Manhattan Island was to be redesignated as the TERROR Group's capital city, and that any opposition to his judgments would be deemed high treason. "Anyone opposed to my supreme understanding of righteousness is an enemy to the order, and shall be dealt with swiftly," he warned.

All Chrysler and Empire State Buildings could do while they witnessed history being rewritten was gaze down at their hardened prisons and desperately wrack their minds for solutions.

Hundreds of miles away, the ever-sentient Lady Liberty felt a sudden and jolting rift in the way of things, and she nearly collapsed in the sand. Freedom Tower, sensing a similar cosmic disruption, helped prop the statue back up. But it was clear to both that time was against them and their friends.

"This plan of ours," Lady Liberty said as she clasped her forehead, "needs to run without a single hitch."

"That is my only aim," the glowing tower replied.

News of the Supreme Chieftain's mad declaration quickly leaked beyond the TERROR Group's territories, and headlines across the planet relayed his words with similar trepidation:

TERROR COMMANDER DECLARES HIMSELF
SUPREME CHIEFTAIN!
MANHATTAN STILL CAPTIVE
AS NATION STRUGGLES TO FIGHT BACK;
LADY LIBERTY AND OTHERS REMAIN MISSING.

While his takeover of the planet's most advanced city already triggered global lockdowns of unprecedented scale, the Supreme Chieftain's new levels of power meant an increase in fear and frustration for governments far and wide; governments already thrown for a loop as it was. In fact, ever since Manhattan Island had been toppled, no other military force had the capacity to challenge the TERROR Group, even with several covert and impractical attempts by national defense teams to try and liberate Manhattan in the days following its hostile takeover. This failure occurred for a variety of reasons, ranging from technological to geographic. Despite their best intentions, TERROR defenses were too well established for incoming challenges to their domain to succeed. Any opponents were simply shot out of the skies with relative ease.

The TERROR Group's future was now in the hands of one lone but determined supremacist, and the Supreme Chieftain wasted little time in laying out the groundwork. From a meeting hall within the island's fiery bowels, the ruler gathered a select number of top donors, strategists, aides, and TERROR Soldiers for what he hailed as an "all-new spiritual mission." His dream of conquering Manhattan was a years-in-the-making undertaking that required unquantifiable amounts of strategy and effort, and the Supreme Chieftain sought ways to streamline this process for when the time came to conquer the rest of the nation. His clever death capsules were just the start of dreadful prospects to come.

"Righteous friends, we stand triumphant in our new capital city, one that serves as a promising gateway into a nation at large. That nation is steeped in decadence and immorality, and is therefore in need of our moral correction."

From their seats within the meeting hall, his hand-picked group clung to the Supreme Chieftain's every word and gesture, afraid to be out of line or to call unnecessary notice to themselves as their leader spoke freely. Such was the level of intimidation and respect that the Supreme Chieftain demanded. They listened in unanimous attentiveness as he spoke, and it was quite apparent that Manhattan's conquest had never been enough for the Supreme Chieftain. Any feelings of victory and contentment earned from his latest victory paled in comparison to the prospect of what lay ahead.

"Being in control of this key location will finally allow our network to spread without a break in the chain," he continued. Rather than swallow up nearby towns and villages, as some of his strategists had suggested, the restless ruler planned the organization's next mission as an ambitious follow-up to "Manhattan's Salvation," one that involved rigorous strategy and new levels of pre-attack infiltration.

"To start," he told them, "we shall hit not one, but *three* 'magnet' cities within this nation, in less than half the time it took to take Manhattan."

In order to emphasize his spiritual mission to his audience, large images suddenly splashed across the hall's darkened walls and surfaces, showing a wide array of targets that ranged from the President's House to a host of other landmarks across three cities. The images beamed throughout the room in collage fashion as the Supreme Chieftain continued to spell out his nightmarish vision.

"In three months' time, after much planning, we shall strike the following targets you see here with swift aggression. So long as Manhattan remains in our possession, lockdown will certainly continue for most other cities, given that they were already less capable of defending themselves anyway. As we've seen, no military power can take Manhattan from us, for the handful of attempts to strike back at us have proved futile in light of our countermeasures in place. This, my friends, is why taking on these new targets *now* will guarantee our stronghold over this nation for decades to come. Once these magnet cities are ours, we will then swallow up more towns and villages to establish a presence of unprecedented scale. The order shall be as immovable as rock, a true manifestation of Pegmatite's graces, and our habit of lying low for generations will be a thing of the past."

The Supreme Chieftain's eyes swelled with passion as he stated his desires. "Now," he concluded calmly, "are there any objections?"

As if any other option was acceptable, praise was unanimous for the Supreme Chieftain's proposal. Once his presentation concluded, the vile ruler dismissed his minions to begin their work, while he sat alone inside the meeting hall, consumed by his thoughts as images of various architectural icons continued to hover across the room.

"A beautiful new world awaits," he said quietly, allowing himself to fantasize. After all, here was a ruler who had been razor focused on righting the wrongs in his own mind, through meticulous planning of his desires until they became his twisted reality. Recapping the recent achievements in his mind, his conclusion was that his strategy was working. The murder of the Twin Towers not only sent a direct message to the world, but also came as a surprise that helped demonstrate the TERROR Group's knack for stealth. Meanwhile, his campaign known as "Manhattan's Salvation" had been executed to the fullest degree, and without a hitch. The Supreme Chieftain used the success in overthrowing his superiors to gain even more power, thereby establishing singular dominance over his entire order. "And it's all mine," he told himself.

But as he stroked his own ego further, the Supreme Chieftain's hubris grew just as much as his success, and it was beginning to affect his judgment. In fact, while the vile ruler had been busy fashioning himself into a clairvoyant figure, he had also allowed higher dependence on machines for protection. Rather than insisting that the surface of Manhattan Island be patrolled by scores of TER-ROR Soldiers on the ready, he opted to keep the majority of them planning, working, and training far below the island's surface. This meant that Manhattan's topography remained bleak, barren, and almost devoid of activity, save for a few Cyclops Bots or Death Rays on patrol.

Per the Supreme Chieftain's orders, most protection came from the network of missile stations that sat just across the rivers along Manhattan's eastern and western boundaries—a practice that didn't go unnoticed by Chrysler and Empire State Buildings, who remained open to any possible escape option.

Empire State Building had been surprised to see so many missile stations pointing out and away from Manhattan Island's interior, undoubtedly ready for any long-distance attack but seemingly blind against anything that made it past their threshold and onto the island itself.

"I think I finally see the Achilles' heel of this whole setup," he whispered to his lover after another long moment of studious observation. "Those missile stations, you see, don't seem to account for any kind of close-range ground assault."

"So, what you're saying is that it's possible for anyone to slip right under those missile stations' noses?" Chrysler Building asked.

Her companion nodded. "As much as I hate to imagine that playing out, should Lady Liberty and the rest manage to bypass that defensive wall's line of sight, then yeah, it just might be possible."

True to the captive towers' suspicions, it wasn't long before Freedom Tower, Lady Liberty, and the other survivors had come to think along similar lines.

But as the ragged, sand-laden yet determined survivors advanced within two hundred miles of their intended destination, a faint whirring sound began to infiltrate the dusty skies above, and it was getting more noticeable by the second.

"Quiet everyone! What is that?" Rockefeller Slab said with alarm. Startled, his friends stopped in their tracks to survey their surroundings.

"Everyone, assume shelter positions on the double, and make sure Manhattanites keep away from your windows!" Freedom Tower ordered as she made out the hazy sight of three aerial TERROR Cruisers on the prowl, just coming into view. "Scouting crews heading in our direction," she warned.

"Wonderful," Rockefeller Slab said as he and other towers bent down to shelter the smaller buildings.

"We've gotta take 'em out before they report us!" UN Building added.

"I will do that. Inform everyone to turn off all their lights." Lady Liberty motioned as she knelt, closed her eyes, and tried her best to summon the ability to fly once again. Her thoughts disjointed, however, the statue struggled to achieve her goal, and blaster fire came in from high overhead, hitting no one but indicative that their location had been breached.

"What do we do?" Rockefeller Slab asked.

"They're zeroing in on us ... Lady Liberty, you've got to fly up and dispatch them before it's too late!" UN Building urged.

"I ... I cannot," the green lady admitted with regret, her best efforts to recapture some long-lost magic failing them all.

"Let me handle this one," Freedom Tower said. "But we should not shelter here any longer, UN Building. Help Lady Liberty up and get everyone behind that high dune to the north. Keep your lights off and get low to the sand as soon as you reach it. Go now!"

Following a much closer round of firepower from above, Freedom Tower and the rest of the group parted ways. To distract the speedy pursuers further, the normally brightly lit tower began to flicker her lights on and off as she moved away from the rest of the buildings, kicking up more dust and hazy glare in the process. The tactic worked, as Freedom Tower could feel her flying predators closing in on her at a furious pace that shook the earth.

"Target identified," the lead TERROR Pilot confirmed. "All units, prepare for my order."

"Come and get me," Freedom Tower muttered as she approached a flat desert valley, sandwiched by dunes on all sides. Seeing that her efforts had attracted all three of the pursuers, she stopped near the center of the open area, angling her gaze up at the sky as she waited for the pursuers to catch up.

"What the hell's she doing?" UN Building anxiously asked from the group's semi-protected perch behind one of the sand dunes. The other towers watched with dread as they barely made out the scene from afar.

"There's our sitting duck," the lead TERROR Pilot said with glee as Freedom Tower came into range. "I've got this one locked on target. Should be no big deal. Prepare to fire."

Just as the three cruisers began their descent, Freedom Tower increased the lumens of every single light within her vast structure, and she beamed so brightly that the glare disoriented her pursuers.

"I can't see the target!" panicked one of the aviators.

"Same here ... target lost," the lead TERROR Pilot confirmed as he tried but failed to lock back onto Freedom Tower's exact location. "All units, just fire ... fire now!" he said, sending a blaze of missiles raining down on their target with mighty force.

Just then, Freedom Tower was suddenly swallowed up by a whirling dervish of sand and dust that sucked her down into the earth below, right before the missiles blanketed her location in a massive burst of explosions.

"Pull up!" the lead TERROR Pilot shouted, as smoke and shattered earth intercepted their flight path, causing one of the speeding cruisers to spiral out of control and crash, while the others cleared the chaos just in time to avoid the same fate.

"Target destroyed," the lead TERROR Pilot said, and he and the remaining cruiser flew up and away from the area.

"Are you sure we hit it?" the other Pilot challenged.

"I *said* the target was destroyed!" his infuriated superior snarled before recomposing himself. "Nothing could have survived that barrage of missiles. Now send my message to base so we can get out of here."

Once the remaining TERROR Cruisers had flown away and out of view, Lady Liberty feared the worst. She and the others abandoned their hidden perch to make their way down to the wide-open valley where Freedom Tower was last seen. The statue and UN Building were the first to reach the flat area, and they were taken aback by just how blanketed the site was with craters of blackened ash and smoldering embers.

"How could anything have survived this?" UN Building quietly asked, feeling hopeless that their new friend could have withstood such an onslaught.

"It cannot end like this. She has to be alive ... she just has to!" Lady Liberty proclaimed, her voice sounding hoarse from the choking smoke.

"I don't know," UN Building said with doubt as he continued to survey the devastated landscape.

Following an eerie and empty silence, more towering giants began to congregate around the area, appearing mournful and solemn.

"She was our final hope," Guggenheim Museum said. He rested his weary frame against Puglia Ristorante's equally bruised and battered brick façade, but the restaurant seemed distracted by something else.

"No, she *is* our final hope!" Puglia Ristorante suddenly said. "Lady Liberty, everyone, come see this!"

Before long, a crowd grew around the two diminutive buildings, and Puglia Ristorante gestured toward a glowing object jutting out from the charred ground at his base.

"Can it be?" UN Building wondered.

"It surely can!" Lady Liberty confirmed.

They watched as Freedom Tower's glowing spire began to rise straight up and out of the scorched earth, forming a mound that forced the observers to clear the way. In moments, there she stood before the survivors, seeming to be unfazed by the recent missile attack.

"She loves doing that, doesn't she?" Rockefeller Slab said.

As the dust settled and the smoke cleared, Lady Liberty approached Freedom Tower and pressed her copper palm against the building's glowing facade. "Warm to the touch," the statue said with relief, hoping to confirm that Freedom Tower was indeed alive and well.

While survivors continued to look up in wonder and relief, Freedom Tower wriggled about, trying to ensure that every last grain of sand was removed from her momentous structure. She cleared her vocal passages soon after that, her thoughts and desires focused only on what lay in front of her and her friends.

"Well, that takes care of that," she said. "Now, let us get home."

The emboldened buildings shook off the experience and pressed forward, and Lady Liberty took in the glowing sight of Freedom Tower, smiling heartily when she realized that the Twin Towers' gift to them all had just passed her first major test with flying colors.

The remaining TERROR Pilots, lucky to be alive, were miles away from their recent mishap against Freedom Tower when a call suddenly came in.

"Please inform your superior to hold for the Supreme Chieftain," a no-nonsense voice on the intercom instructed.

"Oh! Understood," the Pilot on the receiving end said. "Boss, there's a call for you. I'll patch it through to your ship."

"What? I told you not to pick up any calls until we land," the suddenly fearful lead TERROR Pilot said from his cruiser.

"I think you outta take this one, boss. I'm told *he* wants to talk to you," the Pilot reported.

"Fine ... just put him through."

Seconds later, the Supreme Chieftain's voice filled the lead Pilot's cabin with a booming intensity. "What happened out there, Pilot? I'm getting radio silence over here. No good, my friend."

"Apologies, Excellency," the lead Pilot began. "It's been quite chaotic. We did find one survivor, but its defenses were such that we had to destroy it. We even lost one of our crewme—"

"You had to destroy *what?*" the vile ruler interrupted.

"The building, sir. We had to destroy the building."

"You destroyed a building in pursuit?"

"We had to, Excellency. I ordered the hit, a direct one by all accounts, and the target was swiftly neutralized," the lead Pilot elaborated, inaccurately.

"Oh," the Supreme Chieftain said coldly.

A noticeable pause permeated each cruiser's cockpit.

"Are you there, sir?" the lead Pilot asked.

"Yes, I'm here, but I told you to bring any survivors back to me alive, did I not?" the Supreme Chieftain pressed.

"You did, sir, but the enemy was overpowering, and we had to resort to other measures. I'm sorry, Excellency," the lead Pilot replied, already sensing what was to come next.

"No, my friend," the bereaved leader said. "I'm the one who's sorry that you couldn't comply with my simple order. I thought I was clear. Oh well, go and be with Pegmatite now."

"No, no wait!" the lead Pilot pleaded, following his master's casual write-off.

And with one equally laid-back push of a button with his spindly finger, the Supreme Chieftain triggered a self-destruct mechanism on both TERROR Cruisers, turning each into violent plumes of smoke and flame that careened into the dunes below.

Following their close call with the by-now doomed TERROR scouts, the journey toward Manhattan took longer than anticipated for Freedom Tower and her friends, thanks to a succession of blinding sandstorms. In due time, however, the hopeful emancipators finally reached the rim of dunes that led to the mouth of the Hudson River, and the island just beyond.

"This place has 'hotspot' written all over it. Now is the time for every tower to shut their lights off again, and crouch down as low to the earth as possible, just like we practiced, to avoid detection," Freedom Tower told Lady Liberty, who relayed the instructions down the line.

As she studied their surroundings, the green lady pointed out Manhattan Island's shadowy, beleaguered profile off in the distance. "I can barely make it out against the smoke and haze, but there it is," she told her friend.

"That island cannot be more than a mile away," Freedom Tower suspected as she sharpened her focus to survey whatever defenses lay along the river's edge. "And I see very little activity happening on its surface." After careful observation, she landed upon the very same theory that Chrysler and Empire State Buildings had entertained.

Signaling to Lady Liberty, Freedom Tower identified a potential weak spot in the TERROR Group's security system as UN Building joined them by the frontline.

"Those missiles only point outward and up to the sky, and they look long-range at that. The gaps between each station are inconsistent because of the varied topography, and I think those blind spots may just be enough to allow us through."

Encouraged by the prospect, UN Building was wary nonetheless. "We'll need all the topographic cover we can get, though," he cautioned.

Freedom Tower considered UN Building's point and zeroed in on a tall rocky area near the southwestern region of the island—by far the most-shielded zone.

"Look down there. Given that area's high cliffs, if we make it past its one adjacent missile station, we can reach the island before the other stations in the network notice us."

"Yeah, and then what?" UN Building asked.

"And then we just charge onto the island with force, dispatching remaining Manhattan Military tanks the second we reach dry land," she explained.

"Getting across that river will be treacherous, though. And what about those other missiles? If they spot just one of our antennas peeking over the cliffs, then we're as good as demoed," UN Building cautioned.

"Just wait for my signal," Freedom Tower replied. "I can see from here that the missiles scan from side to side every few minutes. This coordination happens in unison, so once they all point away from our target, we need to head down as quickly as possible."

Lady Liberty's tone signaled her concerns about the sizable distance between the start of the river and the island's shoreline. "How much time will we have?" she asked.

"Five minutes, maybe six," Freedom Tower estimated. "But if we make it, we will have already reached the island before those other missile stations suspect anything."

Lady Liberty and UN Building looked at each other wearily in the face of such an immense undertaking. Taking a deep breath to compose herself, Lady Liberty looked around to gauge everyone else's morale, knowing they had just one shot to make the whole thing work. As she observed her fellow towering giants, the green lady caught Trinity Church swaying ever so slightly, his old frame worn by their journey, but still seeming composed overall. So, too, were the other taller structures, like Rockefeller Slab, Ladder Tower, and the rest. Shorter ones like Guggenheim Museum, Masjid Malcolm Shabazz, Puglia Ristorante, Apollo Theater, and even Wall Street Tower appeared primed and ready, each carrying a certain "can-do" spirit in their body language. They'd all come too far to quit at that point.

Such an overall assessment comforted the statue, and she turned her gaze back to Freedom Tower. "I think we are ready to do this," she said.

Nodding, Freedom Tower then emboldened her daring band of rebels to prepare for their imminent assault. "Autocracy should never outweigh liberty," she began. "But remember that liberties and freedoms are earned, which is why we are back here. What was lost could be regained if we stay focused and sharp. For those who wish to stay behind for some reason, you shall not be judged, as the task ahead is a daunting and dangerous one."

The tower paused to give them the chance to stay behind, and it became obvious that nobody intended to run and hide. "Very well," Freedom Tower said. "There is one more thing. I spotted your two friends—Chrysler and Empire State Buildings—who are being held captive near the center of the island. They look to be waiting for a miracle, so whoever gets to them first during our advance should try to free them in any way possible. With that, let us get into our designated groups as I keep an eye on the missile stations. We can do this. Lady Liberty, UN Building, prepare for my signal."

While everyone shuffled into position, Lady Liberty and UN Building did a final inspection. "Manhattanites, be sure that all working windows in your buildings are closed, and that you keep as far away from them as you can. Adults, shield your children, and make sure to hold onto something before we start our charge," the statue instructed, hoping that no deadly scenarios would occur for the brave but fragile humans within. "Our hearts beat as one now," she assured Manhattanites young and old as they took their positions.

Every so often, a building would glance toward Manhattan Island in the distance and be reminded of just how rapidly their once polychromatic city had devolved into a place so bleak with disparity. Ladder Tower, for one, couldn't help but think back to a landscape once brimming with rich magentas, vivid crimsons, and sky blues; a magical world where the sea often blended into the sky. "Everything seems so ... off!" he said. To take in such a place in its present condition, ensconced by thick plumes of ash, impacted the slender tower, as it did his neighbors.

"You're right. I recognize nothing," Guggenheim Museum admitted grimly as he, too, took in the dire scene. After the city had built itself up over generations, it was apparent to all that a twisted embodiment of a once-great dream was all that remained. Even if Freedom Tower's plan were to play out perfectly in their favor, the only certainty that ran through most buildings' minds at that moment was that Manhattan's recovery would be long and arduous. Still, they had to fight for their homeland.

Freedom Tower stood like a determined warrior as she kept a keen eye on the missile stations' movements. Anyone who managed to sneak a peek for themselves saw a tower totally invested in her work and her promise. But as far as Freedom Tower was concerned, she was simply doing the Twin Towers' bidding of getting their friends back home. Whether they weathered the incoming storm or not remained to be seen, though it was clear to the survivors that she already managed to reawaken their morale. The idea that the island's fate was dependent on their actions only helped embolden each building further as they awaited Freedom Tower's go-ahead, like soldiers eager to charge from the trenches. Soon the air grew heavier with ash as remaining remnants of sunlight were all but swallowed up, as if the entire planet was battening down the hatches.

"Just a few minutes more now," Lady Liberty said softly as she suddenly felt an opportunity emerge from the atmospheric rift, sensing something ethereal in the works.

Realizing the time to act was fast approaching, Freedom Tower began a countdown. "We charge in twenty… nineteen… eighteen…"

While towers large and small prepared for their offensive, Lady Liberty closed her eyes and pointed her torch to the sky, chanting softly with long lost ancient spirits of Schistian yore. She had struggled as of late to summon such supernatural capabilities, but this time was different, and buildings saw the sky open up directly above them but nowhere else. Seconds later, ashy vapors surrendered to a quick flash of brightness that struck the green lady like a lightning rod.

Freedom Tower, trusting that Lady Liberty's actions aligned with her own, kept the countdown steady. By the time she got down to ten, Lady Liberty's rusted and battered torch morphed into a blinding white flame. By the count of eight, her eyes had reopened and appeared to be glowing as much as her torch. By five, surrounding buildings gasped when Lady Liberty's feet rose off the ground, putting to rest any doubt that she'd ever fly again as she hovered over the crowd with renewed agility.

"Three … two … one!" With a blinding glow of her spire, Freedom Tower triggered the wave of towers to hurtle down the sandy cliff and to their destination. As the earth trembled and shook from the momentous movement, the buildings came within a few hundred feet of the targeted missile station in good time, and Freedom Tower then pummeled it with enough force to catapult the deadly weapon right into the Hudson River. With that act, the TERROR

Group's wall of defense was broken, and the buildings traversed the river with all the pent-up strength that they could muster, creating a thunderous crash among the waves. The violent commotion caught the attention of several patrolling Cyclops Bots that then rushed to face the incoming horde of towers.

"The battle is on!" Freedom Tower called out to the emboldened group of survivors-turned-warriors. Showing swift agility, the buildings lunged headfirst into the incoming Cyclops Bots, stomping and plowing their way over the mechanized beasts with overwhelming force, while Manhattan Military tanks deployed from frontline building lobbies in high gear, firing their weapons the second their wheels hit the ground.

As that first wave of towers advanced, Lady Liberty signaled the second group to follow her lead. Guided by her torch, the green lady flew through the air with dexterity as the stampede charged below.

"Come on!" she bellowed with a warrior's confidence as more towering giants poured onto the island. All told, it was a violent scene of a skyline in motion like never before.

While the green lady continued to twist and turn in the sky, UN Building spotted an incoming aerial threat from his vantage point below her.

"We've got company. About nine cruisers comin' in hot at twelve o'clock high!" he warned loudly.

"I will deal with them. Keep pushing our ground forces northbound," the statue shouted back, her eyes focused on their opponents.

***

Amid the growing commotion, unsuspecting TERROR Soldiers began to feel faint rattles pervade their chambers within Manhattan Island's caves.

"What's going on out there?" one Soldier asked uneasily, ordering his assistant to check the nearest security monitor.

"Looks like about a dozen or so buildings, and they're uprising, sir!"

"Preposterous!" his superior blurted out before becoming humbled by the footage he saw on the screen.

Just then, two more troopers burst into the room with an alarming report. "The enemy is advancing quickly in our direction! They already bypassed our missile system and are plowing through frontline defenses left and right!"

"Unbelievable," another Soldier said. "Alert the Supreme Chieftain at once."

But such an alert came too late, as tremors had already begun to disrupt the Supreme Chieftain's meditation within his private chamber, and his hellish red eyes opened abruptly as the rattles increased.

"Why have I been awakened?" he barked over his intercom.

A Soldier's voice responded dutifully. "There's been a reprisal, Excellency! The buildings have staged a counterattack."

"Really? And just how did two *imprisoned* buildings manage to break free, may I ask?" the confused leader mocked.

After a long and jarring pause, the Soldier clarified the matter. "Our prisoners are still in custody, Excellency. I'm referring to the rest of them."

Upon hearing this, the Supreme Chieftain slowly stood up from his seated position, sliding his tongue over his razor-sharp teeth as he processed the Soldier's words.

"So they've come back to us, have they? I was told earlier that only one survivor had been found and dispatched, but I guess my scanning crew couldn't even manage to hit their target properly," he muttered as he watched the action unfold on his projection screens.

Speaking closer to the intercom, the ruler directed his troops with renewed composure. "Very well, let us give them what they deserve, Soldier. Awaken every last one of our beasts from their slumber. I want all units to report to the surface and a phalanx of Cyclops Bots to stretch the entire width of the island. You will then advance southbound to intercept the path of these perpetrators. Finally, at my signal, you will wipe out all traces of the enemy, leaving nothing standing. No prisoners this time, is this clear?"

"It is clear, Excellency," the voice obliged.

Upon the Supreme Chieftain's order, legions of TERROR Soldiers, Cyclops Bots, and Death Rays emerged from the ground with fervor—each intent on defending their occupied island to the last.

Following suit, the Supreme Chieftain uncovered his "Staff of Righteousness," that sacred weapon once bestowed upon him, he was reminded, by predecessors whose fates had since been sealed on his account. "Only *one* steers this ship now," he said in a self-aggrandizing tone while he gripped the weapon tightly between his claws. "Bless my actions, mighty Pegmatite. I beg of you." He then spoke to compel his dark forces, took a long, deep breath, and headed out of the chamber to join his army.

Back on Manhattan's surface, the uprising raged and Freedom Tower and the rest gained ground. Explosions rang out everywhere more frequently by that point, while dust and ash minimized visibility. But the buildings and Manhattan Military tanks fought through it all.

Despite periodic damage to the buildings from the Cyclops Bots and their blasting arms, it was far from enough to slow their stampede, for the time being anyway.

"Keep pressing upward and follow me!" Freedom Tower encouraged with might, desperate to keep momentum in the buildings' favor. Whether swinging, trampling, or kicking, each towering giant did their best to be a formidable and consistent foe, fully aware that their collective choreography was what kept the offensive alive and their enemies guessing.

As far as the TERROR Group's leader was concerned, the battle was far from over. Emerging from the belly of Manhattan Island with a clear lust for blood in his eyes, he perched himself atop the cave's smoky entrance to face his troops with a demeanor that suggested victory was already theirs. While he stood there, smoke and flames billowed from behind him, creating a portrait of a feared figure ensconced by his own dark legacy. From his position, the Supreme Chieftain assessed the situation and realized that his army had a lot of acreage to take back. Peering toward the southern portion of Manhattan Island, he made out the silhouettes of the advancing towering giants in the dense smoke and dust, taking account of their success thus far.

"This is bolder than what I imagined. And just what have we got over there? Someone *new* in our midst," he said as he laid eyes on Freedom Tower's luminous form for the first time. Moments later, a whooshing sound caught his ear, compelling the Supreme Chieftain to look up. He spotted Lady Liberty soaring high overhead as she maneuvered around dark clouds and dodged enemy fire from TERROR Cruisers in hot pursuit. Watching her perform a series of dynamic twists and turns, the Supreme Chieftain smirked at the sight of Lady Liberty's stealthy aerial gymnastics, which disoriented the TERROR Cruisers so greatly that they soon crashed into one another. With those violent bursts of flame punctuating the somber and gray skies, the last of the TERROR Group's active aerial fleet was taken out.

"Bravo, Lady Liberty, bravo!" the vile ruler hollered with enough amusement and erratic verve for his closest aides to glance at each other uneasily. Whatever his mental condition at the time, the feared leader switched his attention to instruct his army in waiting.

"It sure looks like our enemies are having all sorts of fun out there," the Supreme Chieftain said before shifting his tone. "Let us have ours now. Soldiers, it's time we put an end to this little soirée." He raised the "Staff of Righteousness" high over his head, before summoning his bevy of troops to move in strict formation toward Manhattan's southern acreage. "Be they large or small, crush 'em all ... crush 'em all!" the vile ruler shouted as his army emerged from the smoky cave in marching unison.

Despite looming dangers, the buildings' coordinated effort to retake Manhattan's southern acreage proved successful, and with a short respite from the violence, Freedom Tower seized the moment to regroup and assess everyone's condition. In her opinion, any weariness or exhaustion the buildings might have felt wasn't reflected in their warrior-like stamina, which seemed strong and capable still. Most importantly, not a single soul had been lost so far. But she also knew the time to celebrate wasn't yet upon them, before Lady Liberty swooped in to report her latest findings.

"The TERROR Group has activated its ground-based reinforcements, and from what I saw from up high, they appear to be approaching in tight formation from the north," she said. Both Freedom Tower and UN Building nodded tensely as they processed the statue's ominous update. "We have little time to proceed," the green lady added.

Such news hit the rest of the towers with unwelcome force. They had already fought so valiantly, only to learn they faced yet another looming threat.

"Understood," Freedom Tower acknowledged before turning to face the suddenly weary crowd. "There are plenty more of them out there," she said, "and they remain hell-bent on stopping us. So, we can either take the fight directly to them by forcing ourselves uptown, or we can stay and defend this land we already earned. I shall not judge either way, nor would I judge any decision to retreat into the dunes and leave all this behind for good. We could start fresh elsewhere, for the point, you see, has been made loud and clear to our perpetrators. You *were* able to defend yourselves after all, and the Twin Towers can now rest easy. Anything further, I leave up to you."

The towering giants looked at each other with a combination of dread and desire. While fear certainly moved through the crowd like an ill wind, so too did feelings of hope and rebirth, the very motivators that had brought them back to Manhattan in the first place. For all her wisdom, Freedom Tower understood that any further move was just a simple matter of which road they wanted to go down.

To break the tension, Rockefeller Slab stepped out from the crowd to share thoughts likely felt by all. "Your words have gone a long way since you first greeted us among the dunes, Freedom Tower, and your actions went even further. As far as I'm concerned, you fulfilled our twin brothers' wishes by bringing us back home." He paused for a moment before adding more. "But I say we try to give this battle the send-off it deserves."

The rest of the buildings nodded in unison.

Lady Liberty, moved by such strong conviction, took in a deep breath and glanced up at Freedom Tower.

"Then in that case, I will stand with you all to the end," Freedom Tower stated with certitude, knowing that despite any present fears, hope had won out.

In no time, each towering giant stood by as one united front, ready to face whatever opponents were coming their way. As the warriors reassembled, the Manhattan Military likewise prepared its remaining tanks for the next wave of action.

"Our strategy will be as before, but with greater ferocity," Freedom Tower urged. "Meaning we just charge with enough force to penetrate their offense head on."

By that point, tremors could once again be felt in earnest. As visibility temporarily cleared by a hot gust of wind, it revealed incoming TERROR forces stacked four deep, stretching almost the entire width of Manhattan Island. Leading the phalanx was a row of Cyclops Bots, followed by two rows of TERROR Soldiers at the ready, their electrified staffs primed. Backing them up was a row of Death Rays, their serpentine eyes as hellish as ever. To the towers watching, it was a grand display of the TERROR Group's intimidation factor.

"They're just machines … They're just machines," Guggenheim Museum reminded himself as the shadows of the enemy drew nearer.

"And they're no match for any of us. That includes you," Puglia Ristorante comforted him in jest, despite his own trepidations.

"Let's just take these bastards down and be done with it!" Rockefeller Slab yelled with confidence.

"Okay. Everyone, be ready on my watch," Freedom Tower signaled.

As the TERROR Group moved within thirty yards of them, the time came for Freedom Tower to initiate their second charge, and seconds later, strategy became action again as Cyclops Bots unleashed their firepower, intent on laying waste to anything that moved.

"They're much stronger this time!" UN Building noted with alarm, and almost immediately, the machines' rejuvenated offensive caused the cluster of buildings to separate and scatter in all directions.

Rockefeller Slab was among the first to feel the TERROR Group's wrath. "I'm hit ... Look out!" the building screamed as his concrete and steel midsection burst into flames and sent the tower careening into the ground, alive but incapacitated.

At his location several hundred yards away, UN Building was the next to be targeted as he tried to veer around the eastern edge of the attackers, a move that sent concentrated firepower his way. Quickly, the Cyclops Bots' raging blaster arms pierced through the building's upper stories with an impact that blew out much of his façade and sent dozens of Manhattanites and thousands of glass shards crashing to the ground.

The onslaught continued all across the island as towers large and small did their best to outsmart the incoming inferno. But as Trinity Church and others tended to the aid of their injured colleagues, it was obvious the game had drastically changed.

Such devastation forced Freedom Tower to change strategy before all hope was lost. "Move in diagonals to avoid as much direct firepower as you can, but try to penetrate that phalanx, no matter what!" she said. But the scene further deteriorated into a chaotic jumble of broken TERROR factions and individual towers running every which way, and the once-uniform row of Cyclops Bots splintered apart while buildings charged in.

TERROR Soldiers on the ground found themselves pitted against buildings much sooner than anticipated, which gave the towering opponents a slight advantage as they stomped and slammed their enemies to the ground with the full weight of their structural frames. Despite their gains, however, it was still a physically taxing endeavor for the buildings, and it couldn't last forever.

"We need more help," Freedom Tower cried out, as if calculating the gravity of a situation that would eventually result in the buildings being toppled by their stronger and more unrelenting opponents.

"Give us one last push, please," she appealed to the skies above, and nearby buildings watched in suspense for whatever was about to transpire. Indeed, just when it seemed like their progress would plateau, a sense of rejuvenation took hold of each towering warrior, as if momentarily releasing them of their ailments and strengthening their capabilities.

"Thank you," Freedom Tower acknowledged softly, and the revitalized towers seized upon their sudden momentum with everything they had. They continued to wear down their opponents with bludgeoning force and gained noticeable ground in the process.

"This is our shot!" said Ladder Tower, rallying the crowd. He and a host of buildings large and small smothered all the Cyclops Bots in their midst, piling onto each with much more crushing force than before.

The buildings' counteroffensive was growing. Guggenheim Museum rolled about, Puglia Ristorante pummeled and pelted, Apollo Theater stomped away, and even reserved sacred structures like Masjid Malcolm Shabazz, St. Patrick's Cathedral, Central Synagogue, and Trinity Church defended themselves and all they believed in with renewed agility. Despite TERROR Soldiers climbing atop many of them like a swarming army of ants—clawing, jabbing, and sending electrical jolts into their windows and other openings—the emboldened buildings responded by rocking and swaying themselves out of danger, squashing or disorienting their attackers in large numbers.

Such efforts allowed the towering giants to stubbornly press forward, and for the once-impenetrable threat of the Cyclops Bots to wane. The machines clamored to land accurate hits onto their architectural targets, and the TERROR Group's deadly phalanx, so reliable in the past, became drastically hindered. Despite the carnage, it was apparent that the tide of battle was on the buildings' side, and soon enough, Freedom Tower and her friends secured Manhattan's central acreage.

Like it always seemed to do, the sky reflected the conditions below, with winds picking up and whisking away the thick ash that had plagued the island and its outlying regions. This provoked the sun to push through the dense smog and make itself known once again, and waves of illumination dappled the charred landscape.

Even as they continued their fight, the buildings couldn't help but stop to notice the phenomenon occurring overhead. Nor was this change in climatic fortune lost on the Supreme Chieftain, who gazed at it with agitation while he waited for his army to return victorious. But with each passing moment and receding cloud, it became more apparent that the ruler's expectations were not lining up with reality.

He monitored the battle from his location outside the cave's portal, and witnessed the horde of buildings continue to outsmart the order he'd spent his life grooming into perfection. Despite the seeming impenetrability of his TERROR forces, including their intimidation factor and long list of past conquests, this new battle had come down to *heart*, and the buildings had more of it.

The vile leader's frustration reached a boiling point. "What happened to my phalanx? Why aren't my troops obeying my orders for attack?" he shouted at his closest aides, all the while sensing their growing doubts about his leadership abilities.

"Judging by your timid expressions, I wonder if you mistake me for a weak leader. Is that the case?" he asked his subordinates. "Is that the case?" he repeated in a fierce tone.

As the Supreme Chieftain's composure continued to spiral, most of the aides fled to their caverns below the surface. "Where are you all going, to run and hide? No, no, you stay here and watch the show, you fools!"

The Supreme Chieftain grabbed his nearest aide by the head, intent on forcing the captive to watch the far-off battle against his will.

The vile ruler's erratic behavior soon drew the attention of the armed guards standing watch over Empire State and Chrysler Buildings from a thousand feet away, and each left their post to see what the commotion was about.

As soon as they walked away, the imprisoned buildings knew it was time to act, since they had been watching the battle unfold.

"This is our one shot," Chrysler Building said, and the two towers began to flicker all of their working lights on and off, desperate to grab the attention of a far-off building. At the same time, they kicked their lower stories side to side within their hardened cells, hoping to finally wriggle free or weaken their encasements from inside.

Amid his tirade, the Supreme Chieftain happened to glance in the direction of his prisoners, grinning at their impromptu escape attempt.

The distracted guards who were supposed to keep watch over the prisoners soon came within range of the frustrated ruler. "Is everything okay here, Excellency?" one of them asked.

"All is fine, but what I don't get is that you've left your post. Oh well, I guess I'll have to handle this matter as well," the Supreme Chieftain stated. Calmly, he drew his pointed staff, activated its blue electric charge, and drove it through the bodies of each guard with inhuman strength, incinerating each with a burst of electricity that killed them instantly.

"Never leave your post," the murderous ruler added in an icy voice.

"He just killed them. This is getting bad ... Try to break free!" Empire State Building said while he and Chrysler Building continued to pry themselves loose.

The Supreme Chieftain, breathing heavily, began to walk toward them. "If I go down, so will you two," he shouted as he came within a few hundred feet of the captives.

Despite the commotion all around her, Freedom Tower caught a glimpse of Chrysler and Empire State Buildings' flashing lights. "They are not too far off!" the tower said, just as a fresh horde of TERROR Soldiers climbed atop and jabbed at her from all directions with their weapons. The onslaught forced Freedom Tower to have to fight off her attackers one by one.

Lady Liberty, low on energy, had grounded herself to regather her abilities. But when Freedom Tower put out the call to rescue the buildings, she heeded it.

"I see them! Everyone, stand clear!" she said, and closed her eyes to summon her remaining energy, more intent on rescuing her friends than anything else. "Grant me your will once more, Great Spirit," the statue prayed. Sensing a feeling of rejuvenation from deep within her structure, she focused her mind fully on the prisoners' location, knelt on one knee, and prepared to thrust toward them with all her soaring speed.

Zeroing in on his captives with vengeance in his eyes, the Supreme Chieftain's profile drew upon Chrysler and Empire State Buildings like a looming shadow as they continued to flicker their lights and kick back and forth, only to cease from the fear of his presence.

"What do you two hope to *gain* by doing this?" he asked with cynicism while he slowly encircled them. "I thought we had an understanding that you would accept your place in life, and that I would have dominion over your kind!"

The Supreme Chieftain continued to mock them, but the captive towers did their best to pretend not to notice a glowing green ember hurtling toward them at full speed.

"It's time to meet your maker then," the unaware Supreme Chieftain concluded. He readied his weapon and aimed it at Empire State Building's upper stories.

"You first," Chrysler Building spat at him.

Caught off guard by her remark, the vile ruler had little time to turn his head before Lady Liberty rammed into him with enough force to send them both careening directly into Empire State Building's lava prison. The impact allowed the tower to finally break free, and any lingering TERROR personnel to scatter in fear.

Freed from his bondage, Empire State Building could barely make out Lady Liberty's location in the crash site's smoke and debris at first. After shining his antenna light upon the hazy grounds, he finally spotted the statue's unconscious body lying on its side and smoldering from the collision.

"Help her first!" Chrysler Building shouted despite her ongoing struggles to break free of her bondage.

"Okay, but I'll be right back!" Empire State Building called out to her. With great difficulty, the tower then rolled Lady Liberty away from the imminent danger of a lava stream bubbling nearby. Once the green lady was moved to a relatively safer area, he then turned to try and free his lover.

"Let's get you out of here," he said.

Both buildings soon realized that the Supreme Chieftain was nowhere in sight, while the surrounding area began to glow with a new kind of hellish hue, making it difficult to see anything.

Chrysler Building tried to pinpoint the vile leader's where-abouts, when the earth began to rumble and split into jagged shards and sections, sending fresh molten lava oozing up to the surface.

"The impact must have triggered something below. We don't have much time here!" Chrysler Building shouted, fearful of what could happen if they stayed where they were.

"Just hang on! I'm getting you out of this thing," Empire State Building said, despite the lava creeping in ever closer. Using his top-most floors and antenna to hammer into Chrysler Building's rock-hard prison with all his might, Empire State Building shouted in desperate frustration. Chrysler Building noticed a shadowy presence lurking closely behind her companion as he struggled.

"Look out!" she screamed, right before the Supreme Chieftain jabbed his staff into Empire State Building's lower floors. Following a loud shriek, the tower plummeted to the ground in dizzying pain. The vile ruler then released his weapon from the building's façade and limped as he made his way to his victim's upper stories. Watching the horror unfold, Chrysler Building saw that the monstrous figure's left arm was missing, though it was apparent that he was agile enough to finish her lover off.

"I want you to *feel* this," the Supreme Chieftain said as he readied his weapon, intent on delivering a death blow right into Empire State Building's Schistian-rich steel spine. Luckily, the ground beneath them shook and disrupted the vile ruler's balance, sending him and his intended target rolling into a smoky abyss. Shaken by the sight but determined nonetheless, Chrysler Building tried once more to free herself, but to no avail. She heard the two struggling, grunting opponents somewhere out in the distance, but couldn't see them.

Lady Liberty awoke from her crash landing in a daze. Strug-gling to regain her footing, the statue looked around her hellish environment that was fast becoming consumed by more smoke and fire. Once she slowly stood up, the earth below separated further, and the green lady nearly lost her balance. Despite bad visibility, the statue managed to make her way toward Chrysler Building.

"It's too late for me. Just get out of here while you can!" Chrysler Building said in a panic while lava started to consume her hardened prison.

"Stay still," Lady Liberty instructed before jabbing her glowing torch right into the hardened encasement. To Chrysler Building's delight, this act was enough to undermine large portions of the rocky shell from within, enabling the tower to finally break free. The two quickly moved away from the area, right before lava swallowed up everything where they had just been standing.

"I owe you one," Chrysler Building said.

"It was nothing," the statue quipped, before sternly adding, "but where is your companion?"

"I don't know, we got separated. He's somewhere down there," Chrysler Building replied, using her gargoyles to point toward the smoke infused abyss beyond. "And the Supreme Chieftain is still alive."

They brainstormed their next move, but noticed a soft white glow begin to permeate the dense smog around them. "We will deal with that Chieftain accordingly," a voice said, and Lady Liberty and Chrysler Building turned to find Freedom Tower emerging from a wall of smoke with resolve in her sway.

"Manhattan has been liberated," the glowing tower reported. "But we lost some Manhattanites, and several buildings sustained injuries. All told, though, it was a battle well fought."

"Thank you, stranger, but this battle is not yet won," Chrysler Building said. "We've got to help Empire State Building stop the Supreme Chieftain before he has a chance to escape!"

Lady Liberty wholeheartedly agreed with Chrysler Building's wishes, but was doubtful given her own failed attempt to subdue the vile ruler. "We must be cautious, for this villain wields powers we have never encountered before. And I lack the ability to fly again," she admitted with sadness.

Listening intently, Freedom Tower sensed her friends' undying collective determination, and knew just the right words to say to keep their morale up.

"Fear not, Lady Liberty, for your torch and my light will guide us," she said.

Lady Liberty and her friends began their pursuit into uncharted and smoke-clogged darkness, but Empire State Building and the Supreme Chieftain had already descended deeper into the fiery abyss. With each passing moment, the warring opponents rolled and tumbled freely down a scorched, jagged patchwork of hardened lava, engaged in a fight fit for two leaders of starkly opposing ideologies.

In the midst of their battle, both opponents appeared worse for wear. Empire State Building's façade had become riddled with gashes, shattered glass, and crumbling chunks of limestone and concrete that exposed many of his floors within. The Supreme Chieftain's body, meanwhile, appeared even more mangled and prickly than before, and his limbs, spikes, and bones intersected in new and unnatural ways as he fought on.

Empire State Building managed to use his antenna as a lashing device quite effectively, though his overall design limited his fighting abilities, especially against such a flexible opponent. After several more agonizing exchanges, the Supreme Chieftain soon gained the upper hand and managed to pin the building into a giant rock cavity. Just behind them, lava swallowed up what seemed to be the only way out of their hellish surroundings.

"You should've let me kill you earlier, Empire State. Would've been far less painful than this," the vile ruler taunted, raising his weapon once again in order to send it piercing into the building with full force. But just when his staff came within inches of its target, the ground rumbled and shook mightily. The Supreme Chieftain lost his footing and his weapon sailed from his grip.

Seizing the opportunity this change of fortune offered, Empire State Building pried himself loose from the rock, and after gaining his footing, knocked the Supreme Chieftain to the ground with all his might. This sent a colossal wave of rock and debris to fly in all directions. However, Empire State Building failed to see that by using such force, his judgment was fast becoming clouded by his own hatred.

As if sensing this, the Supreme Chieftain began to cackle with glee.

"You've got innocent blood on your hands ... I'll kill you for that!" the building shouted, and began to pummel his opponent harder with his uppermost floors.

In spite of the damage being inflicted upon him, the Supreme Chieftain's jubilation only grew, infuriating his opponent more.

"Hit me! Yes, and again! Good! Oh, I'm so proud of you," the vile leader said in a sardonic tone.

Aided by the tower's rage-fueled assault, the Supreme Chieftain's body wasn't weakening. In fact, it regenerated with each passing blow, because unbeknownst to Empire State Building, his hate fed right into Pegmatite's hand by actually *rejuvenating* the Supreme Chieftain. In no time, the vile ruler's limbs, spikes, and muscles reformed and expanded.

Even so, the tower doubled down on his efforts to weaken an opponent that simply wouldn't falter.

"You're doing well. Keep going," the Supreme Chieftain said. His voice now deepened to a lower and far more menacing register—a monster reborn was he.

Amid his aggression, Empire State Building managed to catch a glimpse of his friends, who'd finally located him among the jagged and smoky topography. They stood beyond a ring of lava surrounding the tower and his opponent, and their sudden appearance was just enough to take Empire State Building out of his dark mindset, which allowed him to maturely reflect on his violent actions.

"You were not built for this purpose," Freedom Tower called to him in an effort to bring him further out of his black hole.

"She is right, Empire State. Look where your anger leads you. Stop feeding it!" Lady Liberty said.

The Supreme Chieftain's mockery subsided due to this sudden turn of events. "Don't listen to those fools. Finish me off!" he shouted in the face of Empire State Building's waning hatred.

"You're right, my friends," Empire State Building realized, and he took a giant step away from his devilish foe. Moments later, however, large booming sounds permeated the air and the ground broke apart all around them.

"This whole place is going under. We need to leave!" Chrysler Building said while her partner took one last look at his opponent.

"It's over, Supreme Chieftain. Your influence is finished. Either you come with us and face justice for your crimes, or you stay behind and perish," said Empire State Building.

"Finished, you say?" the Supreme Chieftain asked. He stood back up to display his regenerated form, which brought him nearly eye-to-eye with Empire State Building for the first time. "I'll show you what finished looks like!" He looked around to locate his weapon, which lay jammed in a nearby rock cavity.

"Forget it, just come on!" Lady Liberty said to Empire State Building. She outstretched her arms in order to help him leap across the widening lava stream.

"Unrighteous fools!" the Supreme Chieftain roared while attempting to pry his weapon loose. But he struggled and strained, and the staff began to dissolve into an ashy vapor.

"What is this?" the Supreme Chieftain asked in alarm as the buildings watched from a distance. Suddenly, the ring of lava that encircled him rose on its own to a tremendously great level, and formed a colossal wall of fire that then seemed to zero in on the Supreme Chieftain with predatory focus.

"Mighty Pegmatite, what are you doing? I don't need you here. Let me take back what's mine!" the Supreme Chieftain shouted in anger to the fiery presence, his self-conceit emboldened and defiant. But as he gazed up in resistance, the Supreme Chieftain's eyes shone with the reflection of a reluctant presence staring back down at him.

"Pegmatite," Lady Liberty whispered fearfully as she watched the scene unfold.

"No, think otherwise," Freedom Tower said, alluding to the fact that Schist—not Pegmatite—had arrived.

"I am not the one you speak of, and I grant you no such request, for you have betrayed the gift of life," the fiery shape boomed in a deafening tone.

"What do you want from me?" the Supreme Chieftain asked to little avail, as his expression quickly turned to worry. Schist then let out one last fiery moan and crashed down upon his prey in an engulfing wave. The ruler's violent and turbulent life had come to a smoldering end.

"We really have to get out of here!" Freedom Tower said. After she and her friends took in the momentous event, they fled the trembling danger zone. Much of the area left behind caved in on itself, and rock and earth imploded and buried any lava that remained exposed.

"I can't believe it, Lady Liberty. Despite my growing rage I was still rescued," Empire State Building said after he reflected on the events that had just transpired.

"You abandoned your rage just in time, my friend. Such abilities are Schist's blessings, which are present in any season," the green lady said, her sage advice always on the mark.

"Indeed they are," he agreed, knowing that the experience would affect him from that day on.

Upon navigating out of the thick smoke and to a much safer part of the island, Freedom Tower, Lady Liberty, Chrysler, and Empire State Buildings emerged from the ashes with not only a newfound bond with one another, but also with gratitude that their lives had been spared.

"What's with the happy disposition all of a sudden?" Puglia Ristorante asked his mate from their location atop Manhattan's liberated soil.

"Well, I do believe we've come out the victors in this whole affair," declared Guggenheim Museum, gratefully.

"You just may be right, my friend. You just may be right," the restaurant seconded as glimmers of newfound optimism sprinkled his own thoughts.

Signs of victory indeed permeated the island and all of its battle-worn towering giants in the aftermath of their fight. With recovery efforts now underway, some spent their time tending to other injured towers like Rockefeller Slab and UN Building, while the Manhattan Military began to carefully assess the damage to the island. These efforts were just the start of things to come, of course.

Lady Liberty and her friends rejoined the rest of the survivors for a long-overdue moment of reconnection, embracing buildings and greeting every Manhattanite they saw, while all across the island, spontaneous cheers erupted.

"I'm fine. Just make sure that anyone who needs care gets it on the double," Empire State Building told his able-bodied contemporaries, before he took in the landscape for himself.

Welcome for all was the sight of daylight that poured over the towers with cheery radiance in the aftermath of the battle, causing the last vestiges of dark clouds to drift away. And with nothing to fuel them further, the lava streams that had crisscrossed the island so treacherously began to flow into the sea and cool down, their bubbling demise a telling sign that Manhattan had already begun to heal itself.

Chrysler Building moved in close to her companion as he surveyed the barren and charred surroundings. "What happens now?"

"You mean, what of this place we still call home? It's simple, really. We rebuild, my love, only stronger and wiser than ever before," Empire State Building said.

"All this thanks to our old friends," Chrysler Building pointed out as she looked toward Lady Liberty, UN Building, Rockefeller Slab, and others, before a new thought entered her mind. "And now we have a *new* friend, don't we?"

"We do," Empire State Building replied.

Lady Liberty and others then joined the two in what became an impromptu show of appreciation for Freedom Tower, their new friend. In a show of the city's utmost gratitude, Empire State Building offered a long-overdue thanks to the radiant giant.

"I hear they refer to you as Freedom Tower, yes?" he asked in a playful voice.

"Not officially," she replied, only half joking.

"Hmm, let's just go with it. I think that name suits you considering everything you've done for us," Empire State Building said. "On behalf of everyone here, welcome to Manhattan, my friend. We're grateful you're with us."

"But will you *remain* with us?" Lady Liberty asked, speaking the question on every building's mind.

Freedom Tower was content to reply in the only way that felt right. "I just may, Lady Liberty, for as the Twin Towers had told me, there is something about this place that resonates like no other."

"Well, wherever they are," the ebullient statue said, "they must be pleased to know their wish has been fulfilled."

Cheers from nearby buildings and Manhattanites once again erupted all around, as everyone became overjoyed by the glowing tower's decision to stay with them.

With everyone now on board, a collective comeback was set to be in order for the city, its buildings, and its people. Spurred on by the immense and daunting challenges that lay ahead, this new chapter in Manhattan's story involved momentous infrastructure changes that were unmatched by any in its long and storied history.

MANHATTAN LIBERATED!
EMPIRE STATE, CHRYSLER TOWERS ALIVE;
SUPREME CHIEFTAIN DEFEATED;
TERROR GROUP DEALT MAJOR BLOW.

Word of his organization's demise spread across all media outlets, and the Supreme Chieftain's death officially ushered in the

TERROR Group's changing global fortunes in the aftermath of the city's rescue.

"That monster's lust for authoritarian rule turned out to be his biggest folly," UN Building boldly stated as he stood alongside Empire State Building. While each was still recovering from their injuries during the crucial days after the island's emancipation, both were focused on getting Manhattan up and running as soon as possible.

"What has been the global reaction to his defeat?" Empire State Building asked.

"Well, I've got reports coming in from all across the planet that TERROR factions and outposts are surrendering in earnest due to what's happened here, and as such, most of their remaining adherents will be tried by local courts."

"I see," Empire State Building replied. "So is it safe to say the threat is shrinking like the Manhattan Military predicted, and that our island contained the largest share of TERROR forces?"

"Absolutely," UN Building confirmed. "And it's shrinking to a degree that we haven't seen in generations, especially with no Chieftains or Commanders at the helm. I'm also told that governments worldwide are announcing far more aggressive efforts in stamping out remaining traces of the TERROR Group ideology."

"Peacetime is fast upon us, then," Empire State Building said before adding one other observation. "You, my friend, are gonna be busier than ever around here as everyone tries to stitch diplomacy back together. What do you think about that?"

"What do I think about what, retirement? Ha! Forget it," UN Building said.

The towers soon caught the watchful gaze of Chrysler Building as she approached to check in on her recovering fellow giants.

"Will you two ever stop with all the admin talk?" she joked, as if already knowing the answer to her question.

"He started it," Empire State Building playfully said, motioning his antenna toward UN Building.

"Oh I did, did I? Then in that case, my work is done here for now. I'll, uh, leave you two alone," UN Building said before strolling away.

Chrysler Building turned her full attention toward her waiting lover. "I suppose secretarial duties and politics are what you were designed for, anyway. Am I right, Mr. Mayor?" Chrysler Building flirted with him now, at peace with the notion that Empire State Building wasn't about to forego his civic duties.

"Yes, but they're not the *only* things I was designed for, if you recall," he reminded her. "Speaking of which, I'm scheduled to survey the damage in the Manhattan Forest this week."

"Oh yes, I've heard of that place," Chrysler Building said coyly.

"You could, um, meet me up there when the work is done," he sheepishly proposed.

"Why not?"

Despite their rekindled but welcome romantic banter, both towering giants nonetheless understood the magnitude of their situation.

Meanwhile, the antagonists responsible for countless acts of destruction, brainwashing, and ecological turmoil over many years had lost their potency as a viable threat to cities, towns, and villages worldwide. Following the TERROR Group's dissolution, lands were reclaimed, restored, and returned to the descendants of their original inhabitants. Cultures and governments everywhere, inspired by the efforts of Lady Liberty and her friends, fully embraced diplomacy in order to repair any lingering points of contention with their neighbors, ensuring that groups like the *Territorial Reclamation and Restoration of Righteousness* would never have any reason to manifest again.

EPILOGUE **THE WONDER CITY**

IN THE MOMENTOUS PERIOD that followed, the utopian notion of *a brighter tomorrow* became more tangible, and plans for Manhattan's redemption were, naturally, set to be historic, ambitious, and daring. While there was much work to be done, the island's rejuvenation signaled a collective promise made to both itself and to the planet that the best years were still ahead, a point echoed not only by Manhattanite authorities, but also by towering giants like Lady Liberty and Empire State Building during sequential Manhattan Building Conferences.

"After all, the memory of those we lost drives our need to rehabilitate a certain generational continuity here and inspires us to deliver a city of the future with full credence," the green lady proclaimed to the masses during one such meeting a week after the island's emancipation.

In light of the city's rekindled desires, the effort became more than just a grassroots campaign, and news of its intent to rebuild spread quickly around the planet. Millions everywhere remembered Manhattan's unique place in history, embodied by its legendary towering giants, its open-mindedly cosmopolitan ideals, and its cultural contributions. Grateful citizens from across the world banded together in an extraordinary relief effort, contributing aid and supplies worth hundreds of millions of dollars, for however long it took the city to get back on its feet.

These early efforts boosted the city's morale as it began its long and arduous reconstruction, and also helped put Manhattanites in a position of restoring their own self-sustaining agrarian practices much sooner than expected. For instance, Breuckelen, totally ravaged by the TERROR Group, was the first of the outlying regions to be completely restored and prepped for new farming and cultivation methods, and soon staples like cotton, corn, and a multitude of other crops were harvested in profusion again. As a simple but symbolic act of gratitude, Empire State Building called for three million apples—harvested from Breuckelen's vast orchards—to be sent out to every nation that had chipped in to help.

Millions of acres in the Manhattan Forest were also surveyed for damage and then restored, its ecosystem made whole as vast areas of charred and ravaged lands were fertilized and replanted. Nature, of course, took it from there. For buildings who either viewed the great forest as the backbone of their own physical being or as a romantic hideaway, it was a relief to know it would still be there to provide stone and steel for the *next* generation of towering giants.

Per Lady Liberty's request, not one aspect of the island's rehabilitation went overlooked, and the whole place was a frenzy of activity. Even in those early days of reconstruction, as buildings assumed temporary roles as makeshift hospitals and first responder units for the multitudes of injured Manhattanites, elsewhere on the island, huge chunks of debris were routinely hauled away and disposed of.

With the building boom in full roar again, ironworkers poured in from far and wide to heed the call. These dedicated human laborers brought to the city a simple and vivacious desire to clean up the mess and return the place to normalcy, removing tons of shattered steel, hardened lava, and truckloads of earth as they reawakened the land beneath their feet.

To speed up work even more, Empire State Building publicly supported the reestablishment of a workers' union that hadn't been active since the darkest days of the last depression, many decades back. This human union, known as the Civilian Conservation Corps, or CCC, took to Manhattan with the same verve as children with shovels on a beach. Just like long ago, the CCC consisted of ironworkers, architects, builders, contractors, engineers, scientists, construction crews, and designers of every kind. Many of its ranks were also composed of previously unemployed or homeless citizens displaced by war.

"The work happening all around is just the spark Manhattan needs in order to take its comeback to the next level, and the perfect economic and social catalyst to drive the city's new look and feel. This means that we buildings will be renovated and renewed like never before," Empire State Building publicly announced as he attempted to elevate the CCC's role in the minds of towering giants everywhere.

Coordinating with existing committees set up by both buildings and Manhattanites, the CCC was an organization created by the city and for the city. A revolutionary master plan was drawn up in no time, and new towers came to live side by side with pre-existing ones, continuing the island's pursuit of social harmony set forth so long ago by Lady Liberty's creators. Undoubtedly, the skyline became a chameleon of monuments young and old, each one claiming their place among the recharged and whimsical bouquet.

The CCC's infrastructure checklist was momentous yet manageable. Cranes and scaffolding seemed to dance along the city's rooftops in enthusiastic, rhythmic fashion, their mechanical sounds singing a healthy tune of progress to everyone's ears.

Three years after the TERROR Group's defeat, Manhattan's skyline became ever more promising. The efforts put forth by the CCC delivered a fine return on investment, for it was truly a living skyline once more. While buildings of every type continued to sprout, surviving towers, too, basked in their new restorations. Wounds of the past healed to respectable scars, and in due time, Empire State and Chrysler Buildings, Lady Liberty, and the rest, were all in peak working order. An exciting air of rejuvenation existed among the buildings who'd seen and been through so much, and they were proud of what they had to overcome in order to reach this point.

Like many others, Empire State Building couldn't believe the dramatic turnaround of the city around him. Standing side by side with Chrysler Building one fine morning, his glowing companion through it all, he found it hard to escape the irresistible feeling of being reborn.

Chrysler Building—her crown shimmering more brightly than ever—looked at her lover with new desire in her heart. Words were unnecessary with such devotion, and the two towers remained linked forevermore. Some things were only natural, after all.

Indeed, stories of revival came in from all throughout the city. As gashes in Rockefeller Slab's upper floors were sealed up with new steel and concrete, delicate stained-glass clovers on St. Patrick's Cathedral had been lovingly repaired. So too, were the proud domes atop Guggenheim Museum, Central Synagogue, and Masjid Malcolm Shabazz. UN Building, meanwhile, received extensive updates to his glass façade, whose green-tinted radiance shone more brilliantly in the sun. And once the city's fractured grid was repaired, Times Square's neon towers were fully recommissioned, illuminating the sky with the soft glow of their billboards and news tickers for all to see. Even Lady Liberty's base, long dilapidated in the middle of the harbor, was painstakingly restored to its former glory—a proud perch to again welcome visitors from far and wide.

Manhattan, great phoenix that she was, emerged from the ashes with a renewed purpose. Buildings were able to return to tasks they were previously accustomed to, citywide employment reawakened, and Manhattanites all across town began their new jobs with pent-up verve.

Building occupancy also rebounded to record levels, made evident by the variety of sounds of human activity that increased within each towering giant's floorplates. As they enjoyed the rhythmic sensation of working elevators that went up and down within them like a steady tide, lights flickered on and off like clockwork, and doors opened, closed, or slammed shut, depending on their human user's intent. Whatever the case was, the buildings welcomed it all as a sign that they were back to peak working order.

Once Manhattan's economy was pulsing again, focus turned next to restoring the island's key civic amenity: Central Park, that great green expanse once situated near the heart of the island. The original park was lost during the recent war, buried and irretrievable from under thick layers of hardened lava, but its successor was intended to sit atop the old location like a layer-cake. Among the hundreds of design entries, the winning proposal called for a large and beautiful urban oasis, featuring specific plants, memorials, and other amenities evocative of a rejuvenated city at large. This *New Central Park* would be one for the ages, the grandest and most bucolic statement of idealized landscape anywhere. And in the eyes of the CCC, it was the symbolic cherry on top of everything they were working on so diligently.

Following a ground-breaking ceremony witnessed by thousands of Manhattanites and a great majority of the city's buildings, hundreds of acres at the island's center were sealed off from the public. Shortly thereafter, CCC construction crews moved in, carrying out an immense site excavation to remove any wartime remains. Huge masses of hardened lava, far too expensive to relocate, were artfully sculpted and left to jut out of the earth, similar to how the island's bedrock was once exposed in the original park. With the help of dynamite, ponds and streams of varying shapes and depths were then formed throughout the site.

In response to the new park's completed survey and earth moving work, millions of tons of fresh soil, a gift from different places around the world, were delivered to the site. This allowed for grassy lawns to be freely created in accordance with the new park's varied topography, turning it into a spontaneous landscape that offered inspired views of the city all around. After that came a plethora of pedestrian bridges, pathways, playgrounds, and at least one carousel, all lovingly designed and built by the most talented laborers, sculptors, and craftspeople the CCC could provide.

Once the park's construction neared its final stages, many plants were added, which included thousands of cherry trees whose brilliant blossoms illuminated the landscape with radiant pink bursts. In juxtaposition to the vast green backdrop of the park, these young cherry trees provoked a visceral experience all their own. And with time, their steady passage to maturity would recall the island's blooming redevelopment at large.

Plans also called for areas of the park to feature trees that had been donated by other nations. The CCC, in conjunction with both UN Building and Lady Liberty, helped to orchestrate the immense effort of shipping the specialized memorial trees to the site.

"These particular trees," Lady Liberty explained one day, "are to stand as living gifts from many cultures on Earth, a lasting sign of Manhattan's importance in the hearts and minds of places beyond our shores."

Anticipating the significance of this gesture, the park's design called for featured memorials at all four corners. Incidentally, these would also be the first areas of the new park to open to the public, and upon completion of these "Global Corners," as they were soon called, thousands of visitors came to leave flowers and other mementos beneath the trees every day, a tradition to be repeated for generations.

New Central Park was arriving in a big way, and after count-less months of construction, this bold new people's playground promised relief for eager Manhattanites peeking through the fence to stay on top of its latest developments. Considering the defin-ing moments already occurring on its vast acreage, there was little doubt in the new park's ability to capture that same communal air that its predecessor had achieved. Thanks to countless hours and efforts, Manhattan's green heart—an important component to its identity—was revived and well.

Despite the psychological obstacles that the wrath of terror once wrought, the island of towering giants had regained its foot-ing by the time New Central Park was nearly completed. Likewise, the firmament of this latest version of Manhattan bore renewed vigor in the hearts and minds of those who called it home, and the changes were apparent everywhere—an island reborn, renewed, and eager to take on the next chapter in its immeasurable life. To the multitudes who had moved back to the place they'd once called home, what a long-awaited vision it was.

"I think we need a party—one to celebrate the seismic changes occurring all around us," Lady Liberty suggested one fine morning while she continued to survey the city's revival. Her idea landed on receptive ears.

Days later, plans were put in place to mark the progress that occurred over the past three years, and city officials worked out all the specifics. Ultimately, it was decided to have a ticker-tape parade on the twelfth day of September, appropriately enough, and when that morning arrived, Manhattanites and buildings everywhere awakened to a paid work holiday that had been issued citywide. So, aside from some ongoing construction work happening in New

Central Park, and a few final panes of glass that were being affixed to UN Building's gleaming exterior, everyone else—buildings and people alike—spilled onto the streets with glee.

The sights and sounds were memorable in a million ways that day. Clothing was as festive as carnival costumes, with carefree Manhattanites showing up dressed as everything from Lady Liberty to Santa Claus. Choreographed marching bands trotted down the gleaming avenues, their instruments in full force. Towering floats of cartoonish sea creatures, ice cream-carrying minions, and caricatures of Manhattan's own iconic buildings all brushed up against actual buildings with playful buoyancy. Tanks from the Manhattan Military rolled along in peacetime formation, their gun barrels stuffed not with munitions, but rather with flags that proudly proclaimed, *WE DID IT!* to excited onlookers. Specially rigged searchlights, meanwhile, caressed the clouds as they beamed skyward, marking the historic occasion for hundreds of miles beyond the city's borders. And all the while, ticker tape generously floated down to the streets from open windows above, as if everyone had come to the consensus that it would just get cleaned up later on.

The parade gave Times Square's towers an excuse to showcase something beyond just the latest lipstick or soft drink, and their billboards borrowed instead from timeless songs like "Give Peace a Chance," "Heal the World," and "Smile." Such gestures were momentous in their own right, for gone were the days when Uncle Sam loomed over the city to sound the drumbeat of an impending war.

However much of an excuse for self-indulgence this parade was didn't really matter, since no critic could argue that such boasting had been in lasting supply over the past few years. Besides, this parade was something more than just another party. It became a perfect amalgamation of all things joyous, for all kinds of buildings and people. It was as if Manhattan's generational layers, as ancient as the glaciers that once formed the island, had been reopened and allowed to permeate the present.

The city celebrated its right to thrive once again, and the press took note of how churches, mosques, and synagogues stood side by side to happily watch the festivities and floats going by. Freedom Tower beamed extra brightly as she shared the sky with the equally ebullient Chrysler and Empire State Buildings. And nearby, the repaired Rockefeller Slab winked at the streets below as searchlights playfully bounced off his exterior, illuminating the building in a brilliant glow. Even the divisive Wall Street Tower carried a different demeanor that day—one that seemed to forego any traces of bad blood between him and his fellow buildings. In fact, the once-bitter political opponent to Empire State Building had been seen working with him on financial matters in the days leading up to the parade. Quite the sea change, indeed.

As the parade moved uptown, Apollo Theater's namesake marquee burned brightly for the crowds, not a bulb busted. Among others standing close to the theater was Ladder Tower, whose exterior rungs became a popular seating option for daring Manhattanites seeking a better view of the festivities. Lady Liberty stood a short distance away, her torch of white flame resting casually in her well-worn hands as she watched the parade go by. Her expression reflected her demeanor, and it was described by the press as one of calm admiration, with an ever-so-slight grin on her face that mirrored the joy felt by everyone that day.

The green lady and other towering giants continued to gaze down with appreciation at the crowds that careened along the wide and glimmering avenues. In turn, those throngs of Manhattanites of every shape, color, and creed reciprocated the buildings' affections as they waved and cheered away. To any visitor, it was as if all tensions and prejudices between the various groups that called

Manhattan home had long been forgotten, for all one had to do, it seemed, was to be oneself.

In addition to the extraordinary civilian turnout, multitudes of firefighters and other first responders came out in droves, as did numerous Manhattan Military personnel. These battle-weary heroes had experienced pain, loss, and anguish beyond measure over the past few years, but the parade was a chance to let them know that it was once again okay to return to a peaceful way of life. In no time, the warriors found themselves cheering and laughing just like all the other Manhattanites.

The marvelous mayhem lasted well into the night, fueled by champagne breaks, mountains of ticker tape, dancing both within buildings and out on the streets, and enough live music of every genre to go around. As dusk began to blink, crowds had decided it was time to disperse, leaving behind a ticker tape-littered pile in every nook and cranny of the city. While the party to end all parties eventually came to an end, its songs of joy lingered in the hearts and minds of those lucky enough to have been there for quite some time. Indeed, the parade would long be remembered as the official moment that put Manhattan's soul back together.

Much like her peers, it wasn't until late in the night when the parade had stopped that Lady Liberty could even *begin* to think about catching a few winks. As she crossed the Hudson River and climbed back atop her perch at Liberty Island, it dawned upon the green lady that, for the first time in a long time, her exhaustion was the result of something joyous rather than something distressing. Such a realization put her mind at ease as she prepared to settle in for the night.

Before surrendering fully, though, the statue took one last look at the rippling tides that absorbed the vibrant rays of the skies above; skies fit for a painting as always, she observed with fondness. Beyond the tranquil harbor tides, she took in the island's skyline of resting towering giants, friends old and new. Out in the distance, faint noises from the city streets soothed her mind, for they were the sounds of remaining parade-goers on their way home. Free then to take in a full and deep breath, Lady Liberty did just that while cool harbor breezes brushed gently against her sides.

"Such a time and a place to be alive," she said softly to the skies above. Then, knowing that a new day was waiting just beyond the horizon, the statue saw fit to close her eyes, clear her thoughts, and dream away.

AFTERWORD and ACKNOWLEDGEMENTS

Writing this book was an adventure that followed me across two states, with many years of dreaming and determination holding it all together. Coming from a background in painting and architecture, I approached my writing no differently than if creating a complex painting or architectural rendering. That is, I broadly conceptualized each scene before refining it to the point that the composition felt, well, natural.

Obstacles were plenty, and often came as dogging questions in the middle of the night. How would I give life to the inanimate with enough serious conviction that readers wouldn't mind if the main characters were talking buildings? What would each building's personality and character traits be like? Were there ways to weave key moments from Manhattan's actual history into my fantasy-driven drama? Lastly, how could I rework ever-evolving ideas of terrorism and authoritarianism into something otherworldly and appropriate to my narrative, while still echoing real-world villains from both the twentieth and twenty-first centuries?

There have been countless literary tales about Manhattan. Here, I wanted to portray a city both familiar and yet wildly unrecognizable—an alternate vision of an already well-documented place, recreated and repackaged through my artistic perspective. In fact, this is a story with origins stemming from a series of acrylic paintings I began in 2002 and completed in 2020, which makes this book a companion piece to those works, one that had to be true to the source material even as it expanded well beyond the painted images. In the end, the paintings and novel could work hand in hand by telling the story of a progressively open-minded and utopian community on the brink of annihilation by a raging and destructive force.

Taking all this into account, I view my story as an ode to Manhattan's infinite ability to overcome obstacles. I would like this book to be seen as not only a celebration of the city's famous architectural icons, but also as a tribute to its remarkable human diversity.

Constant companions that aided my writing included Ric Burns' PBS series, *New York: A Documentary Film*, Pete Hamill's *Forever*, N.K. Jemisin's *The City We Became*, Neal Bascomb's *Higher*, Eric W. Sanderson's *Mannahatta: A Natural History of New York City*, as well as many episodes of "The Bowery Boys Podcast." Countless other sources, from *Star Wars* and *War of the Worlds*, to the Biblical account of David and Goliath and Madelon Vriesendorp's anthropomorphic illustrations for *Delirious New York*, fed my imagination as well. Needless to say, living in New York City for seven years helped a great deal too. All the while, countless hours of music from many different talents poured into my ears as I wrote away.

Acknowledgements are in no short supply. I thank my parents, Belle and Sal Sr., for their unwavering promotion and support of my various dreams over the years, including this one. I'd also like to send a shout-out to Coco at Beta Reading Services, whose reactionary feedback to my writing helped immensely in those critical later stages. Next, I owe a debt of gratitude to Michele Chiappetta and Andrea Neil at Two Birds Author Services, who helped me carve this story out from a bulbous block and into a more polished creation. I'm also grateful to Lauren Smith for some much-appreciated coaching along the way. Lastly, a huge thanks to Carla Green of Clarity

Designworks for capturing the essence of my paintings in the book's final design. Thank God for each of you!

Finally, I should acknowledge the *actual* Manhattan, the creativity it brings out, and all the people—past and present—who've made it such a memorable place on the map, for four centuries and counting.

ABOUT THE AUTHOR

SAL COSENZA is a painter, design educator, and former architectural designer, whose work often depicts anthropomorphic characterizations of famous buildings and other iconography. He is the creator of over 100 paintings and several acclaimed artwork series, including the award-winning *Manhattan, Monuscape,* and *Domestic New York* collections, while his short stories and illustrations have been featured in the widely-circulated Commercial Observer real estate publication. He currently lives in Arizona. Learn more about Sal's ongoing and ever-evolving creative process at www.salcosenza.com.

The best way to thank an author is by leaving a review
on Amazon or wherever you buy books.